MIRANDA

a novel

MIRANDA

a novel

SHEILA SHEERAN

Translated by: Hilda Naranjo

MIRANDA

This is a work of fiction, a product of the author's imagination. Any resemblance to reality is purely coincidental. The author owns the copyright to this work. Total or partial publication or reproduction of this work without permission is prohibited.

Translated by Hilda Naranjo

Original tittle in Spanish: ¿Te acostarías conmigo?

© 2013 Sheila Sheeran
Interior design by Sheila Sheeran

Cover art © Sheila Sheeran / fotolia.com
All rights reserved
Registered United Stated Copyright Office as
¿Te acostarías conmigo?
Registration Number: TXu 1-861-072 August 2013
Translation registered United Stated Copyright Office as
Miranda
Registration Number: Pending, July 2015 Case: 1-2498211371
ISBN: 0990613038
ISBN-13: 978-0990613039

To my husband and daughter:
The immense love that you give me clears the limits of my imagination, and even without reading my stories you are always my #1 *fan*.

To my parents:
I love you.

To life:
For allowing me to live so many experiences, see the world, and placing wonderful people in my path.

MIRANDA

It is this struggle in my heart that makes me love and hate you...

Chapter 1

*T*he way the faint lamplight near the bed reflected off his skin aroused me. It made him look hot… smoldering… desirable. His delicate hands roamed my legs. Each time, they dared explore more of my body. I couldn't resist. My toes would curl while paying homage to his touch.

Ahh, mmm. This one must be handsome. A body like this must belong to only one face: that of a God.

Our silhouettes connected and I could feel the weight of his desire. The dim light slowly revealed his identity… Norman!

Norman?

My eyes opened wide open and pulsated at the beat of my agitated heart. It was before sunrise. The cell phone rang like it was deranged, and maybe somewhat jealous. I didn't know whether to be annoyed or to thank it for bringing me back to reality–for saving me from a sin. Although, on second thought, a dream can't be sinful because it's involuntary. It's only a dream.

Damn it! Where did I put you? The screen's light gave away its location. There it was, on the nightstand, beside the lamp of sin. The chill of the sheets clung to my skin as

13

I reached for the cell across the empty side of the bed.

My eyes, blinded by the bright green light of the numbers on the phone, could barely see that it was 2:47 in the morning. *Who the hell is calling at this hour?* For a few seconds I hesitated to answer.

"Hello?"

"Miranda Wise?" Judging by the seriousness in his voice, it was something important.

"Who's calling?"

"I'm sorry to bother you." Well at least he apologizes. "This is Detective Hernandez from the Investigation Unit of the Police Department. Are you Miranda Wise?"

"Yes."

"Do you know Norman Clausell?"

"Yes." I spoke in a barely audible whisper. Now I was worried. It seemed like the room was getting colder.

"All right, I'm calling to inform you that Mr. Clausell has been in an accident and is receiving medical treatment in the trauma center of the local hospital." It is imperative that you arrive soon."

"Okay." The call ended.

Okay? Is that what I said? I had not realized how much my hands were trembling. *Is this part of the dream?*

Some threads of light that streamed under the door lit the floor of the room in darkness. My legs were shaking so much that I almost fell when I jolted out of bed. My brain had not yet processed whether it was real, another dream, or a nightmare. My eyes turned to the cell. No, I wasn't dreaming. I had to hurry.

I don't recall having changed from my pajamas into

jeans or having driven to the hospital. I remember only that I was there, standing before two enormous sliding doors. When they opened, they let out a blast of cold air, a smell of industrial cleaner, and, no doubt, the departing souls of those who previously had come in alive.

I followed the posted directions that lead me to a counter with an "Information" sign. The guard sitting behind it greeted me.

"Good morning. May I help you?" he smiled.

"I'm looking for Norman Clausell. I think he was admitted a few hours ago. A police detective called me. He said he was here..." I said in one breath. It was impossible for me to minimize the despair that came over me.

The man picked up the phone in front of him and said to the person at the other end of the line:

"Norman Clausell?"

For a few seconds, the silence was deafening. The man waited, making a strange, rhythmic tapping noise with his shoes, and hung up.

"Miss, I'm told you need to go to the waiting area. In a while, you'll be given more information."

"To the waiting area?" I asked to make sure that I understood what he said.

"Yes. Follow the hall to the left and you'll find it there at the end."

"*Hall, left, hall, left hall, end, hall, end...*" a voice repeated over and over again in my head while I ran. I slowed down as I approached the entrance, but I didn't enter. Through the glass, there were multiple scenes with different characters and the same script.

The people waiting had the same expression that revealed anguish and despair. I stood right there where I had stopped, leaned against a wall, put my trembling hand in my purse, and fumbled to find the phone. As always, it seemed like that damn purse had swallowed it. After finding it, I dialed the detective's number.

"Detective Hernandez," I cleared my voice. "Hello, it's Miranda Wise."

"Who?" I was surprised that he did not remember me after having interrupted my sleep and calling me at such an unusual hour. I paused before answering, "You called me not too long ago to tell me about Norman Clausell."

"Ah, yes, of course." There was plenty of noise on the other end of the line.

"I'm here, in front of the waiting room."

"Perfect. I'll be there in ten minutes."

Those ten minutes were really about fifteen, which seemed eternal. I couldn't find a place to rest my eyes without tripping over a face in distress. I was staring at the floor when I heard a voice authoritatively calling my name.

"Miranda Wise!"

It was definitely an order: *Miranda Wise, here, now!* There was no other way to interpret his words. When I looked up, I found a pair of blue eyes gazing at me, waiting for my response. I took two steps toward him, and he did the same. He reached out to shake hands, and I reciprocated. Once again, my words were rushed.

"Hello. What happened? How is he? No one has said

16

anything to me."

As I bombarded him with questions, Hernandez motioned for us to move to a more secluded spot, but where we could still see doctors go in and out of the waiting room.

"Thank you for arriving quickly," he began to say, I was thinking: *Forget about the thanks and get to the point, since you still have about fifteen questions to answer...*

"How is he?" I blurted out.

"I'm sorry. I'm not authorized to give you information about Mr. Clausell's condition."

Perfect! He had asked me to come to not give me information?

"What *can* you tell me?" I asked in a tone of irony. The detective noticed it immediately.

"I can tell you that Mr. Clausell was in what appears to be a traffic accident. In fact, a very serious accident," he stared into my eyes without blinking.

"But how? Where?" It seemed like my questions didn't make him as uncomfortable as not being able to answer them.

"We are still investigating. Several investigators were sent to where Mr. Clausell was found in his car." The ease with which his words came out increasingly exasperated me.

"What do you mean 'was found'? Was he alone, or with someone?" I was tempted to push him against the wall and make him spit it out all at once.

What is wrong with you, Miranda? You shouldn't lose

control so easily!

"We found Mr. Clausell because we received an anonymous call alerting us to an apparent multiple vehicle collision." Little by little, and consciously, he eased his tone. "When we arrived at the scene, we found Mr. Clausell's car and him inside, in very bad shape. The car was unrecognizable."

"Wait, stop. I don't understand. Just one car? And the rest?"

My concerns were not assuaged. The more information the detective provided the greater my confusion.

"We are not yet able to determine what happened."

The pair of blue eyes diverted their attention from me. He turned away.

A woman was heading towards us. She was wearing scrubs.

"Doctor," said the man.

"Detective," she responded. They shook hands.

"She is Miranda Wise, Mr. Clausell's emergency contact."

The doctor reached out to greet me.

I took advantage of the situation to ask abruptly, "How is Norman?" while shaking her hand.

"Hello, I'm Dr. Martinez. I'm tending to Mr. Clausell."

I took refuge in a strategy of insistence.

"How is he?" I was referring to Norman.

"He arrived in critical condition. He suffered fractures to his femurs in both legs. We can repair them in surgery. However, what worries us most right now is the intracranial bleeding that we have not been able to control and is causing dangerous pressure levels on his brain. We are still very cautious about his prognosis. We've placed him in the intensive care unit and we'll keep him in an induced coma until the pressure on his brain has been alleviated. Later we can discuss the surgeries to repair the fractured femurs."

In summary, Norman was in very poor shape.

"Is there something I can do?" I asked as tears welled up in my eyes.

I knew nothing of medicine. I had spent years working in the healthcare industry, but not on that side. The naïve comment apparently was a bit humorous to the doctor, who half smiled.

"For now, pray a lot. He needs it."

"May I see him?" My face echoed the supplication in my words. I needed to see him.

"Not at this time, but if all goes well, perhaps during morning visiting hours." The doctor's gaze shifted to the watch on her left hand. "In other words, in four hours you'll be able to see him. Although, as I already explained, don't expect too much from the visit. He'll be under sedation as long as is necessary."

"Thank you," and I said nothing more.

This truly was very serious. Norman was in a very precarious situation.

How did you get into this Norman?

The doctor vanished, I blinked and she was gone.

Once more, the blue eyes watched me with some authority.

"Will you be staying here?"

"Until I can see him, I don't have any other choice." The sudden changes of intonation in my answers did not seem to bother him.

"Will you have coffee with me? I would like to speak with you. You may have information that could help us understand what really happened."

What could I know about Norman that could help solve the case?

All I knew about him was related to us and Medika, his company. Outside of that, he was unknown to me.

"Could I get in trouble for talking to you?"

The seriousness in his eyes turned into a grin that managed to calm my anxiety.

"No. You don't need to call a lawyer, for now." He pointed the way with his hand, in a way I thought was polite.

"In that case, I'll join you." I batted my lashes and turned toward the slabs that marked the path to be followed.

Are you really flirting with this man?

For some time, my hormones had been suffering from insomnia and had invaded my dreams. There were still after-effects from their last showing before the inspector woke me.

We walked down the same hallway that had led me to the waiting room. This time, instead of turning right and heading to the exit, we continued on our way to the cafeteria.

"With cream?" his voice sounded friendlier.

"What did you say?" Hernandez's question made no sense. I was obviously on another planet.

"How do you want your coffee?" The detective, who was used to dealing with people, realized that I wasn't in full control of all of my faculties. I wasn't there, even if my body was.

I displayed a timid smile that I felt take shape on my face–a reaction, perhaps involuntary, to apologize for my cluelessness.

"Oh! Yes, with cream and two sugars." Still confused, I didn't even make a gesture to pay.

Hernandez took care of the bill and headed to a table that was secluded in a corner of the cafeteria. As in any other hospital, even that space was good for getting hypothermia. My body reacted immediately. The hairs on my arms stood up and I shivered a little. The detective poured the sugar in my coffee. He watched every detail… every move I made.

"Why were you surprised that Mr. Clausell listed you as an emergency contact person?"

Until then, I had not realized that my tone and response to receiving the phone call had been thoroughly studied. I thought it had gone unnoticed. In seconds, I checked each of the personal files I had in my mind before answering. I found nothing that could make sense of what was happening. I looked the detective in the eye. I was honest.

"I really don't know."

"You don't know?" he asked, and I realized that I

did nothing but think about Norman giving me one of his usual smiles. That was all I had in mind.

"I don't quite yet understand." Those cop eyes didn't reflect any emotion.

"Let me see if I can help you. How do you know Mr. Clausell?"

The story of our lives crossed my mind at lightning speed. A sigh gave way to my answer.

"He runs the company where I work."

"Your boss?" He took a sip and jerked the cup away from his mouth, his face contorted in pain. The coffee was hot.

"Are you okay?"

"Yes, yes," he replied. He pressed a napkin against his lips. "This always happens to me. I love this stuff so much that I always forget that they serve it hot enough to skin a chicken."

His candidness was endearing. A silent smile allowed me to relax for several seconds. The man liked my reaction, but did not want to risk straying from the conversation.

"You were telling me that Mr. Clausell is your boss," he commanded me to continue the story with his eyes.

"Yes."

"And what is your relationship to him?"

The interrogation began to bother me.

"I already told you: he's my boss." That was another

half answer. *We've known each other for over twenty years.*

"And where do you work?"

"Medika," I drowned the name in a sip of coffee.

Abruptly he moved the cup away from his mouth, but this time not because he had been burned.

"Medika? The pharmaceutical company?" The questions came out in a mild stutter. "Is he *the* Norman Clausell, the chairman and C.E.O. of Medika?" The way he pronounced the pronoun "he" made me understand that until that very moment, Hernandez had no idea who exactly the victim in this case was.

"Yes, yes, and yes." I noticed that the detective was as surprised as he was disappointed to not have realized which Norman Clausell was in such serious condition sooner. I almost read his mind. *How could I miss such a detail?*

He leaned forward to face me up close. If the table had not been between us, my personal space would have been invaded.

"And what is your position at Medika?"

"I'm the Director of the International Business Division," I answered automatically, without even noticing the responsibility that entailed. He narrowed his eyes and forced his eyes further into mine. I thought they revealed an air of astonishment.

"It must be a position of great responsibility for someone who looks so young..." he remarked with the intention of giving leave to continue talking. I don't know how he dared make such a remark if he also looked too young to be a detective.

"I've never been bored with my work, and about being

young, well... thank you for the compliment. Let's just say the years have treated me well." If his questions made me uncomfortable, his scrutinizing eyes were worse. He crossed the line that delineated what he should be allowed to say and ask professionally. "I don't think the questions related to me are going to help determine what happened to Norman." I risked speaking to him that way to divert his attention from me. *How stupid of me. How could I think of doing such a thing?* He didn't expect the comment, but clearly, it encouraged him. I knew it as soon as he scowled.

"I think you're right, Miranda," he breathed and began to speak again. "Miranda, right?"

"That's right." A thought crossed my mind: *I can't believe it worked.*

"I *should* talk to a relative. Do you have the contact information for any of them?"

"No," and I thought: *He is all I have and I'm all he has.*

"Do you at least know where I can get it?" He leaned back in his chair. "Wife, children?"

"No. Norman is still married, but I've never met his wife, much less his son." I took another sip of coffee. "I believe his son lives in Europe."

I stopped talking because it occurred to me where the detective could contact the woman that was still his wife.

"Do you have any paper?"

Hernandez pulled out a small notepad and pen from his jacket and placed them on the table. I reached out. With a look, I asked permission to take them. It wasn't until he agreed with a nod that I moved them towards me. I wrote down a name and a number with my best handwriting.

"This is Norman's attorney. He may be able to help

you contact his family." While reaching out to take the pen and pad back, he brushed my hand.

God, these hormones are driving me crazy.

"Thank you. I hope you don't mind if I contact you again, if necessary."

Another unwelcome thought. *Why would it bother me that such a handsome man contacts me?*

"You're welcome. I'd be happy to help you with whatever you need." I made sure he understood that I was at his complete disposal, *for whatever he needed.*

He again reached out to say goodbye. I did the same and, for a second, I sensed that his eyes were like an open book, and just when I thought I could read them, the book closed again. It was as if he had realized his misstep. Then I felt guilty about thinking how attractive I thought he was with his tanned skin, when the real reason I was there with him brought me back to reality... Norman.

I thought of calling someone... someone else from the office, of course, because they should know what was happening. I thought that a call at that hour would upset anyone, so I decided not to. I left a voicemail message with Medika's corporate counsel, and Norman's attorney, Ethan.

I walked towards the waiting room. There were seats available now. I entered and sat down.

Chapter 2

$\mathcal{I}$ awoke to the ring of the cell phone. Yawning and anxious, the cell that I had in my hands fell to the floor. I answered with a raspy, cracking voice.

"Miranda Wise, hello."

I recognized Ethan's voice instantly.

"What the hell is going on?" Tactfulness had never been one of his strengths. "Where the hell are you?"

I had forgotten my executive voice and used a more calm and informal one.

"In the hospital waiting room," I rubbed my eyes in an attempt to feel my body's reactions and make sure that it was still there. If only there was still hope of waking up from a bad dream.

"What happened? Are you okay?"

"Yes. It's Norman. He had an accident a few hours ago." My voice cracked the moment I said *accident*.

"God! What happened to him? How is he? How is Norman?"

My silence aggravated Ethan's usual characteristic anxiousness. He asked me again how our friend was. I explained briefly, without embellishing the situation: "It's bad."

That instant, only silence came across the other end of the line. Then, a moment later:

"I'm on my way. You can explain in person." The called ended.

The cell's screen backlight had barely shut off when I heard a masculine voice above all others.

"Relative of Norman Clausell!"

I felt like they were calling me, like I was that person, even if I wasn't. I looked up and saw a nurse in blue clothing, standing below the "authorized access only" doorway. The man saw me and, noticing my anguished expression when hearing Norman's name, knew that I was the one he was looking for. He waved me toward him using the papers in his hand, opened the door a little more, and indicated the way with his other hand.

"You may see Mr. Clausell now."

I followed the nurse through another set of doors with a sign that read *Intensive Care Unit*. We passed three cubicles and arrived at Norman's. It seemed like there was no hospital equipment that wasn't connected to his body. I watched him carefully. His face had suffered enough: his cheeks were swollen and purple, and the inflammation in his right eye was worse. The impression this made left me standing at the foot of his bed staring with a lump in my throat, an upset stomach, and short of breath.

"You may stay for a few minutes. Dr. Martinez will come to speak with you soon."

I approached Norman. With every step I took, I seemed to feel the pain of his wounds in my own flesh.

MIRANDA

My legs couldn't stand it anymore and there, next to the bed, I fell to my knees. I took his pinky between my hands. I began talking to him the way he always spoke to me.

"I don't have time for this, Norman. You better get out of here quickly. This is no time to be taking a vacation. Leave that to others." I could barely hold back my tears. I couldn't help but think of our last conversation, less than twenty-four hours ago.

Norman had been leading a campaign against me. He was determined that I devote myself to living. He would say that I spent too much time studying and working–that at thirty-two it was time for me to do something more with my life.

Did he sense that something would happen to him?

I felt a stare at my back. I couldn't lift my head. The weight of profound sadness from seeing him this way was too much. A woman spoke from the doorway. It seemed to me like she didn't want to see my reaction to the bad news. She must have learned that was the best way to deliver it: without looking people in the eye.

"I'm not going to lie to you. Mr. Clausell's condition is very serious. The next forty-eight hours are going to be very important to making a prognosis."

Dr. Martinez approached me. She helped me up off the floor. I dried my tears and turned towards her. I could only speak in a low whisper. "What's supposed to happen during these forty-eight hours?"

"His body needs to start the healing process: the intracranial bleeding must stop, and the pressure against the walls of the brain must diminish. If that happens, it would be a good sign."

I paused the conversation briefly.

"What's the worst that could happen?" I asked, without really wanting to know.

"That the bleeding doesn't stop or increases, and that it causes permanent brain damage, or even worse, that Mr. Clausell's body goes into shock and cardiac arrest."

The summary I imagined seemed more appropriate: *stated simply, he could die any moment.*

"Is there something I can do besides praying?"

It goes without saying how helpless I felt just waiting and doing nothing, at the mercy of whatever his body decided to do.

"Yes, you can do something more." A feeling of hope came over me. "You can help us contact a relative, wife, perhaps children–someone to consent to the surgeries to repair his broken bones."

The sense of hope dissipated.

"And if no one shows up?" I asked without analyzing what she might think.

She looked at me a little confused.

"In case no close next of kin can be reached, we can proceed with the necessary treatment to ensure Mr. Clausell's health, but we're required to document that an effort was made to contact them. I'm certain that Detective Hernandez will take care of that." She approached Norman and began to inspect the intravenous medications that were being administered. "What is your relationship to the patient?" she asked as she moved slowly towards the monitors that displayed every sign of life still left in him.

"Mr. Clausell is a good friend..." my words were interrupted by a sigh. *Why do I give these people details?* I asked myself. "And my boss," I added anyway.

As she listened to the explanation, the doctor flashed me half a smile. With my last three words, she had come to her own conclusion. I imagine that with so many years of practicing medicine, she's heard so many stories that one more didn't surprise her.

I couldn't stay with Norman much longer. On my way out, I ran into Ethan. Protocol wasn't necessary.

"He's fucked up. Right?"

I nodded while looking to support myself against the wall. I needed something to share the weight I felt inside. He spoke again.

"A little fucked up, very fucked up, or too fucked up?"

Ethan's personality forced people to believe that he never took things seriously, even if that wasn't true. If I had been an outsider, I would have thought so.

"Very fucked up, Ethan. Very fucked up."

I started crying, then felt relieved that I could do it on a familiar shoulder. He hugged me with one arm for a couple of seconds and that was it. He had never been empathic.

"What the hell is going on?" he asked as he pushed me away from his shoulder. He had fulfilled his consolation quota. I told him that it wasn't clear. I repeated the same story the detective told me–that another car was involved and that the driver had not bothered to help Norman–and that filled me with incredible rage. I'm certain that my cheeks were red with fury. I noticed Ethan's eyes when

I mentioned the possibility that the other car had run off.

Nor will they find him was what I seemed to see in Ethan's eyes.

"What's wrong, Ethan?" I asked.

As soon as he realized that I had noticed that part of what I was saying didn't surprise him, he took refuge in his attorney's mask... in his poker face. I knew that face very well. It had been ten years that I'd known him and worked with him daily. I knew that something in my story had not surprised him, but I could not figure out what. An unexpected cold traveled from my spine to my neck. This must be how it feels to lose trust in someone–a very unpleasant feeling to say the least. I was left staring into his eyes.

Spontaneously, we began to struggle to see who could stare the longest without blinking – who would blink first. Knowing that Ethan would win wasn't new to me. He had been trained for it. It ran through his veins with generations of lawyers and prosecutors in his family. I accepted defeat.

"You must contact his family."

"Why?" he asked in a defiant tone.

"Doctors need permission to perform surgery."

"They can proceed without consent," he exclaimed without me having finished speaking.

That was very true. He was right, but why not contact the family? If someone could find them, he could, but his interest was absent.

"What's wrong, Ethan?" His attitude was now
32

irritating me.

I crossed my arms.

"What's wrong with what, Miranda?" he asked, and then he made a mistake.

He hid his hands in the pockets of his slacks, a habit he had to hide the involuntary movement of his fingers when he was lying or hiding something. He had forgotten that he had once confessed that weakness to me.

"Why don't you want to contact his family?" I insisted, because it seemed he was forgetting that I had been his student, and that he had taught me various tricks and ploys that he had mastered so well.

I took several steps back.

"It's probably not what Norman wants us to do," he shrugged.

"What makes you think that?" Tension could be felt in the vacuum created by the pauses between our words.

Ethan exhaled and grimaced. It seemed as if his chest deflated.

"Miranda, in all these years, how many times has he mentioned his wife or his son?"

I didn't want to admit it, but Ethan had a good point. I allowed my mind to wander to the past. On two occasions, I had heard Norman mention his wife's name, but his son's, never. "Eliezer" was the young man's name. At my continued insistence, Norman's assistant, Margaret, told me one day, but not without first making me swear that I would never tell anyone.

Ethan faced me head-on. He came so close that I felt

33

uncomfortable.

"You're right about that, but we can't burden ourselves with something that is not our concern."

Although I was very surprised by his behavior, I didn't show it, nor did I back down. I remained defiant and poker faced.

"That's why. It's not up to us. Let the police do their work."

A third voice interrupted the conversation–a wish come true.

"Sure, that's our job."

Hernandez had approached from behind Ethan, hearing our clumsy challenges. Ethan turned towards Hernandez after first giving me a look that said: *Why the hell didn't you warn me?*

The detective, who must have been working since early morning, had a fresh look on his face. He held out his hand.

"Detective Hernandez."

Ethan pulled his right hand out of its hiding place.

"Attorney Valdes."

Hernandez pulled out the piece of paper on which I had written the information for Norman's attorney. He unfolded it, glanced at it, and a smile spread across his lips–some very desirable lips, indeed.

"Did you say, Valdes?" he asked Ethan, thanking me with a smile.

"Yes," replied Ethan.

"Then, I think I'll do my job. Are you Norman

Clausell's attorney?" Hernandez looked relaxed. He was enjoying the moment.

Ethan gave me another look of disgust, asking I'm sure, in his particular style: *How the hell does he know that?* Being a good student finally, I kept the poker face.

"I'm Medika's corporate counsel, Mr. Clausell's company." He stressed "corporate." Being a man of few words: that was another one of his distinctive tricks.

"Counsel, lets skip the technicalities. We need to contact Mr. Clausell's family. Can you do it or can you facilitate an arrangement?"

Ethan was sly. He knew better than to arouse suspicion or make an enemy of the detective.

"I don't have any contact with them. Nor telephone numbers. Many years ago, Norman gave me an address. I don't know if it's current."

The detective smiled.

"Perfect! We have to start somewhere. I'll see you at your office after lunch."

Ethan took his other hand out of his pocket and made a motion with it in the air.

"That's not necessary, detective. I can send it to you in an e-mail, if you give me your information."

I found this classic encounter between a lawyer and policeman entertaining. Ethan, who thought himself such a tough guy, knew how to pick his battles. Unfortunately, with the police officer, he couldn't even score a point in his favor.

"Don't bother, counsel. I have to go to Medika

anyway."

Ethan didn't like that. His hands returned to their hiding place. Hernandez, on the other hand, looked satisfied with what he had accomplished.

"If you'll excuse me, I'll leave you now." He turned his head, excusing himself, and walked away with that hurried gait with which his legs moved. Before he could leave, I called out his name. He stopped and turned towards me.

"Yes, Miss Wise."

"Any news about the accident?"

He could smell my anxiety. He shook his head.

"I hope to have more news soon." This didn't comfort me, of course. Even so, I thanked him anyway, as a courtesy. "You don't have to thank us. It's our job." He looked at Ethan. "Isn't that right, Counsel?"

The detective had chosen Ethan as one of the battles he had to win.

"Yes, yes," he replied without taking his eyes away off Hernandez, who then turned around and continued walking.

As soon as the police officer left, Ethan approached me and squeezed my arm.

"Thanks, Miranda!"

"Thanks, for what?" I tried to sound like a naïve girl.

"Because now I have that bloodhound on me." Ethan was definitely upset with me. I removed his hostile hand from my arm and backed up a little. Having him so close bothered me like never before.

"And how is that my fault? Where in the hell is it written that in case Norman has an accident that results in a coma, I can't help the police and give them his attorney's phone number?"

He moved in so close again that I could feel the warmth of his breath as he spoke.

"It's called having common sense, Miranda!"

"Go to hell, Ethan!"

Chapter 3

*T*ears tangled in my eyelids, I left the hospital at the same hurried pace as Hernandez with Ethan with words still left unsaid. When I got in my car, I hit the steering wheel and screamed.

As I was leaving the hospital for home, the cell phone rang. I parked by the side of the road and had to search for that damn phone which had disappeared in my purse again. This time I saw that Ethan's name was on the screen.

"What do you want?"

"Miranda Wise, as Medika's corporate counsel, I order you to limit your communication with police and to not make any statements to the press. I'll be the one in charge of issuing statements to the press and releasing information."

I smiled.

"Don't fuck with me, Ethan! You must be joking."

"That's an order, Wise. If you don't follow my instructions, you will face the consequences." He swallowed and took a breath. "You know you're exposing yourself. Understood?"

Ethan was serious and although the pedantic tone

he used bothered me, I understood that he was just doing his job.

"Understood," I whispered.

"Good." The call ended and then there was silence.

***

I arrived at home and forgot about the bath that I so wanted to take. I lay down exhausted on the bed to recharge, wishing everything had been a dream... a terrible dream and nothing more. *It's not, Miranda. It's ugly and it's real*. With that thought in my mind I fell asleep... who knows how.

***

A little later at noon, I arrived at Medika. I came in through a rear entrance, which was meant only for board members. I wanted to enter unnoticed. I wasn't in the mood for explanations or questions, which surely would be asked. Anyway, I had no answers.

As I was about to enter stealthily, a voice called out my name. There was no escape. It was Alex, my assistant. Drafting corporate press releases and memos was one of his duties. If there were someone with whom I should share what had happened, he would be the one. Even so, it weighed heavily on me to repeat what little I knew.

"Are you okay?" I noticed concern on his face. He took my purse and the portable computer from my hands. He always did the same thing.

"Yes," I lied. He approached and quieted his voice, to avoid being heard by someone else.

"Is it true about the news?"

"I don't know what you're talking about," I said.

MIRANDA

It surprised me that rumors had apparently ignited like gunpowder by way of the national media. If the press knew, the next thing for them would be to seek a reaction from Medika.

"About Norman," he said in an even softer voice.

It wouldn't be good to hide the truth from him. Not from him. We met each other back in college. At first, his closeness was the result of sexual attraction. I must confess that I didn't have any other intentions toward him either. He had always been an attractive man.

His skin was tanned by the sun, and he would wear his hair long–long enough to make it curl. He made all the girls go crazy... even the female professors, I'm sure. They gave themselves away with their furtive glances and drooling when he would interact with one of them. Alex sported that eternal surfer look. And yes, we romped, but just once. It never happened again–not because it didn't feel good, but because it wasn't right. Within a few months, the attraction faded, but our friendship had become very strong. In short order, that we would be friends mattered more than sex. When I began working at Medika, Alex already had my trust, so when Norman gave me the opportunity to hire my own team, the first one I hired was Alex.

"I don't know what the media is saying," I began to say, whispering just like he was. "I spent hours at the hospital. Come. Let's talk in my office."

Alex closed the door and sat in one of the black chairs that faced my desk. I was surprised that he didn't choose to use the elegant sofa that was his favorite piece of furniture in the entire building. Sometimes I would let him put his feet up on the sofa, as long as they were clean enough.

Faced with this unusual behavior, I didn't use my chair either, but sat instead in the one next to him and rested my elbows on the wood.

"Norman had an accident."

"I know that already. How is he? What's going to happen to him?" His anxiety was overtaking him as mine was. I too wanted to know how he was really doing, and if he would be able to survive this.

"Not very well." I turned away to look at the floor. "It's bad, very bad. Now that this news is public knowledge, I'll need your help." I looked at him again. "We must send out a memo which briefly states what happened. Also, we must stress that any request for information from the media must be routed through you."

Alex nodded. There was no time for lamentations–only work. *The show must go on.* That's what Norman would have ordered.

"Make sure not to communicate anything to the media without having it first approved by Ethan and I. If the police visit Medika, Ethan must direct all interaction with them."

Alex said nothing. He looked at me as if he didn't understand the instructions... as if he were waiting for me to say something else, or that I would provide a better explanation.

"That is all," I concluded.

Alex is not easily fooled. He is my only friend and the only one who meets the requirements to hold that title. He knew I was nervous, and when I get like that, I sometimes don't act normally. But he is also a good communicator. He knew I was hiding something in between all of those instructions.

"What's going on, Miranda?"

He was looking at me with those pleading little eyes that made me lower my guard. Speaking grew more difficult.

"I don't know. I really don't know, Alex, and until I know, it's best to follow protocol. Something isn't right, but I don't know what it is yet."

That was enough for him. He got up out of his chair and walked to the door.

"I'll go write the employee memo," he announced.

He came back inside almost as fast as he left. I was still seated with my face in my hands.

"Detective Hernandez is in the lobby. He's asking for you."

"For me?" I asked him, as if I didn't already know the answer.

If I was not mistaken, Hernandez was coming for the information Ethan would be providing. Why would he come to see me too?

"Do you want me to call Ethan?"

Those were the Ethan's exact instructions: that he be called. That would be the only proper way to handle the situation.

"Tell him I'll be there in a few minutes. I'll take care of Ethan."

I picked up the phone to let Ethan know about the police presence in Medika's facilities. The anger I felt towards Ethan made me disobey his instructions. Besides,

I wanted to know more about the case.

Alex, who still hadn't left the office, saw that I hung up the phone and smiled knowingly.

"That's what I like: for you to be a good girl and follow instructions."

***

Half hidden behind a large column, I watched Hernandez. His brown hair was somewhat disheveled–that's how he looked since the early morning–an additive to the air of intrigue that exuded from his pores. The cream colored jacket he was wearing showed signs of light wear at the elbows, which revealed that it was his faithful companion during work hours. Even with the high heels I was wearing, Hernandez was taller. He had a mole on his right cheek. Every now and then, that mole caught my attention more than his stunningly blue eyes.

The detective was playing with some key in his hand. Sometimes a peculiar tic of making noise with his shoes would show itself as well. When he was bored of staring at the wall or the ceiling, he would stretch out his neck to look beyond, perhaps with the hope of catching a glimpse of me among so many employees. Suddenly, it occurred to me that with the nervous act as a cover, he was actually photographing every detail of our facilities that he could with his eyes.

"Good afternoon, detective." We shook hands.

"Good afternoon Mrs. Wise."

"Miss," I corrected his mistake. Once, it's a slip; twice, he may begin to believe it. His eyes sparkled and he smiled.

"How can I help you?"

He insisted that we go somewhere where we could

speak privately. *Of course, there are many places here where we can speak and do what you want in private,* was the answer I gave him in my mind. What was the source of such lusty thoughts for him?

"We can speak in my office."

The receptionist had a "visitor" nametag ready. I gave it to Hernandez and asked him to put it on.

My office was next to Norman's at the end of a long hall decorated with abstract oil paintings. The detective walked slowly, examining each work in detail.

"They are very impressive. Whose are they?"

I scanned some of them with my eyes before answering.

"Mr. Clausell's."

He looked at me disapprovingly, as though I didn't have to be formal with him.

"Norman's," I corrected myself. Then he corrected himself too.

"I meant to ask who the painter was." He stepped back to get some distance and to better appreciate the paintings.

"Oh! I don't know. From what I understand, they are by an anonymous artist." I joined him in contemplation. I did just that every afternoon before going home. "Norman is mildly obsessed with them. They are magnificent, yes, but for some reason, they make me feel... uncomfortable."

I decided to keep my mouth shut. Why was I telling him how a few abstract paintings affected my mood? He didn't miss the opportunity to throw out some questions.

"Really? Why is that?"

"I don't know... perhaps they make me feel sad? Sometimes I imagine that the artist is a very solitary, melancholy person." I didn't want to add the following truth: that, one way or another, I saw a reflection of myself in them. I didn't always understand why, but there I was... alone, every time. I knew many people, and only a few of them were part of my life–my inner circle–but that did not mean that I was a sad person. Really? No, I wasn't a sad person. Sadness didn't have a place in my life. At least, not until I was looking at those paintings.

"Do you really want to know why they make me feel that way?" I stopped in front of the painting that hung facing the door to Norman's office. "This painting expresses the pain... the fury when someone betrays you."

Hernandez lifted his head.

"I think that someday I may request your services for an investigation. I think your interpretation is very astute. I'm amazed."

I let out a laugh that provoked an even bigger one from the detective. Between laughs we arrived at my office. He sat in the same chair in which Alex had been sitting just a few minutes earlier. Again, I used the chair next to it.

"I came here because I wanted to know how you were, Miss Wise. I know that all of this has been quite overwhelming for you."

"I'm somewhat tired, but fine. How can I help you?" I insisted.

"The detectives have finalized the search for evidence

where we found Mr. Clausell."

The silence was uncomfortable. I swallowed hard. My heart was beating forcefully.

"And what news do you have? What happened?"

Hernandez sighed.

"This is not an official version, because these things don't work that quickly, but I can say that this does not seem to have been a traffic accident... with other vehicles."

Suddenly it seemed like the detective had stopped speaking English–like he was speaking French or Chinese, or maybe some kind of jargon.

"What makes you think that?" I was able to verbalize.

"There is no evidence that shows that the car lost control before hitting the fence."

My mind went blank, again without understanding the language he was speaking. Maybe that's how some people feel when they have been told they won the lottery– but I had not won the lottery. I had lost it, and it was as if everything was taken away abruptly... even the air out of my lungs.

Little by little, I figured it out. If it had not been a car crash, then what was it? I dared not ask for fear of what I may hear. That he shared those details with me made me curious. As is usually the case, my mouth reacted before my reasoning.

"Why are you telling me this?"

His eyes turned into question marks.

"Why am I telling you what?" He asked, knowing the answer and trying to conceal a very indecent desire to laugh.

"These details! Aren't you supposed to keep them under wraps until everything is solved?"

His face lowered its guard.

"Miranda," he spoke gently, with total kindness. "May I call you Miranda?"

"That's my name," I stressed.

There were no warning signs left on his face.

"Miranda, I think you've watched too many movies and TV series," he couldn't hold back his desire to laugh. We both laughed at the same time. When we managed to calm down, he added, in a more realistic tone, "I think there may be something behind Mr. Clausell's accident."

What ability he had to change topics within seconds! Of course, pure strategy to cause confusion and identify lies. He was going to say something when someone knocked.

Through the glass door, I saw Ethan. It must have been very difficult for him to not interrupt without permission, as he always did. No doubt he wanted to show the manners that, truth be told, he lacked. Without waiting for an invitation, he opened the door and walked in.

"Detective Hernandez, good afternoon. Please forgive the delay." He gave me a look that did not seem to mean anything, but I knew what it meant.

Then I remembered who had authorized Hernandez' visit.

"Don't apologize, counsel. I've taken advantage of the opportunity to speak with Miranda." Ethan hid it to perfection, but I, who had known him for a long time, knew he was about to boil. I had disobeyed his instructions... *and it felt so good.*

"Please come with me to my office and I'll happily provide you with the information that is pending."

Hernandez got up.

"Miranda, have a wonderful afternoon. We'll keep in touch."

The greeting and farewell with a handshake was now a habit–a habit that made me feel very good. His hand was delicate, so delicate that I couldn't imagine him shooting a gun with it.

"Likewise," I answered in a casual tone to completely unhinge Ethan.

I moved on to sending some emails. I wanted to leave the office before Ethan could finish his business with the detective, but because I waited to review the employee memo that Alex was preparing, I was not able to leave on time. Ethan returned to my office before I could make my eager escape. He remained standing at the doorway with the door shut behind him. I had no escape for what awaited me.

"So then, Miranda?"

"Did Hernandez leave?"

He raised his tone of voice.

"Why didn't you follow my orders?"

From inside, a muffled giggle escaped. *So they weren't instructions, but orders.*

Ethan's attitude really bothered me. It was time to clarify our roles in this new state of affairs that was unfolding. I got up and leaned on the desk, stopping right in front of Ethan, who was watching every step I took to get closer.

"I think I need to remind you of a few little things, Ethan. I am second in command at this company. So, I decide how things will be managed while Norman recovers." I would never have wanted to be so rude, because I was not that kind of person. I've always been peaceful and calm, but he left me no other choice.

"Damn it, Miranda! You have to understand. That's the reason I want to protect you." He lowered his voice by several decibels. "You must not involve yourself with what happened to Norman. It's not good for the company."

"What are you saying?" Although we spoke almost simultaneously, my voice could be heard over his. "What do you know that you're not telling me? And how is it that you also know what's good for me and what's not?"

"What questions you ask!" Now it was I who invaded his space, and he didn't like it. "I don't know anything about anything, Miranda." He stepped back and raised his hand to his forehead. I knew that gesture inside out. He was weaving a story–the story he wanted to sell me. He began the act calmly: "Miranda, my job is to look after the company's interests. You, more than anyone, know how hard Norman has worked to build this. He wouldn't want Medika to be affected by his personal situation."

I relaxed my jaw and shoulders and moved away a few inches.

"Yes, yes, Ethan. Whatever. You're not going to convince me with that story. You know or you at least have suspicions about what happened to Norman. What kind of trouble are you both involved in?"

He voice went up again.

"There's no trouble here! I already told you. I don't know anything. I just do my job: watch over the interests of the company. I recommend that you lower you guard with me, Miranda. Don't forget, I'm your ally, always! I'm not looking to cause you any harm."

I made a disrespectful display of false reverence.

"Whatever you say, *ally*." A look of anger accompanied the brief silence. "I would appreciate it if you review the employee memo that Alex drafted. If you approve it, authorize its distribution."

He dared question me when he saw me taking my purse and cell phone.

"Where are you going?"

I stopped right when I was about to open the door. I turned and responded, because answering his questions must have been included in his *instructions*.

"Hell!" I opened the door.

"I hope it goes well!"

The uproar behind me left him speechless.

Eliezer

Why do they think that it matters to me that he's dying? If they only knew that is what I've wanted my whole life...

Chapter 4

$\mathcal{O}$ne week after the accident, Norman still wasn't showing signs of improvement. I signed in at the intensive care unit window. That night, a nurse whom I had not seen before was in charge of issuing visitation authorizations.

"Name of patient?"

"Norman Clausell." She directed her attention to the endless list of patients. A friendly smile formed on her face.

"You can see him now."

It wasn't until I had signed the paperwork she handed me that I rethought her words.

"What do you mean I can see him now? I know what the visiting hours are. Has someone else been here?" I was the only one authorized to see him.

"Some time ago, yes, a young man was asking about him."

"A young man? Who?" My face must not have conveyed friendliness.

"He left without telling me his name." She blushed. "He was very handsome, and he had light colored eyes."

The answer she gave me didn't seem very professional.

I was left with questions in my mind. *Who could it have been?*

"Thank you." I entered the doorway to the rooms.

In Norman's room, the medical devices created a terrifying symphony of sound. *A handsome young man was asking about you.* I couldn't stop thinking about that while looking at his swollen, injured face. *Could it have been Hernandez?*

I pulled up the only seat in the room and sat next to the bed. I had too many questions, and the only person who could give me answers was temporarily silenced.

"What have you done, Norman? What have you gotten into? What happened? When will you wake up? You need to organize your office, fire a few idle employees, fix your life and your affairs..." My sermon continued until a voice interrupted me.

"That's good of you to do. He needs a familiar and friendly voice, even though I fear that, for now, he won't wake up." She checked the IV line. "He's still under sedation."

I dried my tears.

"His progress is very slow, but look: the good news is that he's making progress."

I couldn't handle the joy I felt when hearing those words. I looked at Norman's face and smiled. New tears rolled down my cheeks. The doctor continued chatting, looking at me with a certain distance. As long as she was giving me news about Norman, I would put up with all of those looks and daily dramas that were certainly products of her imagination.

"The bleeding has stopped. Giving you a prognosis

would be very premature, but it's undoubtedly a good sign. If it continues like this, and if his brain swelling continues to improve, we can proceed with the operations to repair his bones."

I lowered my head as a gesture of appreciation. The doctor marched off and I went back to looking at Norman, combing his unkempt hair a little. He always liked looking presentable.

Two weeks passed with no change in routine. Norman's progress was slow–very slow. At first, the nursing staff almost kicked me out when visiting hours were over. A few weeks later, they would become my friends. I would bring them doughnuts, coffee, and chatted with them. I could enter and stay as long as I pleased. Surely they thought I was his fiancée, or his lover. Why would anyone else stay by their boss' side day and night? I asked myself what kinds of rumors were spreading: their conclusions had to be unspeakable. No one knew the truth. No one knew our past. Doctor Martinez had the questions of a gossip written in her eyes. I never wanted to provide more information than she already had. I never felt like giving her an explanation.

Even though Norman was a very successful man who had accumulated a great fortune due to his extraordinary capacity for business, he never lost his way: although his negotiation skills earned him many enemies, he contributed to improving the lives of whomever would cross his path. Nevertheless, according to Norman, the only real enemies a person could have are poverty and corruption.

And there is something more that attracts me to this man, but I wouldn't know how to describe it...

***

Sleepless nights at the hospital were taxing. Fatigue stayed with me by daytime and not even a ton of makeup hid the darkness that seeped through under my eyes. Luckily, I no longer saw the detective, apart from the two times that we met and he updated me on the steps taken to contact Norman's family. In short, he was unsuccessful.

During that time, Ethan and Alex succeeded in calming the media, who did nothing but attempt to obtain information on Norman's health–perhaps an exclusive would increase their ratings. After a few days, the media stopped trying. Other events in the political realm occupied the front pages of the country. I never thought I would have reason to be thankful for politicians.

Medika projects continued on their way. Decisions that Norman generally made fell to me instead. I must confess: before making decisions, I would go to his room and tell him about proposals, announcements, and requests. I would consult him first, even though he couldn't respond. His space in the hospital was converted into my space for peace, for philosophizing, and for making thoughtful decisions.

When good news arrived that the swelling in his brain had diminished sufficiently to take him off the medication that kept him sedated, it gave me an incomparable happiness and I thanked god a thousand-and-one times.

One of those evenings, on the third day after taking him off the sedatives, something unexpected happened. I had covered his bed with paperwork. I was looking for a way to increase distribution of our products and services.

"Do you think that we should do business with the distributor in El Salvador? I think that…"

He said in a whisper, coughing slightly, "No, no

chance in h...ell."

The emotion was so overwhelming that the shock made me trip on the IV cart. I almost yanked out his catheters. I kissed his hand. I kissed his cheeks. My tears drenched his face.

"Calm down." The cough interrupted him, but I didn't stop hugging him. "For God's sake, Miranda, this is harassment."

We shared a laugh. My much-loved Norman had returned to life. I pushed the nurse call button and the room filled with people in less than a minute. I had to leave while doctors and nurses gave him thorough evaluations. My emotions were so strong that I wanted to share them with someone.

I thought about calling Ethan, but I gave up. Once I lose confidence in someone, it's nearly impossible for that person to restore it. I called the one person I should never have called.

"Inspector Hernandez," he answered. His voice was accompanied by the crazy sound of sirens.

"Hello," was the only thing I could think of saying.

"Miranda?" Did he recognize my voice or did he see my number on his cell phone screen?

"Yes. Sorry, it's that..." I had doubts about continuing the call.

"Miranda, is everything fine?" The tone of his voice reflected consternation and surprise.

"Yes. Norman just woke up."

He fell silent. Only the sound of sirens could be heard.

When he reacted, his voice sounded more relaxed.

"That's very encouraging, Miranda."

"Yes..." I repeated, and I found myself at a loss for words. "The doctors are conducting a routine evaluation on him. I need to hang up. I only wanted to share the great news with someone. Thank you."

He must have imagined that I was smiling.

"No, no. Thank you for sharing this with me! We'll see each other later at the hospital. I still need to interview Mr. Clausell."

When he hung up, a thought invaded my mind and bothered me for the rest of the evening. *Should I have called Hernandez?*

***

I couldn't stand it, when I realized that Norman was fine and that he seemed to be out of danger, I pressed him for an explanation. At first, I did it subtly, with the passing of days there was less subtlety in my insistence. I needed to know what happened. What caused the accident that almost sent him to his next life? He never lost his cool. Every time I asked him, he always responded with the same words: "It was an accident, Miranda. Accidents happen and one happened to me. Let's forget the past and live in the present." There was no trace of worry in his words, so, why should I worry? Probably because there was something in his eyes that I could not decipher with certainty. Could it be guilt?

The pace of Norman's improvement slowed over the passing days. On various occasions I had to inform Hernandez that my friend was still not ready for an interview, and that doctor Martinez didn't approve either.

He surprised me at the entrance to Norman's room where entry was restricted. Hernandez was a lawman, and wouldn't do it without the necessary authorization. You could see determination in his face. His eyes told me that he already had been patient, that he deserved answers and, that morning, he was willing to get them.

"I don't want to intrude, Miranda, but I have a duty to perform."

That sweet voice that he used could easily convince me if I didn't maintain my guard. *If you told me to drop my pants or lift my skirt, I wouldn't think twice.*

"I understand, but..." I paused, "understand me. *My* duty is to look out for Norman's health."

"And why is that your duty?"

A real answer was overdue. Hernandez was another one on the list of those that did not understand what it was that united Norman and I: an intimate relationship, of course, but not *that* kind. It wasn't easy to remain fixed on his eyes, nor confess the truth.

"Because that man is the only family I know. He has looked after me, he has been my mentor, my friend, and almost my father... for more than twenty years." His eyes still looked for another answer. "And no! I am not his fiancée, nor his lover, nor his...!" I didn't say the last word that I was thinking. Even though that was the response that he expected, it surprised him. I felt the presence of some curious eyes on us. I didn't look at anyone. I lowered my voice. "Are you satisfied?" The expression on his face was like gold. The words choked him. "You have no reason to look at me that way. That is the big question that everyone here asks. Congratulations! You have the exclusive. Now, if you'll allow me, I must get back to Mr. Clausell."

Without giving him time to let out the words that got stuck in his throat, I moved away. I expect that he understood that the man who had been on the verge of going to a better place was one of the two people whom I trusted completely, who, as far as I knew, behind all of those machines, had the most noble heart on the planet, who had always believed in me, and had given me opportunities that would have otherwise been impossible if he hadn't been there.

***

Norman spent more time awake than sedated. The surgeries were successful, but the titanium rods in each leg caused him so much pain that they sometimes had to give him powerful painkillers.

"How are things going at the office?" The question conveyed a complaint.

"Why does the office matter, Norman? Everything is under control."

He laughed.

"I know that you must have everything under control. It's just that I can't stop worrying. You must go rest. You know? Look at the time!"

He embellished his authoritative tone. He definitely was getting better every time.

"I'm fine," but the yawn gave me away.

He laughed again.

"Have you seen the circles under your eyes?"

"Thanks for the compliment, Norman. I don't know why I'm inclined to keep you company, if you've gone back to being as insufferable as you were before…"

The criticisms were silenced by a cough and another even more irritating complaint.

"Miranda, go get some rest."

"See? You can't even speak very much. Don't worry. You are the one who needs rest. Get comfortable. Do you want me to look for more blankets? I brought a book to read to you."

This time, he didn't laugh.

"Perfect! Now I am back to being a boy." He was about to lose. He had nothing to gain by arguing further. He had nowhere to go.

Making myself comfortable in the chair that had become my friend, I put up my feet and rested them on the edge of the bed.

"Look, Margaret says that these are your favorites." I showed him the cover of the book that Margaret gave me. I remembered that on various occasions, she mentioned that what he most liked doing in the little free time he had was to enjoy some good wine and read poetry.

"Oh, good choice!" A half smile appeared on the face that bore the marks of the abuse that he had sustained.

"Good taste comes from a good teacher." I shrugged my shoulders, even though poetry was something that generally traveled on roads that were totally alien to me.

I began reading *Amar sin Motivos*, or *Loving without*

Reasons by De Lorenzo Roman.

I have no reasons to love,

I love because I love,

With no reason to hold onto

The passion that I give and don't demand.

***

Loving for something, for a reason,

Is not loving from the soul,

Nor is putting the phrases or their meanings

Where calmness abides.

***

If you ask me why

I would not know how to reply

Because I don't know from where there comes

So much and so much love…

Those were my words, feeling confident with each verse to the end. As I raised my eyes, overwhelmed by an innate modesty, I encountered a man lost and nestled in those words. Seven nights passed the same way while poetry and Norman transported me to another world–the world where feelings became verse.

***

One night, while leaving the office, dead tired, I stopped by the hospital to read to Norman a little. What began as therapy for him transformed into therapy for me. Fatigue was wearing me out. Neither MAC nor Sephora could work the miracle of concealing it. At Norman's insistence, I lay down at his side. The level of discomfort grew and it bothered me until I noticed that a void in me was filled with the closeness. Suddenly, in a hesitant voice, Norman pronounced her name.

"Isabel."

There she was… his wife: a very elegant woman with dark hair, whose features conveyed a fine lineage. Her skin seemed of Lladro porcelain. Her silhouette did not reflect what must have been her age, about fifty-five, and I had her right in front of me, standing at the doorway to the room contemplating the scene: her husband sharing a hospital bed with a stranger.

My heart beat so rapidly that if it were connected to the monitors that were connected to Norman during the first part of his hospital stay, the alarms would have startled the nursing personnel. I didn't know what to do. While seconds passed, I hesitated.

I got up, but I remained seated on the bed.

"Wow, Norman, you really are doing much better." Oh, her tone said it all.

But what right did she have to come here, after so many years? I looked at Norman, trying to anticipate his reaction, which surprised me more than his wife's greeting.

"Isabel, this is Miranda."

"Miranda Wise? The International Business Director?" She asked with a frown, even though no wrinkles appeared on her face. *Could it be the Botox?*

"And a good friend," Norman emphasized.

I extended my hand out to shake hers. She looked at

it and ignored my cordiality.

This was definitely one of those moments that I had to add to the list of the *most uncomfortable moments of my life,* a list I secretly maintained because it inspired me to be able to survive similar events.

I admonished myself: *I am such a fool for trying to be friendly with the woman…*

Just as I reached out to her, I pulled back, and grabbed my purse.

"It's late. Good night." Without caring about what his wife thought, I kissed his cheek.

From the doorway, when turning to catch a final glimpse of the room and those in it, I perceived the anger on Norman's peaceful face.

"Good night to you, Miranda. Rest. You need it." He smiled, and made things worse. "And please, my apologies for Isabel's lack of manners."

I said nothing. I didn't even look at the woman before leaving.

While I was finding my way to the hospital exit, my wandering mind imagined various ways I should have reacted. *Sure, now you can think clearly because you're not under pressure.* Just as I was in the middle of those thoughts, I tasted the cold, humid floor.

I had tripped on one of those sandwich board signs that advise walking carefully around a wet floor. Reluctantly, I got up and continued walking when someone grabbed my arm. It was a rough hand–not at all delicate.

"You forgot your book," said the owner of the hand.

There they were in the palm of his other hand… the

poems that, on past nights, had further united Norman and me.

"It fell along with you," he insisted with an invisible smile.

His voice was rough, deep, and attractive. I looked up to put a face on the voice.

I found myself facing a dark gaze, engraved in the most beautiful green eyes I had ever seen in my life. The features were of a man of strong character, and he had a beard... oh, darn... a seductive beard, one abundant enough for my taste, which highlighted his mysterious pupils even more! I had before me the kind of man that can intimidate with a look, and no one questions what he says or does. The sensation that it aroused in me felt familiar.

"Thank you," was the phrase I could muster.

Under other circumstances, maybe I would have stayed to flirt with him, to read to him, possibly some poetry and, perhaps, something more. The opportunity and the prospect were worthy... *but not today, not tonight.*

Eliezer

I don't know what the hell I'm doing here. She drags me around to where I don't want to be with her damned insistence.

Chapter 5

$\mathcal{M}$y cell didn't stop ringing. Something had happened. I adjusted the air conditioning vents toward me while the stewardesses delivered the pre-flight instructions. I turned it off when it rang again. It was Ethan. I didn't care about what he had to tell me or his recriminations. It took Medika months to arrange this meeting and I couldn't ruin it. This trip was important–so important that, if we got the expected contracts, Medika would be the biggest in the business. More than business, we would be improving access to health services for people who don't have the same opportunities as we do–yes, on this side of the map where we mistakenly take so many things for granted.

It's not every day that one meets with a nation's health minister.

During the flight, the movie that I chose turned out to be boring. Perhaps because the only thing I did was think about the fact that I never got a chance to speak to Norman about his wife's visit. I also didn't feel like I had the confidence to do it. But why did she return? Where had she been for so long? Where had she been for the last two months? Where had she been for the last twenty years?

Did she really think that there was more than a

business and friendly relationship between Norman and I? What did she think of me? What did she think of Norman?

***

It was my second day in a Latin American country. When the meeting was over, I dialed Ethan's number. He picked up, but didn't begin speaking to me right away; rather he apologized to those at his meeting, which wasn't as important as mine, of course.

"Ah! Took you long enough!" I smiled, because he didn't abandon his sarcastic tone even at long distance.

"What's going on, Ethan? I was with the Minister…" He interrupted me.

"I don't care, Miranda. You need to come back immediately!" Something important was definitely happening, and it was not the meeting that he had arranged, that I repeat, was not as important as my own.

"Why? Has Norman gotten worse?"

"Norman has gone crazy! Does that count?" He paused his speaking to think, to explain as well as his stress could allow. "Miranda, Medika has undergone a form of coup d'etat!"

For a few seconds, confusion dominated my thoughts.

"What are you saying, Ethan?"

"Your beloved Norman has named his son, Eliezer, President of the company! That stranger bastard is our boss!" He announced, finally, and because I couldn't seem to react, he started talking again. "The jet is on its way to pick you up. Be sure to be at the airport at six o'clock. Please, Miranda, be punctual."

Alone, my thoughts attacked me. *But what can you do, Miranda? He's his son, and moreover, Norman is the principal*

72

shareholder in the company. He can name whomever he wants to any position, even though that might put his mental capacity in question.

I called Norman.

He picked up on the first ring.

"Hello, Miranda. How are you?"

"I'm fine, Norman." I lied. "How are you?"

I noticed relief in his voice.

"Much better, thank you. Tomorrow they'll be releasing me. They are going to transfer me to the rehabilitation center to begin therapy."

"Then I'm going to come by in the morning to help you." It wasn't a question, it was an assertion.

"No, Miranda, don't worry, Isabel will help me."

Isabel? His wife? It took me a few seconds to continue the conversation. I must admit that it took some work for me to get used to hearing him pronounce that name: Isabel.

"Say no more. Let me know if you need me."

"As I always do, Miranda. Thank you. Thank you very much."

That he would hang up so quickly surprised me. Norman is not one of those people that presses the "END CALL" button while saying goodbye. He likes to take a few seconds, even if only as a courtesy.

He didn't ask me the obligatory question, a habit that, in reality, was his personal way of saying hello. He didn't ask me where I was as far as the country. He didn't say those words that always managed to make me feel at home. "Hello, traveler. In what part of the world do you find yourself today?" The events seemed more confusing

73

to me each time–much more confusing.

***

The return flight was like a dream. It came so quickly, barely the next day after my arrival, at the end of the day of meetings. Everything seemed distant... hazy. It had been months that I hadn't been using the Medika private jet. Commercial flights seemed more pleasant and safe, but I couldn't deny the comfort of the Gulfstream G650. It's not that I'm an expert on airplane models, but Norman required me to memorize the model name so that every time I was overwhelmed by the hassle of commercial flight, I would remember the comfort that I was rejecting. It was a beautiful jet, with a white leather interior, an eight passenger maximum, and four crewmembers. I prefer commercial flights to maintain a lower profile. Norman, on the other hand, would, at times, lose his patience with me for preferring commercial flights. "This toy has cost me sixty million dollars and you prefer the hassle," he would tell me.

I couldn't overcome the exhaustion that had become my faithful companion during the past two months. I remained in the arms of Morpheus until landing.

I awoke with a jolt from an untimely source of turbulence: the plane touching down on the runway. I did no more than step down the small metal stairs and got into my car with a destination fixed in my mind: the hospital.

I wanted to see Norman, and moreover, give him another opportunity to confess the truth about what was happening.

I arrived at his room and he was reading a book at the

edge of the bed. When hearing my greeting, he set it aside.

"Miranda?"

It was so strange! Each time that he spoke my name, it made me feel good, including when the reason he mentioned it was not pleasant.

"Hello, Norman."

The calmness in his voice was confirmation that he felt peaceful… very peaceful…too peaceful… and that scared me.

"Come, sit down." He indicated a space next to him on his bed.

"Are you sure? I don't want to impose on anyone."

"Calm down. If you're saying that about Isabel, don't worry. Come!"

I hesitated, but I ultimately sat down.

"Weren't you in El Salvador?" he asked, putting a hand on one of my shoulders.

Who told him where I was?

"I just landed." I took the book that he had in his hands. *I Won't Go Without Telling You Where by Laurent Gounelle.* "How's the reading?"

"Inspirational." A sigh accompanied his response. "And how were the meetings? How's the Minister?"

"The meetings… very good… productive. We were on the verge of sealing the deal. The Minister is fine. He sends you greetings and wishes for a prompt recovery. He said, by the way, that you still owe him a visit to the ranch. Can you believe that he dared say that he wanted to introduce me to one of his sons?"

Norman laughed.

"That man never changes. Be careful on those adventures. You know how they can end."

That advice was a way of saying, "Don't even think about it, Miranda Wise!" The truth is that it wasn't the first time that I was made that kind of offer in a business context. Norman had taught me to take them as compliments, so that's how I took them.

"You know that I don't play with fire."

"Weren't you supposed to be back on Friday?" He fixed his eyes on mine. He wanted to capture my physical and verbal reaction: the whole response.

"Yes. Some unforeseen events arose and I had to advance my schedule." I tried to maintain my poker face... so *Ethan.*

"Unforeseen events at Medika?"

"No. My own." I had no other choice but to lie. I couldn't tell him that my hurried return was related to the appointment of Eliezer.

"Can I help you with something?" That question seemed more of an assertion that he knew that my return went hand in hand with his sudden decision.

"Don't worry. I have everything under control..." I didn't take my eyes off of his. Knowing him, that would confirm his suspicion.

"They told me that I have a new boss," I let out. I had to say it because, if I didn't, the curiosity would finish me off. I tried not to sound sarcastic. He knew me very well.

His eyes lit up.

"In fact, yes: Eliezer, my son."

It was a strange moment. Perhaps, after all, I didn't expect that answer. It was the first time that I heard Norman utter his son's name. I never opened the door to know that side of him that was so mysterious. The curiosity brought me to ask him about his personal life at least once a year. I always got the same answer: "It would be better to talk about the present."

"And you didn't think of telling me?" It was difficult for me to conceal my disgust.

"I'm telling you now."

There was no reason to argue. Norman already made his decision, and I hadn't the faintest idea why. What I did know was that there was no going back.

My eyebrows rose–an involuntary reaction when rejecting a response... to the thoughtlessness.

"Come, lie down and rest a while."

A-ha! Look at how I lie by your side, Norman. That would not lighten the load of baggage that I carried, nor the fatigue, and would certainly have terrible repercussions if his wife were to spy on us secretly through the doorway. If there were something that he had taught me, it was learning from my mistakes.

I heaved a sigh.

"I have to go, Norman. I have several things I need to do. I'll see you tomorrow evening." I took my purse and began to walk toward the door, formulating my next question without worrying about what his response would be.

"Sure, Miranda. I'll look for you tomorrow."

He really wanted my company. Anyway, I was the only company that he has had in years. Before crossing the threshold, I turned around.

"Only one more thing, Norman. What is Eliezer like? It seems that at the very least you owe me a recommendation."

The man sitting in the hospital bed laughed.

"Understand that I don't know. I think that in time you'll have tell *me*."

That response left me speechless. Those words assured me that I had no idea what he was doing. *How the hell do you leave the reins of your life's work to a stranger?* Although he was his son, Norman didn't know Eliezer. He didn't know anything at all about this man who shared his blood!

What was happening? As much as I tried, I couldn't understand the reasons for the decision. I approached Norman again. I didn't take my eyes off him. I wanted to analyze every clue that his body language could give me.

"What's going on, Norman?" I asked in a calm and empathic tone.

"Nothing is going on, Miranda. It's a decision I made… period."

His face didn't give off even the smallest signal of regret or doubt. *Another one of Ethan's good disciples?*

"Norman, excuse me, but I don't understand. I am trying to find logic in your actions, but I can't. Please forgive my indiscretion. It's that it worries me that you are making decisions at such a vulnerable time."

He signaled to keep quiet with a hand gesture.

"The answers to your questions are simple. I was at death's door. My son reappears in my life, and I want him to be able to have what I built for him. Is it the best decision? I don't know, but I can't run the risk of not doing it while I have this second chance at life."

"I understand," and I said nothing more.

I lowered my eyes so that he wouldn't be able to hear what my eyes were screaming at him: *How wrong you are, Norman. What an insensitive mistake you're making. Why didn't you name me?*

"That's why I need you there," he continued explaining. "You have been with me for so many years. You know the essence of what we want to do with Medika better than anyone: what is our mission, our philosophy, that is, what we want to do other than make money."

I sighed while I rolled my eyes.

"I need you to trust me, Miranda."

Again, those screaming eyes: How can I trust you, Norman? A lie crossed my lips—maybe it was a compassionate lie.

"You know that you have my trust, Norman." A pause brought me to confess part of the truth to him. "Even though I cannot stop thinking that the accident has affected your mind."

"I am very conscious of the decisions that I have taken. I am conscious of the pros and cons. Come, sit with me again."

I neared him and, under protest, I sat down. I felt like

a little girl to whom her father was explaining why he gave her favorite toy to one of her brothers.

He took my chin in his right hand, and with care, he lifted my face, tilting it toward him. I could feel my heart beating stronger and an alarm fired up in me. Something in this scene wasn't right. Although Norman was no more than a father to me, the twenty year age difference, at that moment, didn't seem noticeable or significant. He was an elegant man with fair skin. The expressive lines on his face accented his firm and decisive gaze. The silvery shimmers in his hair were like a painted on armor that made him look invincible. In short order, a sense of guilt overwhelmed me when my hormones gave indications of being affected by him. My wiser self would excuse me, telling me that it was alright, because, ultimately, we were not united by any blood ties.

"I need you, Miranda."

It wasn't right. He knew that I could not, that I wouldn't have the guts to give a negative response to an "I need you" from him.

"You know that I will always be here for you."

He withdrew his hand from my face and put it in my hand.

"Go and rest because tomorrow a new day awaits you."

Suddenly, I stopped believing that he didn't know what his son was like. He knew very well what he was tossing me into, and, in time, I succeeded in deciphering the fight against remorse that he carried on his face.

I got up off the bed.

"Count on me," I repeated, just in case I managed to

convince myself that we were both doing the right thing. "As always, count on me. We'll talk tomorrow. You should rest."

His lips drew out a smile. I reciprocated, but only halfway.

Chapter 6

"*It's* about time you answered," scolded Alex.

"What is wrong with you? I'm not your wife. I don't need to answer after the first ring."

"Did you just get up? I've been calling you since ten o'clock last night and it's eight in the morning." I struggled to understand his muttering.

"Is something going on? Why are you speaking that way?"

"If you read your blessed messages, you would have noticed that the new boss has called for a meeting of the board today at eight o'clock in the morning."

I moved the phone away from my ear to check the time on the screen.

"Eight o'clock? Damn it, Alex! I'll be there in half an hour. Tell them that I'm on my way, and there's traffic. Make up whatever you want!"

I checked the cell phone and it had, indeed, several missed calls from him, and some text messages letting me know about the scheduled board meeting. This was going to cost me. Surely Alex would make me repay him by making me take him to happy hour. Since he's been a married man, Elisa, his wife, wouldn't let him go out with anyone else but me and he had to come back early–so he never wasted an opportunity to do something extra for me so that I would have to pay him back. If it weren't for my eternal savior, Alex, I probably would have slept for several consecutive days. *Stay positive*, that would be my mantra for the day. I got in the shower and I think that I broke the Guinness world record for getting dressed and getting out.

When I got to Medika, Alex was waiting for me in the parking lot, opposite the main entrance. I figured he was alone because the others were in the conference room.

"Hello, Al…"

"You've finally arrived!" Alex told me in an interrupted whisper.

I couldn't contain my laughter. His eyes opened wide.

"Why are you laughing?"

"Your voice." I imitated his mutterings, as if the others could hear me from my car.

"If you could see the man's face, you would swallow that mockery."

"Is everyone there?" I was hoping that I wasn't the only one to arrive late. "I'll buy myself a coffee and I'll go in. Go and ask him whether he wants a coffee."

His eyes opened up even wider.

"Ask who?"

"The boss, who else?"

The morning was too beautiful to ruin my day so early. It wouldn't be the first time nor the last that someone arrived late to a meeting. Furthermore, that someone was not anyone.

"Are you crazy? I don't think that buying coffee would be a good idea. Hurry up!"

"I want to make a good impression. Remember that this new boss thing is new to me."

As soon as I said that to Alex, I thought the better of it. If I would be arriving late, I needed to have enough caffeine in my body to deal with the day ahead of me. I thought about the possible scenarios that would surround my triumphant late arrival, but then I decided that it was not worth worrying about. I wouldn't put even a tiny bit of the stress that I had suffered in the past few months in my system for being thirty minutes more late.

"On second thought, Alex, I think I'm going to need that coffee. Tell them that I'm still on my way."

I got into my car and drove off to get my coffee. When I got back, a change in the Medika parking lot caught my attention. Norman's son didn't have bad taste: he drove a Nissan GT-R. The letters on the back of the pearl white car distracted me. Getting out of my car, I slung my purse over my right shoulder, dragged my computer case with my left hand, and my cup of coffee with the other. I entered at full speed, as always, through the back door. My cell phone rang but I had no third hand to delve into my purse. It was a circus-juggling act: holding the coffee, carrying case, purse, keys, answering the telephone, and getting to the meeting.

"Shit, shit, shit, shit!"

I tripped on something in front of me, and got the coffee all over me. I burned my hands and chest. I looked up and discovered that I hadn't hit a wall, unless the wall had toffee-colored hair, a goatee, fair skin, an annoyed look on his face, and didn't stop saying the word "shit."

This must be Eliezer. But... those eyes? That look?

"Damn it! Look at what you've done!" He shook off the coffee that was dripping from his hands and jacket.

"Oh! I'm sorry!" I apologized while I looked for a wet wipe in my purse to help him clean himself off. *This will solve it and he'll thank me. Who wouldn't sell their soul for one of these when they're in a hurry?* "Let me clean you off."

I lifted one of the wipes up toward his jacket, but he raised his hands as a signal to stop–that he didn't want me to help him, much less touch me. I was dumbfounded. I put the wipe in my other hand, still humid and sticky from the coffee, and began to extend it toward him. He begrudgingly snatched the wipe away from me.

"Really, I'm sorry," I apologized again. "Are you Norman's son?" I asked to slightly lower the tension that my trip had caused.

"Eliezer Clausell, President."

I sensed that his words were more of a scolding than a greeting. Oh, that wasn't good! Half an hour with a title and he was already delineating hierarchical boundaries.

"And you are?" he asked with an apparent intention of delighting in the answer that I would give him. He'd put the name on a personal blacklist.

"Miranda Wise," I looked him in the eye and again extended my hand to consummate the glorious moment of meeting him. My name succeeded in attracting his attention, but it was not enough to avoid having my hand extended and ignored, hanging in mid air. He continued cleaning his jacket.

"International?" A contemptuous tone surrounded the

question. How was I supposed to take that?

"Correct. You can call me International, Miranda, Director of International Business, or whatever you like." I used an informal tone with every intention that he understand that I didn't think much of that hierarchy stuff and treating people formally.

"I'm going to my washroom to see if I can fix this disaster. I want you in my office in fifteen minutes."

"In Norman's office?" I asked, but he stopped and nailed me to the wall with just a look.

"My office," he clarified, and repeated.

Eliezer went on his way to Norman's office that, like any presidential office, had a private washroom. I turned around and made my way to mine.

Alex waited for me by the door. I put my purse in his hands and what was left of my cup of cappuccino. The guffaws were fighting to leave his mouth.

"You fucked up, right?"

"Did you see what happened?" Alex nodded. "Yes, Alex. I fucked up really good."

***

I tried to remove the coffee residue from my blouse and jacket without success. I took off my shoes to clean them and clean off my feet, because the droplets of coffee had gone that far. I was a mess. Alex tried to help me. My anxiety and nerves were obvious. Our hands collided.

"Fine! Then I won't help you." He threw up his hands in frustration.

I sighed and lowered my guard.

"I'm sorry, it's just that it makes me angry that this

was the first impression that he would have of me… as a klutz."

"You don't have to apologize to me. You arrive late on the first day that there's a new boss and this happens. Let's see how you do now…" The answer didn't make me feel better. I grimaced.

"I still ask God why you continue to work with me…"

"Because you adore me," he smiled, "and because I rescue you from every problem."

That was very true. It was impossible to be unpredictable with him. He always had everything 'under perfect control,' like Maxwell Smart.

"And what was it that happened to you? Didn't you see him? The guy is big enough, Miranda. It's impossible for you not to have seen him from the parking lot."

We exploded in laughter.

Eliezer was, in fact, a very tall man, especially when compared to my height of 5 feet 4 inches. The new boss had to be six feet tall. How could he have passed by unnoticed?

I gave up on the blouse. The large brown stains and the smell of coffee might stay with me the whole day. However, I quickly remembered that, in the car, I had a long black dress.

"I still have the luggage from the trip in the trunk. Do you think you could bring it to me?"

It was a chore for him to find the keys in my purse. He complained by the doorway.

"Such a heavy purse, and I bet that ninety percent of

its weight comes from things that you'll never use."

"Get going! That's none of your business!"

He threw up his hands and left the office.

***

Dressed in a black dress, without the smell of coffee and with a notebook in hand, I made my way to Norman's office, or more accurately, Eliezer's. My nerves warned me of their possible betrayal at any moment. It didn't seem possible that one simple coffee would incite so much hostility in a human being. I paused and breathed deeply before touching the door.

Stay positive, Miranda.

"Come in," he ordered upon hearing me knock at the door.

His voice was similar to his father's, but more intense. I opened the door slowly and there he was, with discomfort and annoyance all over his face. He had changed into a short-sleeved shirt. I took a seat at the conference table that Norman had in his office. With a hand gesture, he ordered me to sit at one of the seats in front of his desk. He didn't have the manners to meet with me at the conference table.

In negotiating etiquette, one doesn't sit to speak with anyone from behind a desk, much less for a first time conversation. A desk is a barrier that interferes with friendliness and creates a certain distance. *Unless that's the message you want to convey*, I thought. I made myself comfortable in one of the chairs. Without warning, I apologized for the third time.

"I really regret what happened." Maybe words of submission would help break the ice. "I didn't see you."

"You certainly didn't. It must have been because you

were in such a hurry." He leaned forward, a gesture that seemed inquisitive.

"In fact, yes." I presumed he was waiting for an explanation for my tardiness.

The truth is that I didn't hear my alarm clock. I went to bed late and the fatigue… If you want, I'll lift up my dress right here so that you can spank me a few times.

That was enough! I gave him what he wanted: acknowledging the tardiness.

"I imagine that the reason for your tardiness must have been a priority for you."

And who does this so-and-so think he is? Idiot, what kept me on the edge of physical exhaustion these last months has been Norman Clausell and Medika.

I wanted to tell him all of that. Obviously it wasn't the correct response for the moment. I perceived that Eliezer was testing me and I would not let him take me there.

"Yes, very important," I answered without giving him any more details. "What did I miss?"

Eliezer sat up and his eyes could not hide the surprise that my question and carefree tone caused. He raised his eyebrows–a sign that he didn't understand what I was referring to. Seeing him seated there, I could see how large Norman's chair was for him. He wasn't his father, and thank God, his father wasn't he.

"At the meeting, what did you talk about?" I clarified.

"We agreed that tomorrow at eight o'clock you'll present me with a report on the state of business in the international division." He enjoyed every word. He savored them.

"It would be my pleasure to provide you with the information you're requesting, but having the list ready for tomorrow would be complicated. I just got back from traveling, and I have some pending priority issues to which I have to attend." It was the truth; I didn't make up those issues.

"See? That is precisely what was lost!" He paused, bit his lower lip and his fangs looked menacing. "We lost the opportunity to negotiate such things." His lips twisted in an expression of mockery. I took note that his face had a trace of some of Norman's expressions, but not the arrogance that exuded from his pores.

"So make it tomorrow at eight o'clock in the morning, then."

This guy would not ruin my day. *Who am I fooling? He already succeeded in ruining my day.* I don't know how I would do it–how I would present the information that he asked for on time. I wasn't willing to play his game. It was obvious that, like a dog, he was marking his territory, making it clear who was in charge now.

"Anything else?" I asked, getting up, out of the chair.

It wasn't worth staying in his presence another second longer. I imagined that we wouldn't agree on a single word.

"No. For the moment, that's all."

He didn't look at me, not when he responded, nor when I turned around to leave. He was too occupied looking over his iPhone. I imagined flying over his desk and adorning his face with a slap. I quickly returned to reality.

"I am standing by for your orders for whatever you

need," I announced from the doorway.

***

Never, ever, has anyone treated me so badly. That man was the antithesis of his father: an overbearing, arrogant, calculating idiot—a real jerk.

In my office, the cell phone wouldn't stop ringing. It was Norman.

"Hello, girl." He was in a good mood. That's what he called me when he was. "How is everything going at the office?"

"In short, last night I fell into bed exhausted. This morning, I almost couldn't wake up. Thanks to Alex, I woke up at eight. I arrived at the office late. I didn't make it to the meeting that Eliezer scheduled, and to top it off, I spilled my cappuccino on my new boss. What do you think?"

"That you're a disaster!" Laughter followed immediately. "You know what I think? That you need to go home, rest, and reintegrate into the world in the morning, when you will no longer be a menace to anyone."

Yes, he definitely was in a good mood.

"You know what I think? That I agree with you." I had to pretend that this day did not happen, because it wasn't a day in which I should linger.

"What do you think about Eliezer?" The mood of his words varied. The gritting of my teeth was like a filter against the complaints I wanted to make to him.

"Look, other than the coffee incident, all good." I asked Norman if he had already had contact with him, if he already knew whom he had put in charge. I had to ask.

"Have you spoken with him?"

"No," he answered vaguely.

"That is, before he took his position?" I restated.

"No, I never exchanged words with my son."

Then where did you get the idea to give him that position at Medika?

Norman interrupted my thoughts. He dismissed me quickly because he knew that I would continue insisting on asking questions about Eliezer.

"Go, go home, disconnect and rest. You need it."

"Yes…" A big yawn came out of my mouth. "I need to recharge my batteries. One more thing."

"Go ahead," he protested.

"Tomorrow I need to present Eliezer with a business review. How much do you want me to tell him?"

"I don't understand the question, Miranda."

"How much information do you want me to share with him? Do you trust him enough to share everything about Medika with him?"

His response was delayed.

"Miranda, Eliezer is the new president of Medika, the leader of the company, and as such, he must have access to as much information as he needs and is necessary to facilitate and sustain decision making at the firm."

"I understand." Although he couldn't see me, I lowered my head.

"And yes, I trust him." He surprised me, and although I didn't like hearing him say that, his words reflected confidence.

"Excuse me, only I… it's that…forget it. I understand, Medika must be an open book for Eliezer."

"Exactly. Now, go and rest." With that decree, he used that paternal tone that always comforted me.

I remembered that was the day that they were going to transfer him and that Isabel would accompany him.

I hung up. I would inform Eliezer that I would not be in the office for the rest of the day. After such cruel treatment, I would have to be crazy to stay!

I wrote a note that I left on my desk and took my things.

The note was to Alex:

Dear, I won't be available for the rest of the afternoon…

Eliezer

"This shirt is hopeless. And this is supposed to be easier. However, it's harder than I had thought. Here, time hasn't been passing. It seems like time has stopped at this firm, in this office, where every thing is in the same place... in the same damned place as I remember it."

Chapter 7

$\mathcal{A}$ new day and my batteries were recharged to one hundred percent. I slept sixteen hours without telephones or text messages–with only my bed and me. It was a bright morning, even though there was terrible traffic that was moving a drop at a time. My positive attitude lasted barely a few minutes: only until I remembered with whom I would have my first meeting of the day.

I turned on my cell, which also got its much-needed rest. I got twenty-six messages all at once. Ten were from Alex (letting me know about Eliezer's attitude and the information that he was requesting regarding the financial condition of the international division). There were others from members of my team and some clients. One was from Eliezer.

"Wise, they tell me that you are indisposed. Return my call."

What poor manners! Who does this guy think he is with that haughty attitude? I wouldn't let it bring me down. Nothing nor anyone would ruin my day or drain my energy.

***

I arrived before seven. I wanted to be ready for the

meeting. I didn't have much to prepare. I had the words in my mind. Nine years in charge of the division should be of some use to me.

There were no other parked cars there yet. Neither Eliezer, nor any of the directors had arrived. When I entered, I deactivated the alarm–confirmation that I was the first to arrive. Walking toward my office, I noticed something strange in the air, in the atmosphere, on Medika's walls.

The paintings!

They were gone. The paintings that Norman so treasured were gone! The paintings that bid me farewell every evening were gone!

A terrifying cold froze my hands. *And what if someone stole them? But when? Yesterday morning they were hanging here. Was it in the evening? At night? Impossible! The office alarm was active when I arrived. Who would dare do something like that?*

I jumped when I heard someone approaching.

"Margaret!"

"Good morning, Miranda." She always used the same relaxed tone during all of those years that she was dedicated to Norman, Medika, and me.

Margaret was a calm tempered woman but with an authority about her that was fit for the role she played. She had watched me grow up since Norman decided to take me on. She always told me how proud she felt. It was she who had covered women's issues with me–the real versions, of course, because, at the orphanage, the nuns would give me the moral versions. She kept scolding Norman because she blamed him for my lack of social life. "You give her so much work that you never let her live the life of someone of her age," she frequently told him. I had a lot of affection for her and I lived my life being thankful to her. While I was in school, when getting out of class, Norman, or she, would look for me at school and bring me to the Medika offices. She would take responsibility for helping me with homework and studying. Even though Norman paid her a separate salary for it, I know that she would have done it without compensation anyway.

"Miranda, are you ok?"

I let out a shriek from the surprise.

"The paintings, Margaret! What happened with Norman's paintings?"

"Well, the paintings..." her face said 'I'm sorry.' "Yesterday, Eliezer ordered them removed." From the informal way she spoke about him, I understood that her years of experience wouldn't allow her to feel intimidated by him. Notwithstanding, she removed the paintings. Wasn't that intimidation?

I'm sure that Margaret must have given Eliezer a big fight when he ordered her to remove the paintings. She knew every detail about everything related to Norman, both in his professional life, as well as his personal life. There were no doubts about her loyalty to Norman or Medika. Ethan often called her "the tomb," because she never spoke any more than necessary, nor did she ever reveal anyone's secrets.

"What? Why?" My tone was inquisitive... very inquisitive... too inquisitive. What reason would the usurper have to remove those paintings on his first day of work?

"Believe me. I tried to bring him to reason so that he

would understand what those paintings meant to Norman. He didn't care." She shrugged her shoulders as a sign of impotence.

In that case, the least that I could do was to assure myself that they were stored properly.

"Where are they?"

"In the spare accounting office."

"Can you do me a favor?" I paused to think. She waited for instructions: "Have them hung... all of them... in my office."

Margaret smiled a smile of confusion.

"You want the paintings to be stored in your office?"

"No. I want them to be hung on the walls," I said as I drew out the outline of a wall in the air with my hands.

"Let's see if I understand, Miranda. You want... all of the paintings... hanging in your office. All ten?" She verified the instructions with an incredulous tone.

"Yes, all ten." I confirmed.

Margaret said no more. She turned her back to me and walked toward the spare accounting office. I said her name and she turned around. I could read on her face that she was waiting for me to change my mind. She never was a woman for conflict or rebellion.

"Yes?"

She shot that look of consternation at me that conveyed how unfortunate the consequences of my insolence would be.

"Thank you."

Eliezer didn't have the faintest idea of what those

paintings meant to his father. To tell the truth, nor did I. One of the many times that I asked Norman about the paintings' origin and significance, he told me that they were a sort of compass that kept him going in the right direction, not by indicating the way he had to go, but by showing him the way not to go.

The paintings also had a certain value for me. If I had been born with the ability to express my emotions on a canvas, I would have painted those very ones. The dark colors, the whirlwind strokes, and the abstract forms frequently reflected my sentiments and moods. Every painting translated a specific sentiment, including even similar events that were encompassed in one sentiment: deception, passion, fury, sadness, loneliness, melancholy, and defeat.

The panorama of my professional life looked more difficult every time. Contrary to what I had first thought, when Norman decided to appoint him, I thought that Eliezer's path through Medika would be temporary and irrelevant. That was another one of my mistakes. From the first day, he made it very clear that he was the new Clausell in charge, that things would change, and that they would be done his way.

At eight o'clock in the morning, the conference room was almost ready. Margaret peeked through the window and gestured to let me know that the great Eliezer had arrived. I prepared myself mentally and asked God for the meeting to flow casually. I owed this to Norman, and it was my intention to be able to pay back my debt, or put more subtly, fulfill my promise.

I was concentrating on an e-mail on my computer screen when suddenly the hairs on my arms stood up.

Something told me that Eliezer was in front of the door. I didn't look up until I felt that he was already in the room with the door closed behind him. He had his jacket on, and that told me that he had not lingered in his office. His face shined with more confidence–he felt at home again.

"International."

For the second time, our encounter didn't start on the right foot. I could sense the condescension in his voice.

"Good morning, son of… Norman." There was very little difference between what I said and what I could have said in that last part of my greeting. He would never hurt me again. I would pay my debt to Norman, yes, but in my way and under my rules.

Eliezer didn't expect for me to respond that way. The half smile that accompanied his greeting had dissipated. He sat in the chair in front of mine.

"I heard that you were indisposed yesterday evening. Too much coffee?" he asked, pointing at my cup. "I see that you don't learn quickly."

"Nothing important," I answered, trying to veer off the direction in which he wanted to take me.

"For having left the office without answering calls, it must have been something important." He resisted leaving the topic.

I exhaled. I had no other weapons to use against him.

"In fact, yes. It was something important, for me." I put a period on the conversation, making it clear that I didn't have the slightest intention to give him explanations. "May I begin the presentation?"

"You have all of my attention," he looked at his watch,

"for now."

I began giving him the background on the international market, and the roles that I had assumed at Medika. For some ten minutes, he listened without interrupting. Notwithstanding, he didn't seem impressed. Rather, he analyzed my words, like a predator that stalks its prey, committing every movement to memory, and waiting for the slightest sign of weakness to attack.

"How long have you known Norman?" he asked unexpectedly, taking me by surprise. I stuttered and I couldn't regain my train of thought. Surely it was a trick so that I would lose my concentration and make a misstep. I responded as well as I could.

"It has been twenty-two or twenty-three years." I looked at his eyes, and I was quickly confused. It seemed like I was looking at Norman and not at his son. Eliezer didn't take his eyes off of me. Neither of us would succumb to the other's mercy. Someone had to give in. I did.

"Did you have any questions related to what I've presented to you up to now?"

"Yes. I have several. Let's see, where shall I start?" He scratched his jaw in a pensive and calculating gesture. "Why do we invest more in the international market than we do in the domestic market if the domestic market is more profitable?"

It surprised me that I considered his question to be a valid one.

"Because we work on projects that, from a long term perspective, bring sustainability to other countries and the firm."

"And why should I be betting my money on that

strategy, since, beyond any doubt, the domestic market still has a lot of room for growth, is less complex, and is more profitable for me?" His eyes returned to being fixed on mine without any sign of retreat.

"Because we have social commitments to less developed countries."

"Social commitments don't generate profits for me." The green of his eyes intensified just like Norman's would when we would argue.

"Social commitments define who we are."

"And who are we, Wise?"

The conversation took a personal turn. I must have seen it coming. One more time he succeeded in taking me off topic.

"Answer me, Wise! What in the devil are you?"

Should I answer? Why do I allow him to address me in such a rude manner?

"I am Miranda Wise, director of the international division. If that's not enough for you, go ask the first person who crosses your path. Certainly, anyone could tell you who I am. Who are you Eliezer?"

He bit the inside of his cheeks. The retort unsettled him.

"I am asking the questions."

A knot squeezed my throat. A void formed in my stomach. My breathing became labored. I didn't know how to respond. I couldn't show him any weakness because he would annihilate me.

"So, Eliezer, tell me who I am." I put the ball in his
104

court without knowing that it wasn't the best move.

"Do you really want me to tell you who you are? Do you really have the balls to hear what I think you are?"

I didn't lower my guard, but the damning violence in his words stunned me. He interpreted my silence as a 'yes.'

"You are no more than Norman's slut."

"What?!"

"You are Norman's stupid slut that he picked up and has used this whole time to serve his self imposed sentence."

The knot in my throat got tighter each time. The insults came without remorse. My eyes watered. What sentence?

It was time to put Eliezer in his place.

"I see that they have told you a lot about me. I confess that it flattered me. It made me feel important. Even so, no one has ever told me about you. Do you really think that I care about what you think of me? Yes, if it makes you happy to think that I am your father's whore, go ahead and think that I'm your father's whore. It doesn't matter much to me." I breathed as little as I could. The air felt hot in my mouth. "You think that I don't feel like slapping you so hard right now that it would make your head spin? Do you think I have any reason to tolerate your insults? You're mistaken, Eliezer Clausell, I am not going to play your stupid game."

He let loose a brief cackle that was dark and cold.

"If you're here, Miranda Wise, you have to play; otherwise, you go. Only, in this game, there are some rules... mine." He got up out of his chair and closed in on me. "Hear me, slut. If it were up to me, you wouldn't be here. I would have fired you even before stepping into this office."

He stopped a few inches from my face. I felt the heat that his body radiated and the anger and rage that possessed him. I lifted my head up to continue looking at him in the eye and seeing how the green of his irises seemed to darken with every word that he seemed to spit at me.

"And if you're such a ringmaster, why don't you fire me?"

He wiped his forehead with his hands.

"You must be very good at what you must do to Norman. You know? The old man gave me the liberty to do what I want with the company, except for one thing: to get rid of you. That's the one rule that I cannot control… for the moment."

He thought so, but he didn't intimidate me.

"Your vulgarities don't insult me, Eliezer. It's evident that you really don't know anything about me. If stay here listening to you speak your strings of idiocies, it would only be for one reason: your father. So we can do this in one of two ways: my way, or yours. My way is civilized and respectful, without taking the low road; or your way, the way of the troglodyte: arrogant and pretentious. If want to, I can be a real bitch. Believe me, it wouldn't take much effort, but that would make me the same as you. And if there is one thing I could be sure of after the few hours that I've known you, it's that I'm not at all like you. The only thing we have in common is your father, or on second thought, not even that. I forget that I indeed have had the privilege of being close to him the last twenty-something years, because I respect, admire, and appreciate him." I paused. "And you, what do you have in common with your father? What do you feel for him?"

I told several lies. I could never be like him. Some of the words that I externalized hurt me down in my soul. His eyes continued to be fixed on mine, but it wasn't me they were observing. They had been lost in an internal trip.

The sound of the cell phone brought him back to life. He took it out of his pants pocket and looked at the screen. He definitely used it as an excuse.

Coward, I was tempted to call him, but I didn't.

"This conversation isn't over, Wise." He looked me over–he didn't do it like a predator, but the way a warrior looks at an enemy when challenging them. I don't know if that fleeting sign made me feel good or bad.

"With pleasure, we'll pick up exactly where we left off, Eliezer."

As soon as he left the room, my legs collapsed and I fell seated in my chair. What the hell just happened? How did we get to this? Should I tell Norman or try to manage the situation. The last thing Norman needed was problems, but who else would open his eyes and admit to him what his imbecile of a son was doing?

***

A half hour later, Eliezer's insults continued grinding away in my mind. With Norman's paintings on the four walls around me, I felt immersed in each one of the sentiments that they expressed, drowning in that sea of torments. I, who was molded to tolerate anything in the business world, quickly felt… different. That protective layer that allowed me to not take things personally had weakened in a matter of less than five minutes. Eliezer really thought that I was his father's lover. He had treated me worse than if I had been, and that, that was personal, and it hurt.

My heart jumped in my chest with the abrupt sound of the opening door. I had my head on my desk, buried in my arms.

"What the hell are these paintings doing here."

Oh, not so fast… no. I lifted my head.

"Decorating, Eliezer, that's what they're doing." A better answer didn't occur to me. "Why are you interrupting me like this in my office? Wherever you're from, didn't anyone teach you any manners?"

I stood up, in my war stance.

He ignored my answer, and continued shouting.

"What are these paintings doing here? Margaret! Margaret!"

I heard the sound of her heels against the floor. She showed up in the doorway. Her face was pale. She, who always showed color in her cheeks, had the face of a corpse.

"Yes, Eliezer?"

He spoke to her amiably and calmly, with a tone of harmony.

"Margaret, excuse me for bothering you, but what are these paintings doing here?"

I would not allow Margaret to take the blame for my instructions. I walked toward them and interrupted their conversation.

"Margaret, you may go. I'll take care of this." I made a gesture for here to leave and close the door. We two enemies were left alone.

Eliezer's face was red with fury.

I spoke in a pleasant tone. Someone had to make peace.

"I ordered Margaret to hang the paintings."

"I want you to get them out of here!" He got too close, waving his hands in the air. I felt threatened.

"Why?" I asked.

He was so angry, he had trouble answering.

"I want these damned paintings out of here."

I crossed my arms.

"Why?"

"Because I'm giving an order!" he screamed. The imbecile screamed at me!

"You know what those paintings mean to Norman?" Now I was the one who got close to him, invading his space and security.

"I don't care what those shitty paintings mean. I don't want them here." He started waving his arms again. I felt like at any moment, he would lose his reason and hit me. I tried to reach his humanity.

"I've been witness to how Norman collected them. He treasures them. He has spent hours in front of these paintings, admiring them, and I'm not going to let you, on a whim, remove them from here. What about these paintings bother you so much?"

He pushed me out of his way with his arm. He began to throw the paintings down to the floor. He took one in his hands and smashed the canvas.

I couldn't stand the pain. In the nick of time I got to the second painting before he could destroy it. I confronted him and grabbed the painting by the other end. We looked like two kids at war over a toy. When he felt my resistance, he froze. I felt like he suddenly regained his reason.

His breathing settled down, the blood accumulated in his face dissipated, perhaps going back to his brain.

My soul was in pieces. I didn't care about showing him weakness. A tear rolled down my cheek.

"Surely, there are people watching and listening. I'm asking you, please, let's calm down."

He yielded. His hands let go of the painting. I let myself fall to the floor, straining to hold up the painting with my hands. Eliezer kept his eyes on me, waiting and wishing for me to burst into tears.

Another tear got away from me. I spoke in a voice that was barely audible.

"If the problem is that you don't want the paintings at Medika, I'll make sure that they won't be here anymore."

I put down the rescued painting and took the torn one in my hands, fumbling with the canvas, as though I would be able to put it back together. I don't know how much longer Eliezer stayed in my office. When I noticed that he moved away, I felt the tension of victory in the air that he left in his wake.

When the door closed, I exploded. I burst into tears. I was short of breath and had a powerful pain in my chest.

MIRANDA

In seconds, the door opened again.

"Miranda…" It was Margaret's voice. "Are you ok?"

"What do you think?"

Margaret helped pick me up off the floor. That was no place for me, it never was, and never would be, despite the arrival of that cursed man.

"What was all of that?"

"I don't know, but one of us has to go or we'll end up killing each other.

"Girl, don't say things like that!"

"That man is a disgusting human being – an animal! He's the living antithesis of his father. He detests me!"

"No, no. You have to give him time…"

The forgiveness that Margaret externalized regarding him surprised me. I grimaced. Tears came forth.

He said that I was Norman's slut.

"God! What are you saying? It can't be!"

She had to sit down to assimilate my words.

"So, Margaret, what do I do? Should I give him more time to find another opportunity to insult me again… or worse? I just met this person yesterday, and today he calls me a whore. To top it off, he tells me that if it were up to him, he would have fired me before setting foot here."

Margaret didn't lose her expression of incredulity and shock. She knew Eliezer, and by the sadness that could be seen in her eyes, I could be sure that I was describing a stranger to her. The seconds of silence allowed her to formulate a way to temporarily relieve the pain.

"Why don't you go on a trip for a few days? That way,

with some distance, things will calm down, and you'll give him space for him to reconsider, be himself, and to settle down."

"Now I am the one who must disappear?" I snapped.

"Miranda…"

Her tone was maternal and friendly. I tried to smile.

"I'll think over what I'll do before running like prey."

***

During the evening, Eliezer and I crossed paths on various occasions. It was a struggle to make eye contact with him out of pure courtesy; he acted as though nothing had happened. He walked around sure of himself. He reminded me of a Komodo Dragon: so toxic… hoping to sink its fangs into its victims so that it can then watch and wait for death to come.

***

Margaret would think that it was because I followed her advice, but no. That same evening I had to confirm a flight to Panama for the next morning. I had to sign a contract with the government in person.

In Panama, Norman called me. He asked me to visit him as soon as I returned. Upon disconnecting, I had stupid thoughts: *What news would he give me now? Who else would he be tempted to install at the firm? His wife, my new personal assistant?*

I laughed.

Eliezer

"That slut has balls. We'll see who has the bigger ones."

Chapter 8

$\mathcal{V}$isiting Norman at the rehabilitation center didn't fill me with as much sadness as when visiting him at the hospital. The center had a positively charged atmosphere. Those who went there had survived some accident that had taken them to death's door. Many needed therapy to regain function in some part of the body. In contrast to the hospital, it was a private institution. The surroundings were well cared for, the spaces appeared very organized, and the aesthetics, in general, were adequate. The design of the rooms provided maximum privacy for patients and their guests. It was so comfortable that each room even had a small living room.

The door to Norman's room was ajar when I arrived. I found him seated in a wheelchair that matched the set of furniture that decorated the small living room. His face showed improvement. He still couldn't walk, which is why he would stay seated most of the day. The intensive daily therapy promised that, little by little, he would recover his mobility.

Norman rewarded me with a smile when seeing me. That smile to which I was accustomed, even with its seductive contours, was the closest I had to the smile of a father. Even though I respected him just like any daughter would respect and love her father, I admit that, on occasions, it was difficult for me to erase how attractive he really was from my mind. In fact, even though there were no blood ties between us, I had spent the last few years fighting with that box where I kept those luxurious and nearly incestuous thoughts.

Reaching out toward me, he ordered me to come closer. We lost ourselves in an embrace. I sighed profoundly and involuntarily.

"What's that about?" His look puzzled me.

"What?"

I accommodated myself in the love seat adjacent to his wheelchair.

"Your sigh... it almost alleviated the weight that I carried." Norman knew me very well.

"Do you think that everyone else has been out shopping while you enjoy a well deserved but forced vacation?" In my thoughts, I added: *Maybe it would be better for us to change the topic of conversation or I'll tell you that your son is the most malicious psychopath in history and that he's unhinging my life.*

"Someone must sacrifice themselves and work."

A smile that was more plastic than Tupperware masked his curiosity. He didn't buy the story, but for all purposes, he dropped his guard.

"I see that your recovery continues progressing. I'm very happy about that... seriously, very happy."

He again gave me that smile.

"I know, Miranda."

"I confess that the night of the accident my hopes

were almost nil." I looked down. "You looked so bad! So wrecked! I thought I would lose you."

A sharp, painful, and suffocating feeling overcame me for an instant. If we made eye contact, I would surely start crying. My family consisted of only one person: Norman.

He put his warm hand over mine, which was resting peacefully on my knee, and he gave me a consoling caress.

"A weed never dies, and if it does, it's reborn where you would least expect."

His joke made me lift my eyes. A damned tear betrayed me. Norman got a little closer with his wheelchair and, with a very delicate gesture, dried what was left of the traitorous tear.

Eliezer couldn't have been more timely. He wore dark jeans and a gray casual buttoned down short sleeve shirt. He looked younger. More normal. Not like an ogre.

"Am I interrupting?" he asked, as always: in his sarcastic tone.

My heart began beating with so much force that if I opened my mouth it would leap out and run around the room. *What's wrong Miranda? The spectacle hasn't yet begun.*

I greeted him the same way one greets a stranger in the elevator because you don't know if the company is a sexual predator, an assassin or the nicest guy.

"Good evening."

Norman on the other hand, swung the seat around, gave him a contemplative look and a smile... one of my smiles.

"Hello, Eliezer. It's a pleasure to see you tonight.

Until that moment, I had not realized that that was the

first time in so many years that father and son saw each other face to face and spoke. The reunion should have been more intimate.

What the hell am I doing here?

"Norman, I'm leaving." Norman took my hand when he noticed I was getting up off the love seat.

"No, Miranda. Please, stay."

At first, I did not understand his insistence but then I thought that maybe he needed my support. Maybe he was more comfortable with me. Perhaps he was afraid that his demented son would harm him, or maybe my presence would serve as a shock absorber for the words that would be said on both sides. I looked at Eliezer seeking approval from him but he didn't even bother responding.

"Thank you for coming, Eliezer. Come. Sit. Get comfortable."

Norman directed him where to sit. His son vacillated for a few seconds whether to stay or leave. I saw the hesitation in his eyes. I'm sure he did not dream to be in the same room with me, much less breathe the air that I breathed, me the intruder who usurped his place. He could have gone. Nothing stopped him. However, he stayed.

There were two seats available, the other side of the love seat and a separate chair away from me. I need not say which one he chose.

The heaviness of the air made breathing difficult. I could hear the tick... tick... tick of a time bomb.

"You look very good," Norman said casually to

Eliezer.

"I can't say the same about you."

The contempt was heightened in his gaze. Norman half smiled.

"True. You should have seen me two months ago," he laughed at himself. "You certainly would have thought that."

I had to contain my laughter. I could not hold back a small squeak and they both turned towards me simultaneously.

Embarrassment came over me.

"I'm sorry."

Norman tried to use that moment to continue breaking the ice.

"Isn't it true, Miranda? Tell Eliezer how I looked a few months ago."

"Terrible," I continued the game. "To tell the truth, horrible."

"Let's save the small talk. It's obvious that you intended for both of us to be here at the same time. What do you want?"

My eyes opened like an owl's. Norman quit the smiles and showed complete control of the situation.

"Well, son, the conversation was becoming entertaining, but since you appear to be in a hurry, let's get to the point.

Not realizing it, the confession infuriated me.

"I know that you have had differences in past days,"

he began to say.

Eliezer looked at me angrily as if I had squealed.

Norman understood that look and explained. He set aside the kidding.

"Don't complain to Miranda. She hasn't told me anything." He placed a hand on mine. I subtlely moved my hand away. Eliezer kept looking at me angrily. Norman sighed. "You are the two highest ranking people in the company. You cannot go on fighting like children. With those attitudes you put Medika at risk and create a hostile work environment. In addition, employees will lose respect for you."

About his words, I thought: *For employees to lose respect for Eliezer, he first has to earn their respect. At the rate he's going, I doubt he'll accomplish that.*

I came back to reality. Another rush of blood flushed my face. What I would have given to make myself very small or invisible! How embarrassing! He's never scolded me like this before.

The lines on Eliezer's forehead became more stressed as he bit his lower lip. I already knew that grimace well. It was only a matter of time and boom!

"Are you done?" he asked and got up to leave.

"Not yet." His voice became deeper. He was not addressing the two of us but rather Eliezer. "I can understand whatever anger you may feel towards me. It's something that we can and should discuss in another conversation. What I don't understand nor will I allow is you lack of respect towards Miranda or any other person at the office. I suggest that you leave your bad mood at home

120

and don't take it to Medika."

He turned the chair and changed his focus.

"Miranda, Eliezer is now the highest authority in Medika, your boss. Although you know the company better than anyone else, you must respect my son and follow his instructions to the letter. Otherwise you would be acting in an insubordinate manner and you would give him the reason that he so needs to kick you out of the company that you have helped me build with so much effort."

Neither one of us made a move in self-defense. With our silence we admitted our faults. The performance had ended for Norman.

"Well, mission accomplished. If you wish to keep me company, both of you are more than welcome."

As I got up off the couch, Eliezer had left the room without saying a word.

I took that opportunity to make a confession.

"What reason is there for me to stay at Medika, Norman? You have been updated on the arguments between your son and I. In case you hadn't noticed, he is not going to change simply because you order him to after disappearing for two decades. And I will not allow him to treat me like trash."

Norman returned to his previous speech.

"Both of you will have to change your behavior."

"We are going to end up killing each other! That's what will happen!"

He lowered his head.

"You can do better than that, Miranda. That is why I

need you."

I took his chin and forced him to look at me.

"Wouldn't it have been easier for you to let me be in charge?"

He let out a sigh like the one that had come from me that he had criticized earlier.

"That part was not negotiable," he grimaced, an assertion that, in fact, he had no other choice. His voice cracked. "It's what I had to sacrifice for Eliezer to come back."

"And why do you want me to stay? You know I don't have a problem leaving to go work somewhere else, with no regrets. I understand your situation."

"Even if you think you understand my situation, it's not like you think. It's more complicated than an attempt at peace between father and son. I need you, Miranda. You are who he should have been." I was insulted and I couldn't hide it: I bit my cheek and my eyes got watery. "Don't misunderstand me, Miranda. I was referring to who you are as a person. You have a noble heart, you're compassionate, and you understand Medika's purpose. On the other hand, Eliezer..." He closed his eyes, in an attempt to get away from reality. "He is selfish, arrogant, overbearing, and pretentious."

I was surprised to hear that he described his son with same adjectives that I would have used.

"I don't know what to do Norman. I really don't know. This is too much..."

Norman approached me and caressed my bangs. He

pinched my cheek. "Just say that I can count on you."

I had no choice other than to tell him the whole truth.

"Did you know that your son thinks I'm... your lover?"

Norman dropped his head back and he let out a laugh. I laughed too. "Well, that is the decent word for what he thinks of me."

"Don't give it any weight. He is very hurt. And if I'm not mistaken, he must also be jealous of you. I don't blame him. Even I would be jealous." It seemed to me as if Margaret was speaking.

"You excuse him too?"

"Not exactly but he is my biological son, Miranda and I have him back after so many years."

I felt how hard it was for Norman to put me in this situation. Even if it upset me, I could understand... I think.

He repeated: "Just say that I can count on you, please."

"And how can I refuse?"

I let the tears run down my cheeks.

"But hurry and get through your vacation quickly, please. You need to manage your affairs. I won't last you your whole life." I smiled at him mischievously. Remember Margaret's words: *The day will come when prince charming steals your heart and takes you away.*

"Yes, yes, yes. And you'll forget about this old man." He smiled and whispered: "But just between us, it's getting late for you."

"Please," my face flushed a bit.

"Enjoy life! Get out! Fall in love! Live once and for

all, please!"

"The injuries have definitely affected your head." That was my good bye.

I took my purse and walked out.

"Thank you, darling!"

His words reached me in the hallway outside the room.

What more can I do to 'live,' as you say? My life, after all is a fairy tale. I've never wanted for anything, thanks to you.

Eliezer

"Leave her alone! Stop! Let her go! Please... Daddy..."

Chapter 9

"*Don't hold back,*" *the male voice ordered.*

It excited me to see his eyes darken with the pounding of my hips. That was my god, and I felt like a goddess on his throne. Ahh! What a delight it was to feel those hands—those hands that roamed from my shoulders to the forbidden part of my back and abused my breasts with passion and fury.

In the middle of the ecstasy, a sudden thought: it's impossible for someone's hands to roam two parts of my body at once!

The intruding hands took hold of my hair, forcing me to pay homage to the erect god before me, miraculously letting his body slam against mine, invading me. Oh! The smell of that skin condensed in the air! Ahh! Ohh!

A second masculine voice interrupted, "Is that how you lust for us, you slut?"

What the hell?

***

That morning Eliezer held an unusual meeting. Medika directors were present. I was the last one to enter the conference room—not because I was late, but because I was the last one to be notified.

How could I look him in the eyes after that dumb dream I

127

had last night?

He had not yet made his spectacular entrance into the room. As I approached the table, several co-workers would ask me if I knew what the meeting was all about. I gave everyone the same muted response: "No idea," as I shrugged my shoulders.

Eliezer arrived like a tornado: walking quickly with his jacket flowing behind him, making noise with the heels of his shoes, with an air of danger, death and destruction. He sat at the head of the conference table, which had another eleven spaces. He did not say good morning.

"I have called you here to make you aware of several announcements related to changes in the organization."

I raised my head. I looked at him with that look that I sometimes throw at Norman when I was afraid of something.

Changes! What changes?

"I have decided that the number of employees has to be reduced to increase operational efficiency. You have fifteen days to present proposals for your respective departments and convince me that they make more sense than mine."

All heads turned towards me, looking surprised, as if I had something to do with it. They were stunned by the words they were hearing. I did not know what to tell them with my glances, since Medika had no vulnerabilities. The company's financial standing was optimal. *On what basis does this damned bastard dare propose these changes if he's only been at the helm for a week and doesn't even know how to do his job properly?"*

"Let's see Eliezer... First of all, when will we see your

proposals?"

The others turned their heads again and looked at their heartless and irrational boss. Eliezer stopped looking at the wall and turned to face me. With a look he told me that he knew very well what the purpose of my question was.

"If you'll allow me, International, I will present them next."

Those present looked at me again with the same astonished looks.

"Miranda, or if you're more comfortable, Wise."

"Yes, excuse me for making you feel uncomfortable. Anyway, don't you manage that division?"

The five seconds of silence that filled the room seemed like an eternity. That was his declaration of war. While the conflict was private, I could handle it, but now he made it public.

"Then, I'll continue…"

He began a parade of proposals, whose goal, of course, was staff reduction.

I could not say they were crazy proposals, because they weren't. It just wasn't the time to implement them. When necessary they could be carried out long term at companies with financial difficulties, but that was not the case with Medika. We had more than two hundred and fifty million dollars in cash flow, and in the last ten years, the business was growing in double digits. Changes were not needed at this time.

I watched as each director's made a face when they understood the impact the proposals would have in their respective areas. After Eliezer presented each proposal, the ones most affected searched my face, demanding help, hoping that, for the love of God, I would say something, but I wasn't the person to whom they should be looking for refuge from the storm. When I heard what Eliezer would do with my division, I did not find anyone to look to for help.

"Eliezer..." I interrupted.

"Yes, Wise," he responded, and apparently he could predict me, because he responded before I finished uttering his name.

"It seems to me that the proposals would be relevant if we were in a difficult financial situation. That's not the case. We have two-hundred fifty million in cash flow."

"Two-hundred forty-nine to be exact." Surprising. So soon and the figures were already clear in his mind.

"Then, what's the purpose of these changes?"

"As I mentioned a few minutes ago, efficiencies. Weren't you paying attention?"

If he thought he would do it, he was wrong. I wouldn't let him ridicule me in front of my co-workers.

"I think that before speaking of changes and efficiencies, you must first understand their potential impact in depth, and even more importantly, understand what we do."

"That won't be necessary. I know enough to make these decisions. Besides, what are all of you here for? It's the responsibility of each and every one of the directors present here to adapt their departments to the new reality."

True. Our responsibility was to adapt our department and make sure that we continue fulfilling our commitments and providing results. Even so, Eliezer was out of touch with reality, with the company's mission, with its true reason for being.

"Let's say that my first action with this adaptation plan would be to extend an invitation to my boss to get to know the reality of my department. We leave in two days." I said that with a smile on my lips.

Everyone present focused completely on Eliezer's face. As much as he wanted to, as did I, he could not say no to my invitation. Suddenly, the idea of being in his company turned my stomach. *How could I ever engage in such madness?* I almost buried my head in the papers on the enormous table.

He stared at me as if his look could destroy me. His jaw shifted. He was about to lose control. It was a matter of seconds before he would explode, but as quickly as it came… it went. He overcame his sudden bad temper. He stopped tightening his jaw and the muscles in his face relaxed.

"Invitation accepted. This meeting has concluded."

The others left the conference room as quickly as age allowed them to, but I was last. I went by him not realizing that I had made a grave error: I let my guard down.

Eliezer grabbed me by the left arm and prevented me from walking any further. He tightened his grip hard until I let him know with a look that it was painful.

"What is your intention, you slut?" he demanded, in a low voice that masked his rage.

I paid him little attention. I looked at his hand, which was hurting my arm more and more. When I looked up, he slowly freed me from the pain.

"My intention is to make the right decisions in line

with the current reality." I raised may hand. I was about to slap him. Instead I gave him courteous warning. "Don't ever hurt me again, Eliezer, or you'll have big problems. And don't ever touch me again, let alone that way."

My words made him reason. He looked at the redness and finger marks on my arm. His expression changed. He understood that he was still screwing up, and that a complaint for battery and workplace harassment would soon be knocking at his door.

The rage that my defiance provoked in him had blinded him. I knew his weakness. I smiled internally. *Is it so easy to make you lose control and explode, dear Eliezer?*

"I'll talk to Margaret and ask her to check your agenda and coordinate the details. I assume that you won't travel on a commercial airline, or am I wrong?" Sarcasm slipped out with the question.

"There's no need to play the common person. Much less in the countries I expect we'll visit." His mouth contorted in contempt as he finished talking.

I was lost in his eyes for a few seconds.

"Too bad that eye color and last name are the only things you share with Norman!"

He was not expecting that comment, but he gave a short dark laugh that ended in a bite to the corner of his lower lip. He glanced at my arm, surely to check that the evidence of his rage had vanished.

"You think yourself quite capable don't you?"

"What do you mean?"

"To take this to the limit." I assumed he was referring

to the declared war.

"I didn't know it had limits." I rubbed my arm, which was still hurting.

Eliezer looked at my arm again.

"Do yourself a favor, Wise. Give up."

"Should I take that as a threat?"

"No because in that case, I'd be giving you a very good reason to screw me over. You should be thankful for the advice, Wise. It's not something I give often." He smiled and his smile was both sarcastic and... pretty? I couldn't believe it was his.

"That's very clear to me. Giving advice is not something you do often. Nor is being kind, respectful, courteous..."

He tired of listening to my string of synonyms and interrupted me.

"Why would I have to be like that with you?"

"I was not referring to me. I could care less about how you refer to me. I care about the others. Since you are being so generous now, I ask that you keep this shit you have against me between us. Don't involve anyone else. Don't fuck with anyone else's life."

"So you mean to say that I'm fucking with your life?" The malice showed in the deep darkness of his green eyes. "This is not going to end well, Wise."

"I guarantee you that it will not, Clausell."

**

I reviewed the events of the morning at the office. Eliezer's strange greeting, his wanting to fire everyone, our confrontation, the invitation, his fingers squeezing my

133

arm, the dream I had just before waking up in the morning.

That man was too… forceful, perhaps? He drained me! I had to choose the words I used with him carefully! His aggressive gesture of taking me forcefully by the arm and squeezing my arm made me feel… threatened… and also… made me ask myself: *How is it possible that someone with eyes like that and a smile like that and skin like that, could have such a cold heart?*

His cologne which still lingered on my arm made me feel like he was still with me, close by. The scent was imposing. I lost myself in intrusive thoughts. *And if… and if… perhaps?*

"Hey! Where are you?"

To not break the habit, Ethan had entered my office without knocking, had sat in one of the chairs, and he had realized that I was not on this planet, but on another. Good thing he did not figure out that the planet was hostile. It wanted to exterminate me and its name was Eliezer.

"What the hell was that show?"

"Before or after?"

Ethan moved forward, he fixed his sleeves and waited for the rest of the story. Since he realized that silence reigned, he asked, "Something else happened, afterward?"

The door opened and Margaret entered. She was carrying a small bag in her hands.

"I apologize for the interruption." She approached my desk. "Here is some ice for your arm."

I looked at Ethan and Margaret. I could not believe what was happening. I could not believe that the madman had told Margaret.

"Eliezer told me that you had hurt yourself with the door and that you would need some ice."

I tried to hide the reaction of disbelief. Besides being an aggressor, he was a liar.

Ethan, a man of experience, did not buy the story. Margaret left and he took advantage of the opportunity to launch his inquisition. He took my arm and carefully analyzed the marks that were still fresh and painful.

"I take it this is what you were referring to."

I moved my arm away from his hand.

"It's not what you think. Nothing happened. I tripped and I hit the edge of the table in the conference room."

"I thought it had been the door."

"Yes, with the door and the table too, before hitting myself on the door."

Ethan let out a laugh, the scary kind.

"Don't tell me he did this to you, Miranda," he looked me the in the eyes and when Ethan looks at me that way I'm, sometimes, unable to lie. "What the hell happened, Miranda?" He kept his tone low to conceal his anger and lessen the seriousness of the situation.

I was surprised by how easily I lied.

"I already told you, nothing happened. If you don't mind, I need to make a phone call. Alone."

I looked at him annoyed to see if he would leave. I picked up the handset of my desk telephone. Ethan grabbed the handset from me and put it back on its base.

He crossed his arms and leaned back in the chair.

"I won't leave until you confess the truth. If you don't I'll go to Mr. Clausell myself and I'll ask him what the hell he did to you."

For a few seconds I hesitated to persuade him. I tried to calm him down. I touched his crossed hands. He grimaced in disgust. I didn't want things to go from bad to worse. I had to lie.

"Ethan, I appreciate that you worry about me, but let me handle this..."

"I don't care what you want nor if you can or cannot handle the problem. That man cannot do that to you. That's abuse. I will personally report him if you don't tell me."

I stopped the soft approach and raised my voice.

"Don't threaten me, Ethan. I already told you nothing happened. I'm handling the situation. End of story."

He remained pensive, inhaling and exhaling deeply, a habit he had to defuse his anger.

"I will keep quiet and calm, but just this time. Do you understand? If I see the slightest sign of this absurd kind of abuse, I'll be the one to call Norman and the police."

"That's not necessary, Ethan. Set aside your distrust. It was an accident. I tripped and hit the table, then I tripped and hit the door. Eliezer was there and he helped me." I told a lie without even realizing it.

Why the hell do I defend this lout? This is the perfect opportunity to get rid of him just the way he wants to get rid of me: a one-way ticket out with no way back.

I placed the ice pack on my arm. I felt it become numb on contact with the cold. The redness of the marks was

136

turning purple. My fair skin did not help the marks look less visible.

I made the phone call that I owed to an upset client, and I don't even remember the agreement we arrived at. All I had on my mind was the way Eliezer tried to cover up the incident.

When I saw him go by my office, headed to his, I followed him. I entered, half closed the door, placed my hand on the doorknob, and turned around.

What the hell are you doing, Miranda Wise? If he dared attack you in the conference room, imagine what he could do here.

He was surprised by my presence… or was it that I was fiddling with the doorknob nervously?

"What do you want, International?"

How should I respond? I myself did not know what I wanted, nor why I was there, pawing the doorknob and possessed with anger.

I walked over to where he was standing in front of his desk. We were face to face. Rather, my face was level with his chest, because even with heels I couldn't match his height. I got even closer, so much so that I felt my body push against his.

"Hear me well, ass, because this will be the only time I say this to you." I poked my threatening finger against his chest. "Don't you ever lay a hand on me. This time I helped cover for you to spare your father any distress… to spare him your greater deception."

My breathing was faster than the flow of my thoughts. Eliezer was staring at me. A trace of shame showed in his eyes. Suddenly history seemed to repeat itself with this scene. He grabbed my arms, but this time, although aggressive in the beginning, his touch was delicate. My involuntary reaction was to push him to defend myself. He let go of my arms, and with the force with which I pushed him, my legs became unbalanced and fell. Eliezer half opened his mouth and bent down. He offered me his help, which I rejected. He didn't care about my rejection. He held me by the arms and stood me up. His voice sounded weak. His face was expressionless.

"That should not have happened." His voice still weak. I moved away from his touch, "I shouldn't have grabbed you that way."

I didn't know how to look at him anymore. Rage was deep within me.

"Is it that hard for you to apologize?"

He continued speaking in a very low voice.

"You really don't know how to judge limits when you see them?"

"Apology accepted," I headed for the door. "See how easy it is?"

I swear that behind so much seriousness in his face an invisible smile was taking shape.

"That doesn't change anything, Wise."

"This changes everything, Clausell."

"Scheiße[1]," he muttered. He enjoyed seeing the confusion on my face because I did not know what the hell he said, nor did I know in what language he had said it.

"Coward..." I answered with an invisible smile under my face overloaded with seriousness.

Before leaving... a thought: "And this door, why is it

---

1   German for shit.

locked? Who...?"

A pause... a headache. *You locked it, Miranda Wise.*

Eliezer

Leave her to me. I'll take care of her.

Chapter 10

$\mathcal{T}$he journey began in Guatemala. It was uncomfortable and there was excess baggage in the main cabin. Eliezer had brought his demons, which gave me more reason to loathe the corporate aircraft. Most of the words we exchanged were silent. A glance here, another there. Actually, that is how we spoke, or rather, we didn't speak during the two days following the slip-up with my arm. He limited the conversations and interactions between us. Of course, neither the silence nor the distance bothered me. I felt I had a little room to breathe, to think. He read during the flight; I checked the agenda again and again and again. I couldn't let anything go wrong, especially not with him as company.

***

In Guatemala, we had lunch with the health minister. The conversation focused on the resources the country needed to take care of the health of its population. Initially, Eliezer continued his usual silence. He spent his time eating and he seemed to pay little or no attention to what I said to the minister.

Once he had his fill, there was a barrage of questions.

I was stunned: first because I couldn't believe that

143

he would have truly enjoyed the conversation that I had started; and second, because his questions were so valid, creative, and interesting that I could hardly say a few short sentences to note, that, although silent, indeed I was still there.

After lunch, we visited several hospitals of the public health system. In Guatemala, as in most Latin American countries, the government is the main provider of health services. These governments have limited resources, so the primary focus is to do more with less, without apparent care for jeopardizing the safety or quality of service to the patient.

We arrived at the first hospital in one of the busiest areas of the city. At Eliezer's insistence, and in keeping with company protocol, we had a driver and bodyguards. They left us at the hospital entrance, next to a staircase that people had turned into seating because of the long hours of waiting. That was only a prelude to the main doors. We made our way through the crowd. Of the six doors, only two were open. One served as the entrance; the other as the exit. Two guards with rifles guarded the passage.

We entered the hall of death. Right away, there were rows and rows of people waiting to receive attention and many more rows of people on stretchers, on the verge of death from untreated wounds or infections or diseases that initially received little attention. Some were barefoot. Others, by their appearance, seemed to have not bathed for who knows how many days.

The undernourished children with sad faces and the atmosphere of certain death caused me to choke up. I looked at Eliezer, for such a horrible scene would have shattered any human soul. I was surprised. He was poker faced. There was no sign of empathy, pity, or disapproval at what he was facing. I felt the words becoming a train with no breaks that would zoom out of my mouth at that same speed. I swallowed them. I swallowed them and said nothing. So what if my bias against Eliezer was such that it prevented me from seeing beyond that?

On our way to the hotel, I remembered that the Minister mentioned the country's current need to help the victims of an earthquake that had taken place a few days ago. Those on the border with Belize deserved special attention.

"How much will you authorize as a donation, Eliezer?"

That was a question I always asked Norman, who without hesitation would give such a high figure that I felt obliged to lower it. Eliezer, on the other hand, looked away from his phone and made a face that I translated as, 'What the hell are you talking about?'

"Donate to whom and why?"

"To the Red Cross of Guatemala."

"And why do we have to give them money? We're not a bank."

His indifference surprised me and it didn't surprise me. One thing was to hate me and resent others, but even the most insensitive human being in this universe would have been moved by the scenes we had just encountered and by the collective grief that the country was suffering, as described by the Minister.

"Let me give you some perspective, Eliezer. Medika, the company that by chance you now happen to manage, has a social mission and supports philanthropic causes as well as charities. With that in mind, how much money will you donate to help the earthquake victims?"

"Nothing." He returned his attention to the iPhone, which he took out of his briefcase. "I won't donate anything."

I let out a hysterical laugh.

"Are you joking?"

He gave me his attention again. His face stiff and firm, unfriendly, did not show any traces of the invisible smiles that I had discovered on other occasions.

"Why would I joke about something like that?"

The driver suddenly slammed on the brakes. My face slammed against the back of the seat in front of me. Eliezer motioned to me with his fingers to adjust my seatbelt. I complied with a litany of profanities in my mind. I could see a curve forming in the corner of his mouth that threatened mocking laughter.

That he worried made me curious. I would not have reminded him of his seatbelt. Perhaps then he would slam his face even harder and disappear once and for all.

"Those people don't have the resources to cover their basic needs, Eliezer. They need clothing, food, water, medicine, a roof, a bed..." The words were taking me to the brink of hysteria.

Eliezer made another gesture with his hands, this time for me to be silent.

"I know, International, but gifting them money will not solve their problems."

I kept silent just as he had asked, until I managed to

calm down so as to not fill the silence with profanity.

"This must be a joke..."

"Have I ever joked around with you?"

Damn him. He was truly serious.

"You've never experienced hardships, have you?" I was attempting to speak in a calm tone, with serenity. I would say *too* calm for this situation.

Eliezer did not respond. He was busy fiddling with the cell phone.

"Do you know why so many misfortunes happen in poor countries? So that people like you, who have so much money that they don't even know what to do with, have fun giving it away to those who most need it."

I managed to get his attention.

He put his cell in its case and turned his head in my direction.

"I have another theory but I warn you that you won't like it."

"Surprise me."

The conversation was getting interesting. It was the first time we spoke of something somewhat unrelated to work matters.

Eliezer reclined halfway between the back of the seat and the inside of the door of the van.

"Let's say God was flushing the toilet."

"What... the... hell?"

My jaw fell limp. My mouth was left open in a giant 'O'.

Definitely, the only thing Eliezer shared with Norman

was a surname… and the eyes… and the cheekbones… and the hair.

"But what kind of contrarian beast am I encountering?"

"Close your mouth and don't say I didn't warn you." He furrowed his eyebrow, enjoying his words and my reaction.

I warned him:

"You should be careful about where you make those type of comments. The media could annihilate you."

"And you think I care?"

Naughty boy. He shrugged his shoulders with indifference. Although on second thought, a child would not have been capable of formulating such theory. My grey matter, still stunned, made my head move unconsciously from side to side, a sign of my refusal to believe what I had heard.

"Tell me what you think, Wise."

"About?"

He smiled. He made that smile which didn't fit his personality.

"About what I just told you."

"About the God and toilet theory?" I bit my lips trying not to return the insensitivity or the smile. "You really want to know what I think?"

"I asked for a reason, don't you think?"

"Later, don't say I didn't warn you, Clausell." I got comfortable in the seat and I mimicked his posture, preparing myself to launch a grenade. "With all due respect, that according to Norman, I owe you, even though I don't agree, I think your opinion is insensitive and repugnant."

"Interesting, Wise, very interesting." He stroked his beard. "Then according to you and your words, I'm insensitive and repugnant."

I didn't respond. *Even if you want to spit it directly into his face, you can't tell your boss that, Miranda.*

Eliezer gave a chuckle and continued the conversation.

"You're very easy to crack, Miranda. You don't have to tell me what you think. I know it. But before you die thinking that way, allow me to tell you some things that support my theory."

I whispered through my teeth.

"I'm all ears..."

"What does a poor person have, Wise?" He asked and I hesitated in responding because I was trying to figure out the path he wanted to take.

"What do you mean, what does a poor person, have? Normally, the poor have nothing."

"You are wrong, Wise. There's a saying: *the poor live off hope.*"

I crossed my arms.

"Well, then let's say that a poor person has hope."

He moved forward, not towards the front seat but towards me, with that peculiar smile on his lips, suddenly very interested in talking to me.

"If all a poor person has is hope, since that is merely an abstraction, at the end of the day, he has nothing." He paused, moved forward, took a cup from the cup holder, and drank the liquid someone had poured. That ordinary action gave him an air of vulnerability to me. "A poor person just has luck, or the bad luck in this case, of being alive. Life is the only thing that can be taken away from him. On the other hand, a rich person has everything. If his bitch of a life is taken from him, well it's taken and that's that. Another rich person is born." He looked me in the eyes, and although that word "bitch" was echoing in my mind, he didn't seem to be ashamed of having unnecessarily used profanity. "The rich are punished differently," he concluded.

He had to be joking. And yet, there was something in his words that made some sense.

"What do you think, Wise?"

"That either way, you shouldn't express yourself that way."

"And of my theory?"

I sighed.

"I'll admit that it was the other side of the coin that I had not seen before." Internally, I was battling myself: *How can you lend merit to such drivel?*

"Do you realize that, Wise? Little by little, we are coming to understand each other." He smiled again his victorious smile.

I laughed. It would be impossible for us to come to understand each other.

"According to your theory, Clausell, how are the rich punished more painfully?"

He was pensive before responding, lost in the blackness of the leather of the seat in front of him.

"The rich are thrown into the toilet but we aren't

flushed. We are left wallowing in…."

"Scheiße?" I completed the sentence.

His eyes gave a sudden leap, an act that made me realize how much I had surprised him.

"That's right, Wise, in Scheiße. That's where we stay. Now tell me, who does God treat better?"

I did not say anything more. I remained unmoved in the perdition of his gaze until he looked uncomfortable and remembered his high-tech tools. He went from the iPhone to the iPad nonstop, without looking at me again.

To my surprise, that same night, he invited me to dinner. It was not a formal invitation, of course, but a necessary one to review some very important bidding documents for El Salvador.

We went to the Italian restaurant inside the hotel. He ordered an Angus steak with a salad. I chose a plate of carbs, which would help me control my anxiety of being so close to that despicable being for so long.

"Do you agree with what we reviewed?" I asked because I needed his backing to finalize the offer.

"What makes you think you'll get that business?"

How I hated when he answered me with questions!

"We have worked for years on this…" Eliezer interrupted me.

"That doesn't guarantee anything, Wise."

"We developed the proper relationships and delivered the proper message at precisely the right moment," I defended myself while chewing on a piece of bread.

"How would you feel if you were to win those eighty

million?"

I looked at him perplexed. *And since when does he care what I feel?* I studied his eyes, analyzed his gestures. *Let's see who lowers his guard this time.* He did.

"What's wrong, Wise?" he asked tactlessly. Although, in any case, it would be difficult for him to even attempt to sound subtle. His voice was too harsh and abrasive.

"What's up with you, Clausell?" The wine was beginning to liberate me with words.

"What's up with me with what?" He took a piece of steak to his mouth. The steak would release juices on the plate every time he cut into it. That simple gesture of taking food to his mouth repeated itself in my mind over and over again. Who knows why?

"Do you always answer with questions or only when you feel threatened?"

Of course, he launched another question.

"Have you been told that you are quite irritating, annoying and inopportune, *wise-ass*?"

"No, this is the first time." I paused. "Nobody has had the ability to irritate me, or of making me annoying, let alone inopportune or a *wise-ass*."

I directed my attention to the pasta. *God! How delicious!* And then...

"Oh! What was that?"

I dropped the fork on the plate and the people at the surrounding tables turned when they heard the irritating sound. I didn't care. My finger was pointing at his face. He frowned and inspected his torso as if trying to understand what I was referring to, why I had been so surprised.

"What?" He moved in a strange way... like was putting himself on guard.

"Was that a smile for a joke of mine, perhaps?"

Yes, that was a smile for me, not against me, and it had just made another appearance. He relaxed his posture. The way his eyes lit up as his face began to show conflicting expressions made me uncomfortable. *Why do I celebrate Eliezer's smiles?* I knew it wasn't proper, but even so, I remarked: "The stingy and insensitive grump has genuine smiles, and he shares them!"

Eliezer took a sip of wine.

"Wise, did you just call me stingy?"

"And grumpy and insensitive."

He smiled again and that smile was indecipherable.

"You better have your credit card with you, Wise."

It was with that comment that the long awaited moment had finally arrived when we both lowered our guns.

Gladly, I would pay for a lifetime, if only you never erased that beautiful smile on your face, if only I would never had to go back to those early days when our meetings were clashes.

The metering needle of the incessant tension between us had been lowered. I paid, yes, but he ordered another bottle of wine, which cost five hundred dollars. At least he would be the one to approve that expense report.

Chapter 11

$\mathcal{S}$ecurity was a very serious subject for Eliezer, although I felt very confident in Panama. Against Eliezer's wishes, I rented a car and I drove to the meetings that were left. I don't know what he was complaining about if he had arrived safely to all his destinations. *What kind of life did he lead in Europe?*

The scheduled meetings included the Minister of Health, the directors of Social Security, and my great friend Dr. Luis Bartolome, whom I had met thanks to my job at Medika, and who, in contrast with other people of influence, had earned my respect and admiration from the beginning.

Curing and helping others was his vocation as well as what flowed through his veins. Passion for medicine was his mission. As one of the best emergency physicians in his country, he dedicated his services to the public sector. A few years ago, he presented a social project to me to take medical services to the needy communities at the far reaches of the city. I remember that when he spoke to me of the proposal, I thought he was joking. It involved establishing a primary care site in a remote town with no roads where the death rate was very high because it was impossible to cross the river to get to a hospital. I still could not understand how situations like that could exist in the twenty-first century. Without thinking twice, I joined with him on that project. I focused my goals on his. Over time, our friendship so blossomed, that on several occasions, during the carnival season, I spent the night with him and his family on a ranch just outside the city.

The visit to Panama also had another purpose: attending the carnival. In Latin America, those carnivals are just tributes to the saints they honor. Lasting up to five days, they paralyze the countries. People from all social classes participate, they mix, becoming one and indistinguishable. That year, besides the promises I had made to my friend during previous months, I had to attend because he had also promised to introduce me to a medical colleague who, according to him, was a perfect match for me. I had accepted the invitation: not because of the prospect, but because of my friend and his wonderful family with whom I always felt at home, like I did with Norman.

"Will you arrive in town or do you need a ride?" asked Luis who was in the back seat.

Eliezer, unaware of my plans and ignorant of the reason for Luis's questions, looked at me from the corner of his eye and raised his eyebrows.

"Don't worry, I'll drive to town," I answered. I looked at Eliezer, who raised his eyebrows even more. "Tonight the carnival begins–the big event." When I looked at him, he smiled a smile of disapproval and annoyance.

"Would you honor us with your presence, Mr. Clausell?" It seemed that, in addition to extending a cordial invitation, Luis wanted to ruin my plans.

"Thank you, but we have a flight to take."

The use of the plural indicated that Eliezer had the nerve of deciding and speaking for me.

"I'm going," I said, looking in the rearview mirror while correcting him. I resumed looking at Eliezer. "Later I'll return on a commercial flight... that is if my boss approves a couple of vacation days for me."

"We'll see," he whispered with a sarcastic smile. He knew that I intended to expose him.

"Perfect, Miranda! So then I'll wait for you. I don't think Mr. Clausell will want you to miss the carnival. It's not held every day, nor in every country."

He had no other choice than to be polite. Perhaps that's why he gave us the most sarcastic and phony smile that I've ever seen in my life. Once Luis was out of the car, I could feel in the atmosphere that peculiar cumulative weight of the words that had been spoken. Were it not for the nerve I had to look him in the eye while waiting for the light to change, he would not have dared to speak.

"So you're going to stay for the carnival," he said as he looked through the window at the cars going in the opposite direction.

"Exactly!" I was loud, but my enthusiasm was unintentional.

"Don't you think you could have mentioned it earlier?"

"I did. Didn't Margaret put it in your agenda? Oh, that's because it was my agenda, not yours. It was the last item and it was not directly related to Medika," I lied and he gave me a look of disdain. "Clausell, my plans don't affect your agenda."

"You're absolutely right, Wise," he admitted.

I thought *who understands him?* Then this came out of my mouth: "They invited you too," I hesitated briefly. Again, my mouth betrayed me. "Have you ever been to a carnival?"

"I've not had the need," and that must have been the truth, because he did not sound interested.

"Why don't you come?"

There was dead silence. My sixth sense made me realize that we both asked the same question. *What are you doing, Miranda Wise?* Eliezer lifted himself a bit from the seat. He fixed his pants and put the cell phone in his pocket. I looked at him.

"That's not in my plans. I will return today. The jet is ready."

It made me uncomfortable that he did not thank me for the courtesy. I'm not someone who extends invitations casually, much less to disturbed bosses who may have been ogres in another life.

"Well, then have a good trip," I mumbled.

"No doubt," he replied with that peculiar smile on his lips.

The conversation ended. I said it in my head: *You're such an idiot, Eliezer...*

***

Three hours later, the elevator door opened and there he was, wearing dark blue jeans and a light blue polo shirt. I left the elevator and, having no other choice, I greeted him with a small gesture, but I didn't stop.

Within seconds, I realized he was walking next to me as if he were escorting me.

"What? Do you need a ride to the airport?"

"No," he paused, dusted something off his leg, "I'm not leaving."

I began to believe that I would never understand a human being by the name of Eliezer Clausell.

"Well, where are you going?" I finished asking following a sigh of discomfort.

"To the carnival, where else? Or did the invitation have an expiration date?"

I turned and looked at him with mouth agape. *To the carnival? Today? Tonight? Why? Why are you determined to make my life impossible? Do you really want to play this hate game all night?* I could not imagine Eliezer among the crowds of people that would surely become unbearable with the music and alcohol.

"Are you sure you want to come?" He stopped walking and so did I. "I must warn you that there will be lots and lots of people. You'll feel hot and suffocated. Your body will rub against other sweaty bodies that may not smell very good, and the smell of alcohol will be nauseating, and you may in fact run the risk of a brawl taking place.

Eliezer tried smiling. I don't know if he was being sarcastic or merely surprised by my description.

"What makes you think I won't be able to withstand a carnival jam-packed with smelly, sweaty, drunk people?"

He used his usual defiant tone. I had to disarm him

159

before he tried to insult me.

"Relax, Eliezer. I've never underestimated you," I smiled.

"Well, then, don't waste more time and let's go."

I complied reluctantly.

***

The trip seemed longer than I remembered. Maybe Eliezer's company had something to do with it. We couldn't figure out what to talk about. Regardless of the subject I chose to talk about, he paid no attention or wouldn't respond to any of my questions, until I asked the question he *did* want to hear.

"Why did you decide to come?"

He bit the inside of his cheek–the face he would make when he was about to lose composure, or when my words bothered him.

"Are you going to persist with this subject?" His eyes remained fixed on the road.

"I'm sorry, Clausell, but you just don't seem to be the kind of person that attend this type of event."

He scowled.

"Let's see, Wise. What answer do you want me to give you to satisfy your curiosity so you can focus on the road again? A week ago someone told me that, before making decisions, I should get to know and live Medika's state of affairs, because any decision would affect the company." He made one of his strange pauses. "Here you have me, Wise, living the entire experience." He opened his eyes widely to emphasize the last word. "Am I excited about being in a loud celebration of strangers in a foreign

160

country? No, I don't like the idea. Nevertheless, I'm here. Can we end this conversation? Can you drive focused on the street and not on my decision-making?"

The ability I had to unhinge him became tempting. It was clear that he was doing it just to prove a point, so that at the next meeting, I couldn't argue against any of his decisions regarding my department. *Why else would he be here with me?*

Chapter 12

The blood had stained the back of Eliezer's baby blue shirt near the left shoulder.

"Take it off so I can see how deep the wound is."

"That's not necessary, Wise. I'm taking a shower." He got up and before I had a chance to respond, he was in the bathroom.

I went to the kitchen. Perhaps my homemade ointments and medicines for these types of accidents had survived the passage of time in the cabinets.

Following the brawl started by two men next to us, the celebrations had stopped and Eliezer ended up with a laceration caused by a broken bottle that was hurled by one of the angry men. The streets were inundated with people. There was no room to move. Coming back to the city was not an option. Luis offered us his home, but Eliezer declined the offer. That's how I decided to go to my favorite spot in Panama, a place far away from the hustle and bustle, a cabin in the mountains: my cabin.

In the beginning, it had two bedrooms but I had asked for the wall that divided them to be taken down and turned the space into one huge bedroom. The living room area and the kitchen were charming, decorated with huge wooden beams that gave them a rustic touch. The balcony was my favorite. I could spend hours... days there in complete solitude enjoying the green countryside and the way the sun would caress the trees when it wasn't raining. It was my refuge and my only private space. Only two people knew of this place: Norman and Luis. Add one more to the list: Eliezer Clausell, my favorite person in the whole world.

I found the alcohol, triple antibiotic and gauze. When I returned to the room, the bathroom door was still closed. I heard the shower was still on. I waited at the edge of the bed. *He's been in there a long time. What if something happened to him? What if he bled to death?*

I jumped towards the door. I knocked.

"Eliezer." He didn't respond. I knocked again. "Eliezer!"

Just when I began to turn the doorknob, I was yanked inside as the door suddenly swung open. I exited as fast as I had entered.

"What's going on?" The shower had not helped quell his bad mood.

"I wanted to know if you were alright. You had been in there a long time and...." As I tried to explain, I got more confused. *What are you trying to prove, Miranda? Forget it.*

"You're not that lucky, Wise. I'm still alive," he said with a sarcastic smile on his lips. I ignored that.

"The shower is still on, Clausell," I said.

His smile vanished. He moved away and he shut it off.

The muscle on his forearm moved when he did that.

"Take these," he said as he threw his jeans, which I

164

was able to catch in the air. Then I realized that his torso was uncovered and the towel only covered his privates. "The least you can do is wash my pants."

"What did you say?" I paused and thought: *He's got to be taught some manners.* "Oh! You meant to ask me to please wash your pants. That's what you meant to say, right?"

I waited for the response of abrupt, unfiltered words–the kind only he can use. The answer never came. It never came because I read in his eyes how uncomfortable he was in my presence. I placed the jeans on the chair next to the wardrobe, and I remembered that somewhere I had seen a pair of pants that he may be able to use.

"I think they may fit you." I threw them like he had thrown his and he caught them just as I had.

Suddenly, thinking I closed my eyes. *What are you doing, Miranda?*

He inspected them for a moment.

"I only hope that the owner doesn't have a broken bottle in his hand when he comes looking for them." His wry tone prompted me to explain.

"They belong to your father." He took the pants and placed them on the bed as if touching them would give him the bubonic plague. "He comes here when he wants to be away from everything."

"You don't have to provide any details, Wise. Let me draw my own conclusions."

It was a confusing moment. I was bewildered by the expression on his face when he heard whom they belonged to, and by the many explanations that I conjured in my mind to make him understand why I had his father's pants in my cabin.

"Sit down. I'm going to check the wound," I ordered with authority. He analyzed me for a few seconds. I showed him the gauze and the bottle of alcohol. "Let this be added to the payment for your heroic deed."

The way in which he rose revealed that his ego had not suffered any damage from the wound. I continued talking because so much silence at such a remote location in his company put my nerves on edge.

"I don't like to admit it, but if it weren't for you, I would have been the one wounded."

His gaze relented when he sat at the edge of the bed. I had to look at the AC panel to make sure it was turned on. The room felt hot… too hot.

"Thank you," I said.

His fair skin radiated light. The sun had not touched it in a long time. Eliezer was not muscular but he had a very well defined physique. I suddenly felt an itching on the tip of my fingers, which I had to relieve by rubbing them against the rifts in his muscle. As I moved towards his back, I was shocked. I couldn't believe what my eyes were seeing. Every one of the images of Norman's paintings were captured in miniature on his son's backside. Silence drowned the moment. Eliezer allowed me the necessary time to contemplate the images. He knew I was overwhelmed with confusion.

"Just one, Wise. You may ask me just one question," he said finally.

"Why do you have those paintings tattooed? What's the relation? If you like them too, why did you lose your mind that time?" Before I was able to come up with other questions, he raised his hand.

"Silence, Wise. I said you could ask me only one question," he warned.

"What do you have to do with those paintings?" I raised my tone of voice, but that did not cause Eliezer to lose the control in his voice.

He sighed with fatigue.

"I painted them when I was in high school. I have no idea how the hell he got his hands on them, let alone on his walls. Satisfied?"

"Satisfied? How could I be satisfied?" That terse answer only prompted more questions that piled up like an anthill. *Maybe after I treat his wounds, he'll feel more at ease and willing to talk about the subject.* I focused on the wound: it was quite deep but only in a small area–nothing that couldn't be fixed with butterfly bandages. The rest was superficial.

"This will burn," I warned him as I poured the alcohol from the container.

"Shit!"

He grabbed my left wrist with his right hand. He squeezed so hard and he did it so aggressively that he pulled me towards him and I ended up right in front of him–very close. The bottle of alcohol fell to the floor. What was left spilled out. I froze at his touch and at the smell of the alcohol. My nerves betrayed me. Our eyes locked, his with anger and mine with fear. I looked down at the hand holding my wrist and little by little Eliezer let go.

I looked at his eyes again. Without realizing what I was doing, I began tracing the expression marks on his forehead with my index finger. His skin was hot. I imagined that those lines were from the memories of a life he had lived far away, a life of which I knew nothing, and that no one really knew what experiences he had. I looked into his eyes and discovered that they looked at me with a certain astonishment and confusion.

"I imagine these were more painful." I couldn't avoid having those words coming out of my mouth.

I prepared for Eliezer to throw me across the room for invading his personal space and making such a comment. That didn't happen. I eased my anxiety by tracing each line with my fingers. Eliezer shut his eyes. His jaw grew tense and he made an intimidating sound with is teeth. Again he aggressively grabbed my hand that was touching his forehead. Again I froze at his rough touch. He opened his eyes. His irises radiated a different green, one I'd never seen before. Unaware of how I had reached that point, I lost myself in them. His chest heaved with every rapid breath.

"Miranda," he paused and looked into my eyes, "move away."

I ignored him. I leaned in and kissed his forehead. His skin twitched as he felt my lips. Words were silenced. Sensations now dictated our course of action.

He stood near the edge of the bed. He held my face with his hands and kissed me. He kissed me and made his way with his eager tongue. He pulled me towards his chest and I felt his heart beating fast.

I didn't close my eyes, maybe that way I could lose myself completely in his... seeing through them and beyond. If I were lucky, I'd be able to see as deep as his memories and experiences that made him who he was. Perhaps, if I continued gazing at the beautiful green, I would also discover why my body felt so trusting and at his mercy; or discover why I was allowing the kiss without trusting him.

I moved his lips away while keeping his eyes locked on mine. He waited for a response... perhaps a slap. My hormones betrayed me. I didn't want to slap him, nor did I want to ask him to move away. I wanted to stay there, in those eyes in those arms. Every atom of my body wanted him, but I didn't understand why. Eliezer Clausell, by all accounts, was the person I most hated in my life, but also, the one I most wanted at the moment.

The lines on his forehead relaxed; his breathing didn't. My hands roamed over his torso. I reached down to his hips, to where the towel that covered his erection was tied. I undid the knot that kept the towel in its place. I closed my eyes.

Eliezer kissed me again–much more forcefully and aggressively than previously. He grabbed the cheeks of my rear, lifting me until his groin met mine. I clung to his body with arms and lips. He threw us down on the bed, placing his body on mine.

He, in full shameless nudity, showed clear signs of how much he wanted my body, my touch, my sex. With one yank, he pulled down my pants and my underwear. A button flew across the room. His heavy breathing was getting more out of control. I was tempted to stop watching him and to try to control mine, which was increasing in gasps. He removed my blouse–not with the care of a lover but with the eagerness of someone who's been waiting a long time for this moment. He tore buttonholes and stitching. I didn't care. My blouse was off. I helped him take off my bra.

I was nude before him. Eliezer was speechless:

dominated by his agitated breathing. He gazed into my eyes, and for a few seconds I thought that he had regained his reason. I thought that, perhaps, damned reason had returned to me as well, that soon, the hate we felt for each other would overtake our desires.

None of that happened.

Eliezer traced the curves of my silhouette with his eyes. He grabbed some of my hair by running his fingers through it, and with it, pulled my head back. He kissed and kissed. He returned to my lips. I kissed and kissed.

Now, it was my turn. I took his face in my hands and licked his neck and then his firm pectorals. Eliezer pulled my hair again, forcing my torso to bend. My firm breasts were at his eye level. He kissed them hungrily with a calm fury, feeling how hot they were for him. I dug my nails into his back, sinking myself into the unbearable pain that he carried on it.

I let out a groan. Eliezer entered me. Short breaths escaped from his half-open mouth. The rhythm of his hips harmonized with mine.

Moving and reaching, longing each time to be deeper in my womb, Eliezer did not stop pressing against me, running his fingers through my hair, kissing the skin of my neck, my collarbone, the lips of the woman he criticized so much. I did not stop caressing his back, which was covered with the emotions that his paintings aroused day after day.

I was not right to surrender to Eliezer. The thought circled my head every time I tried to fill my lungs with the air I needed. When I could inhale it was his breath that provided the air that my mind so needed to understand what was happening. *Is that how an addict must feel when he falls, seduced by his addiction?* Perhaps that's why the pleasure Eliezer awoke in me exceeded any other I had ever experienced with other men in the past.

Eliezer, while keeping the intense rhythm inside me, returned to exploring my breasts with his curious tongue. Sometimes he would look into my eyes, showing me his face contorted with pleasure, those eyes that would lose themselves in mine. Seeing him satisfy his needs with my body caused me to gasp, panting harder, moaning uncontrollably.

He increased the speed at which his hips moved. My breathing kept accelerating. I had to stop so as not to feel as if my heart were about to tear out of my chest. My womb stretched and stretched, enveloping his sex and receiving him completely.

I couldn't stand nor prevent the unparalleled pleasure I felt come suddenly with no warning when my body exploded in orgasm. As Eliezer heard the first notes of my loud and gasping cry, he took my face in his hands, and in the middle of my climax, he was able to increase the strong, rough, and abrupt movements that caressed me from within. His eyes remained fixed on mine as I would alternate back and forth from reality with the rhythm of his penetrations. Drops of sweat caressed his forehead and fell to my breasts.

Still feeling the last waves of my long climax, I could sense that he was ready to experience his own, to lose himself in me. The aroma exuding from his pores became sweeter. The spasms I felt from deep inside my body down to my legs, to my torso, which would curve unwittingly, made me feel alive. Eliezer brought his breathing under control, closed his eyes, and sank his head between my breasts–the perfect spot to silence the sound coming out of his throat.

He moved away too soon, breaking the connection between bodies. We breathed… breathed the heavy air that flooded the room and nothing more.

A loud banging on the door and a deep voice rose above the silence.

"Open the door!"

Both hearts were shaken, but this time not with carnal desire. Our eyes met in astonishment.

Eliezer jumped out of bed and looked for the towel. The bedroom door had been open, and the main door of the cabin that faced the bed was also suddenly thrown wide open. On the other side of the doorway there were two men dressed in black and pointing their guns at us. Eliezer tied the towel around his hips and I grabbed the sheet and covered my damp body.

"What the hell are you doing Donovan?" Eliezer yelled.

It was Donovan, the head of security at Medika. *Swallow me, Earth!*

There was silence in the cabin. Outside, the night was singing; the wind played with the leaves and flowers, a river wound around the rocks.

"I'm sorry, sir. Are you ok? I apologize." Donovan did not know how to hide the embarrassment or how to undo the mistake he'd just made. "We lost track of you at the carnival and thought that something had happened to you. The GPS tracked your cell phone here. Is Ms. Wise with you?"

I reached out from under the sheet with my hand, waving it to convey my presence. Thank God I did not have to show my face, which had turned hotter than an oven at its highest temperature.

"Get out of here!" Eliezer ordered as he shut the door on their faces. When he recovered his breathing, he yelled again, "And prepare the jet!"

Eliezer returned. As he sat at the edge of the bed, he rubbed his face in his hands.

"We must go, Wise."

I pulled the sheets away from my face. My voice trembled as I spoke.

"Where?"

"We must return," he announced sternly. "And don't worry about Donovan. I'll take care of him."

If you only knew that Donovan is the least of my worries. What worried me the most was he, Eliezer Clausell, and it wasn't exactly what happened between us, but what I had felt. *Is it possible to feel that way for someone whom you hate so much? Did I take some kind of drug like the kind they put in beers?* Although I wanted the latter to be true, because it would free me from a huge feeling of guilt, I shuddered at the thought of the sweet poison of his saliva on my mouth, on my breasts.

I really blew it. *Why didn't I remember Norman's instructions this time?*

"I didn't know that security would accompany us to Panama too!" I demanded, my voice having returned to normal.

"Did you think that I would go along with your rules?" He looked at me with his usual look. He was angry.

I decided not to push the issue. I wrapped myself in the sheet and went to take a shower. The lukewarm water would help me clear my thoughts, understand what had happened, and clean the traces of his body from mine. If I had been able to go down into the drain of the bath, I would have done so quite happily. I had a feeling that, from that moment on, things would go from bad to worse. I had served my most intimate treasure on a golden platter to the one who wanted to be my executioner.

"We can forget this," I proposed as soon as I returned to the bedroom.

The lines that adorned his forehead displayed their usual intensity.

"What are you talking about, Miranda?"

"What just happened?"

He was quiet for a number of seconds. He reached for his cell phone. He turned on the screen and looked at me again.

"Nothing has happened here, Wise," he raised an eyebrow expecting my agreement.

"Right. Nothing," I confirmed, my hand trembling.

I walked toward the bed and discovered that he had folded my clothes and had organized them by placing one garment over another so that I could first take my underwear and then the rest.

I looked at him again and the Eliezer that I had known for a few minutes was gone. He was sitting on the other

174

side of the bed, ignoring my semi-nude presence, and looking over his iPhone. He was wearing his father's pants. I felt a tingling in my eyes and a slight pain in my throat. I took my clothing unwillingly and entered the bathroom.

"Can we go now?" he asked when I stepped out. The usual Eliezer was back.

I nodded, whether or not I was ready for what was awaiting me in the near future. The flight to San Juan wasn't very long, but it would not be at all pleasant.

The SUV was waiting at the entrance of the cabin. Donovan was standing next to the passenger doors. He opened the doors to the SUV. I got in first. There were water bottles in the drink holders. I took one and finished it in one gulp.

An awkward silence prevailed during the trip. No one said anything. Not a single syllable. I put on my headphones and looked for one of my favorite songs, *The Ballad of Love and Hate by The Avett Brothers*. What an appropriate song!

There was no way to put my thoughts in order. In my mind there was only room for the image of Eliezer's nude body. I wondered what he was thinking. Judging from his face, he wasn't thinking anything. At least not about what had happened. Definitely, for him, nothing had happened.

Chapter 13

*T*o think we still had to make an even longer trip to Asia....

My head hurt from thinking so much about the unexpected events of that unfortunate night. There was no logical explanation to what had happened between us. Well, at least there was a reason for my behavior: lack of sex. Alex had been warning me about it for some time: "If you let your libido build up, you'll end up with the first one who crosses your path, and you'll regret it in the end."

I had not confessed to my friend that I would receive frequent invitations for sex, but I preferred a less active sex life because I always went to great lengths to act within the limits of what was proper.

Even though they didn't say it to my face, I knew that many people at Medika lived for the day when "Norman's poor charity case" would make a mistake, so I was satisfied with merely fantasizing. It had been a good strategy. I could pleasure myself wherever I wanted, whenever I wanted. With a lifestyle where I needed to go from place to place, it was better to get close to myself than to a different suitor in each country. That was never an option–neither as a woman, as a professional, nor as the lead representative of Medika.

How would I be able to look Eliezer in the eye again and still project confidence? Why did I have sex with a man that didn't even respect me? He could have stopped me. *A man never stops a woman, Miranda...* that would have been Alex's response to my argument. However, I didn't understand one small detail. Why did he go along with my game if it's obvious that I'm repugnant to him? Maybe he needed sex too. With such an unattractive personality, I doubt very much that women would feel suddenly attracted to him. Maybe they would sleep with him only once they found out how much money he had.

***

It was Sunday. To have less thinking to do, I went out for a jog. The fresh air would do me good. While on the track after minutes of jogging, someone was jogging at my side, and at my pace. It was not the first time some Casanova would try to woo me on the track, but this was not the time, nor the day for that.

I slowed down.

The person next to me did too.

I picked up the pace.

The other legs caught up.

¡Ugh! I stopped suddenly.

I took off my earphones and I looked at the person hounding me.

I must have been thinking about him so much that I attracted him...

"What?" I asked in a rude tone.

"Don't stop like that, Wise. You can get dizzy." The

178

warning came late. I was already dizzy and not because of my sudden stop but because of the unwanted company. Eliezer was slowly jogging circles around me. "I'm not lying, it can hurt you, particularly your heart."

I immediately started moving away.

Eliezer caught up.

"What do you want, Clausell?"

"What could I want in a place like this?"

To tell the truth, I didn't have an answer for him, but he did continue observing me. I would have easily shared some of the ideas I had in mind.

"Wise, I want us to talk."

"Can't you wait? We can talk tomorrow at the office, if..."

He stopped jogging. It surprised me that I did the same when I realized that he was not next to me. I walked towards him.

"If I wanted to talk to you about something related to Medika, Wise, believe me, I would have waited."

I began laughing. I know I'm a spoiled brat, perhaps as a result of having been raised under Norman's wings.

"Clausell, you and I have nothing that connects us, much less shared topics of conversation. What do you want to talk to me about on a Sunday morning?" His presence made me feel like something was stuck in my throat.

His eyes half closed. I couldn't figure out if he was trying to control his frustration, anger, or disappointment.

"Well, you sure know how to play the game. Nothing has happened between us? Please, Miranda!"

"I don't know what you're talking about, Eliezer."

He bit his lower lip–yet another mannerism I was unable to figure out.

"I think I got the wrong person. You're not the one I want to talk to."

I got very close to him and looked into his face until I got him to look at me. I spoke slowly.

"Let's get something clear, Clausell. I don't know what happened. I've been spending the last 30 hours trying to understand how I ended up in that bed with you. That should never have happened. Understand? Never! With you, never!" My confidence was displayed in my firm tone, a trick that hid the truth: my body... my body that was filled with emotions didn't agree with what I said. "I cannot take back what happened between us, but I can tell you that it doesn't change anything. Let me warn you..."

Eliezer interrupted me.

"Another warning for the list? What a pity that I don't have anything to write on. There are so many, I won't be able to memorize them." He half smiled–so full of mystery and malice.

"Don't you dare use this against me!" I spoke with my index finger up high.

Eliezer looked at me confused. Instead of smiling, he snorted.

"I had not thought about it. Do you really believe me to be so cruel, Miranda? Sleeping with you was not a trick to fire you... though now that you mention it, it could be useful..."

"Let's just say that we're even," I clarified before he could give it any more thought and come up with a

Machiavellian plan to destroy me. I ran my hand over my forearm, the same arm he had hurt days ago. Eliezer remained pensive. I sensed anger in his face. Once more, he was losing control. I had taken him where I wanted and he had helped me do it.

"We're even, International."

He turned and ran in the opposite direction.

**

I no longer felt like jogging. As I walked home, I reflected on my responses and words. Maybe I shouldn't have indulged in my rudeness. I should have given him a chance to talk, which is the reason he approached me. Perhaps he had come with the intent to apologize. Maybe he wanted to comfort me, telling me not to worry, that he was a gentleman and that gentleman don't boast about their sex life.

My God! If Norman were to find out, he would die of disappointment! He would always warn me: "Miranda, work and pleasure are like water and oil: they don't mix." If Eliezer were added to the equation, for sure you'd get the perfect recipe for an atomic bomb.

I arrived at the rehab center at three in the afternoon. Seeing Norman on that day was like standing before a stranger. It had been a week since I last saw him, and with the twists and turns that life makes, I knew that from here on, he would stop being the man he was. No more Norman the confidant, friend, and father. No more valuable advice for me, a damsel in distress with a mind full of problems, a possible dismissal in the near future, and involved with the worst of men. I had to grow and learn to face the future without him and without help.

When I arrived, Norman was leaving his room. A nurse was pushing the wheelchair. "Time for therapy," she whispered when she saw me. Norman strayed from all decorum.

"Girl!" he yelled, his face displaying happiness to see me. "Please don't go. I'll be back in forty-five minutes. You have no idea about the kinds of things they do to me in there…"

The joke made the nurse laugh. She patted him on the shoulder. I smiled too.

"I live in waiting for you," I let the smile stay with me until they both disappeared through the door at the end of the hall.

I reclined against the door frame of his room, my mind crazy with other thoughts that burdened my heart.

Oh, Norman, what have I done? What have I done?

A voice called out my name. My skin crawled. I turned.

"Isabel?" She was looking at me as if she could hide her hypocrisy and make me believe she was happy about seeing me. I reciprocated. "Good afternoon."

"It certainly is." She placed her hand on my shoulder. She pulled me towards her. "I imagine you're looking for Norman. He just left."

"We met in the hall," I corrected her and dispelled the idea that I had been waiting for Norman.

Isabel smiled at me the same way her son would.

"Come. I want you to join me for a cup of coffee."

I hesitated again. I wondered if the invitation was

sincere. Nothing in that woman seemed to be.

"Thank you, but... I'm on my way out."

I squeezed the handles of my purse and bowed my head to say goodbye. Isabel touched my shoulder again.

"No, you don't have to leave. Do you want ice water? A juice to cool off?" She insisted, and my heart raced.

And what if she knew that I'd slept with her son? Why did she say "cool off?" when that is what I've been trying to do since I had her son in my bed? Could this be just a bad twist of fate and a coincidence?

I decided to give her a chance. Norman once taught me that one should not let one's self be carried away by prejudice alone. Who knows, maybe Isabel is an affectionate woman and could be the best of friends.

"Water is fine."

Isabel smiled Eliezer's smile again.

***

Once in the cafeteria where some children were running in between chairs and tables, she chose a place to sit and indicated where she wanted me to be. That was not a good sign. I hesitated a bit, but to not create any misunderstandings, I obeyed her wishes.

"So tell me about your life, Miranda."

Me eyes opened wide. *Is this woman crazy or is she the witch she appears to be?*

She touched my hand lightly.

"I understand. How are you going to make me your confidant if the impression I made on you was not the right one? I apologize, dear."

"That's not necessary," I said, because, after all, she wasn't. She carried the "wife" title, so she was just following proper protocol. I opened the water bottle and took a drink. I almost choked when she insisted.

"Well, can you now tell me something about yourself?"

I closed the bottle. I swallowed slowly and I moved forward. The conversation was hinting at war.

"What else are you interested in knowing?"

She showed me her imposing teeth again. Her friendliness was alarming.

"How've you been these days? For example, what have you been doing?"

"I've had a lot of work," I summarized.

"Yes, Norman mentioned that. In fact, he said you never stop working. You know, a young woman like you should make time to go out, have fun. There's a saying: 'What's not on display doesn't sell.' Have you heard it?"

So much friendliness and such sound advice could not be a sign of anything good. I folded the napkin that was wrapped around the plastic bottle in four.

"I prefer the one that says: 'Better alone that in bad company.'"

"You're right about that." Again she gave that chilling smile. "Tell me, how is Eliezer doing?"

"You should ask him."

The plastic smile melted and her voice took a tone of rudeness.

"I'm asking you, Miranda." She regained her

composure and softened her voice, "Could you give me your opinion?"

"Eliezer is my boss. I don't think it's prudent to give my opinion."

Her tone of voice went from heavenly to earthly and the red color of her lipstick intensified like flames hungry for destruction.

"Why don't you leave?"

Before opening my mouth in surprise, I took my purse and I stood up. Isabel took my hand and left some marks with her fingernails. I sat down. I heard the reverberation of my heart beating.

"Enough with the games and cordiality, Miranda. Get out. Leave Medika," she blurted out. I understood then what she wanted. I should have trusted my instincts.

"Help me find a reason why I should leave Medika."

Isabel was silent for a few moments looking at me with anger. As I looked at her in such close proximity, I noticed her eyes looked glassy and worn out. The make-up and Botox hadn't succeeded in hiding how horrible she really was.

"Are you as naive as they say you are, or do you try to live up to your name, *Wise*?"

"I live up to my name," I smiled the same way she did, which was the same smile I had learned from her son.

"In that case, Wise, I'll be very clear so as not to leave any doubts between us. For more than twenty years you lived by Norman's side. I imagine that you must be very grateful that he saved you from the life that you would have otherwise had."

She paused and drank her coffee. The brief delay gave me that time to realize that the woman was worse than I imagined. I would also have to deal with Isabel on my own. I had not doubts about where Eliezer got his bad genes. If there was someone in the world more hateful that him, that someone was his mother, the drama queen. *Norman is neither naive nor stupid. At some point he must have realized the mistake he made by marrying this kind of woman.*

"Your time is up, Miranda."

I used her son's words to respond.

"I didn't know I had an expiration date. Norman never mentioned it."

Isabel laughed loudly.

"You're not at all naive, dear."

"I know. By the way, you should verify your sources."

I stood up again, purse and water bottle in hand.

Isabel gave her farewell from her chair.

"Don't cross my path, foolish girl."

I approached her and poured the water in her coffee cup.

"I'm not the one who crossed the other's path."

Chapter 14

A text message was the only communication I had with Eliezer:

I'll see you in the hotel lobby at 7:00 pm.

Eliezer didn't respond to the message. It seemed to me that we were finally, exactly even. We came up with excuses (some made up) to avoid each other, and neither one of us was uncomfortable with the separation.

Following the encounter with Isabel, the last thing I wanted was a 17-hour flight in the company of her adoring son, which is why I was traveling first class on a commercial airplane, and why my rear and back were hurting. There was no first class that compared to the comfort of a private jet. Even so, tired of thinking so much, my mind thanked me for enduring the minor discomfort. Without Medika people around me, only strangers, an internal peace came over me. I felt as if I were losing myself in a deep dream where I was a different person and Medika didn't exist.

I landed in Beijing, after having added eight thousand four hundred miles of flight to my rear. I asked for a taxi to the hotel. At the desk they gave me card keys for my room. They didn't ask too many questions. I opened my purse to give them my credit card and the man on the other side of the check-in desk smiled and said, "Oh, no, no. Your boss already arranged everything for you, Miss Wise. Enjoy your stay!"

I said good-bye with a timid smile and nodded my head slightly. As I crossed the lobby that lead to the elevators, Eliezer appeared in front of me. He prevented me from walking further and checked me out from head to toe.

He showed is habitual mocking smile.

"Welcome to China, Wise!"

"Thank you, Clausell!" I mimicked his enthusiasm with a smile that disappeared in less than a second.

My boss looked rested, and from the soap scent coming from his body, I guessed he had just taken a shower.

Sometimes I hate you more than usual...

I slid to one side to make my way to the elevators. He crossed my path again.

"Where do you think you're going, Wise?"

I yawned casually.

"It's not seven yet, Clausell. Where do you think I'm going?" I waved the card keys I had just received in my hand. "I'll see you then."

He raised an eyebrow and grimaced. He raised the briefcase he was carrying.

"No. We'll review the documents that Margaret asked
188

me to sign *now*."

I let my shoulders drop.

"Clausell, that can wait. I'm tired. I need to recharge."

"Don't you know how to take responsibility for your decisions, Wise?"

There it was: my punishment for traveling on a commercial airplane.

I tried to dodge him a second time. He did not even allow me to try to walk.

"Miranda Wise, I need for us to review the documents. Now!"

"Eliezer Clausell," the tremor that my lips caused when I pronounced his name pleased me, "I'm not joking. If I don't take a nap now, I'll fall asleep, and you don't want me to fall asleep while were discussing important subjects, do you?"

He shook his briefcase as if to tell me that it wasn't his problem.

I sighed. I had made a decision and I had to face the consequences. I would remember this moment the next time I had to travel to China with him and I chose a commercial flight. *Breathe, Miranda. He is your boss.*

"Can you wait? I need to leave the luggage in the bedroom."

He smiled.

"Only if you do it very quickly."

Ugh! Why couldn't he just say yes and leave it at that? Why did he have to be sarcastic or speak with double meanings? My nostrils flared. How I would have liked to slap him at that moment.

"You know what? I've changed plans, Clausell. Let's review the documents now."

"Perfect! Follow me. You'll love the coffee at this hotel."

I rolled me eyes. *As if I'd never been here before.*

Just after six in the evening, between questions, yawns, and coffee cup after coffee cup, I fell asleep on the reclining chair.

"Do you hear me, Wise?"

The question came up following the clattering of cups and plates. Eliezer had slammed his fist on the table.

"Yes, yes," I said, with my eyes wide open and my heart about to jump out of my chest. "I'm sorry, what was the question?"

Eliezer drank some coffee and reworded his question but not before giving me a look of annoyance.

"We have too much money invested in this country. Don't you think it's risky?"

"That's precisely why we're making this investment. It's very costly to repatriate money. The tax rate is about thirty to thirty-five percent."

"We should at least repatriate our initial investment."

"Chinese law dictates that capital funds cannot be repatriated unless the company is liquidated. That's basic knowledge during a first year of study in international business, Eliezer. You should take a short course, at least."

I was hoping to insult him with my comment so that

he would lose control.

His cell phone rang. His expression changed when he looked at the screen. He gave me a look of doubt and excused himself. He left the café to take the call. I was dying of curiosity to know with whom he was speaking. He was pacing back and forth, moving his hands when he wasn't hiding them in his pockets, while every few seconds his eyes would turn to mine.

"Wise! Shit!" he cursed as he stomped back to our table in a fury, while giving me a look such that if the whites of his eyes were to turn red, they would complement the rest of his face. Taking his seat, he slammed his fist against the table again, which made me jump in my chair.

"Go to sleep. Dinner is at eight. Be punctual," he barked.

Dazed and scared I couldn't say anything more. I raised my hand to my forehead and saluted him.

"Yes, sir!"

He made no gesture to help me with my things. With my back to him, while I was picking up the suitcase and laptop case, I discovered in the reflection of the glass table that he had hit so many times, Eliezer's mischievous and mocking smile. He enjoyed torturing me. *Is that possible?*

***

The dinner, although casual, was decisive. We would be closing agreements on a partnership between a Chinese company and Medika. We would put up capital, knowledge, and infrastructure, and although it was a business dinner like many others that I had attended, something told me that this one would have a distinctive touch.

In the room, I was paying attention to details that used to never bother me, such as the fit of the black dress, the soft waves in my hair, the right lipstick that would bring out the subtle color of my eye shadow—and this time I would not be the one who would be late.

To see Eliezer through the tinted window of the car made me take a second look at my cocktail dress, the waves in my hair, and my lipstick. Eliezer wore a finely tailored suit that reinforced the luster of his ego. The sliding doors that were the entrance to the hotel opened for the imposing masculine presence before them. Eliezer exited through them. He looked to one side and the other. The chauffer caught his attention, opened the back door, and invited him to board.

"Hello, Clausell."

He did not enter until confirming that it was I who was speaking. He smiled because he could not hide the (un)pleasant surprise.

"Wise," he smiled at me approvingly, "you're punctual today."

The fragrance of his cologne eased the tension in the air. I tried to say little. I merely told him about the people who would be keeping us company this evening.

Eliezer was paying attention to me. He did not stop looking at me even when the words stopped.

***

The night went just as planned. Dinner lasted a couple of hours. The Chinese left satisfied. There were plenty of respectful bows. The contract was signed to the benefit of both parties.

I said goodbye to Eliezer with a handshake at the hotel. He appeared to be satisfied with the new investment and the course on which Medika was embarking. When he entered the elevator and disappeared from my view, I felt free.

I went to the bar and ordered a draft beer. *Congratulations, Miranda, you shined tonight.* I made a toast to myself and drank.

"Congratulations, Wise."

I didn't realize that my stomach could crawl up my back, but when I heard the voice of my heartless boss, I felt like that's what was happening. I didn't turn to look at him. I didn't even thank him. He, on the other hand, approached and pulled up the chair next to me. He ordered the same thing I was having.

I looked away from him and looked around the place. Besides the couples and friends that were kissing or celebrating, there was no one else that could save me from the discomfort. There was a man at the other end of the bar who did not engender trust. He looked at me like a predator. Eliezer also noticed him, readjusting his own chair so as to block the stranger's view of me.

"What more were you expecting to find here, Wise? The future father of your children?" He took a sip.

I turned to him.

"Did you come to celebrate, give me a lesson, or be like that poor devil?"

Eliezer smiled and bit the corner of his lower lip.

"How difficult you make my life, Wise. Should I

choose one, all, or none?"

He had taken off the bowtie. He was wearing his suit with the first few buttons of his shirt undone and the collar relaxed. I didn't answer. All I could think of was how attractive he looked sitting there, the after-hours executive look, beer in hand, challenging me.

"Don't you know what to respond, Clausell?"

Eliezer got close. He whispered in my ear, "Do it for me."

I let out a short laugh. "That one's on me. Have a wonderful night."

I left my beer and some yuan on the counter.

After a half hour, he was knocking on my door. If it wasn't because he drank both beer mugs, then it was because it took him time to realize, or believe, that I had intentionally left one of the key cards to my room beside the money on the counter.

"May I help you?"

He was silent. He wet his lips with his tongue. He wasn't expecting that I'd greet him in a white *hanfu*. His eyes bugged out.

"You forgot this, Wise." He reached out with the key card in his hand.

"What makes you think it's mine?"

"You didn't seem interested in the guy at the bar," he smiled and clarified, "…the *other* guy at the bar. The idea of going from room to room to figure out what door that key would open seemed interesting, but there was a serious risk that I might find someone dressed… like that."

I returned his lip-wetting gesture, approached him,

and fixed his shirt collar.

"Are you conservative, Clausell?"

His chest heaved as if he were trying to hold his breath and not have to breathe heavily again.

"Cautious."

"Oh, really?" I outlined the shape of his shoulders with my fingers.

Grab him. Kidnap him in your room and don't let him go free until he begs you, Miranda!

I was analyzing the possible consequences of my crazy ideas when he moved his torso into my room and tossed the key card on the nightstand. He placed a hand on my waist and ogled at me from head to toe before leaving.

"Black suits you better, Wise."

Was that a compliment or an insult? I laughed on the inside.

Disappointed with the ridiculous plan of fooling around with him again, I took the card on the nightstand and threw it against the wall. He pulled another key card out from his jacket and walked towards the adjoining room. I then realized that there were two cards and that my room and his were connected by a shared door. The words that the employee at the check-in desk told me that morning were glowing in my mind like a neon sign: *Your boss already arranged everything for you.*

Eliezer Clausell was very cautious, no doubt. He wanted me to follow the rules of his game. Whatever would happen, would happen in his room, not mine. I stood there, in front of the door: was it the entrance to heaven, or hell? *Miranda, this can't be given too much thought.*

Do whatever you want, but do it now!

I unlocked my door and slowly turned the knob. Just as I imagined, his door was open. There was the cautious man, waiting for me. He was removing his shoes at the edge of the bed, looking toward the door with a slight smile on his face.

"You forgot this."

I leaned over and placed the card on the line between the two doors, a neutral spot.

Eliezer chuckled. He had unbuttoned his shirt and was not wearing pants. I looked at his crotch and gave him a look of pleasure. Alex was right. I needed sex more often.

"You couldn't have left it under the door, Wise?"

"I prefer to leave it at the door, Clausell."

He finished taking off his socks and walked toward me, up to the dividing line and observing me with caution.

"What level of risk do you want to assume tonight, Eliezer?"

He brushed his hair with his hand and said in a whisper: "The one that you can't use against me later."

If he wasn't willing to run a risk, why should I? We were even.

He took me by the waist and held me against the doorframe. On the dividing line… that is where Eliezer, the cautious one, wanted us. Our chests connected at the rhythm of our agitated heartbeats. He let his heavy gaze fall into my eyes to see if he could find the answer to the obvious question: do you have any idea what we're doing?

No, I had no idea; and apparently, neither did he.

"I told you that you should have left it under the

door," he said as he wet his lips.

"You still don't get it that I don't like following your instructions?" I finished the sentence in my head: *Unless you command me to surrender at your feet...*

He tilted his head. He wanted to read between my lines. He moved his face close to my ear and breathed.

"I insist that black suits your better."

"That's can easily be solved."

I undid the belt on the *hanfu* and it slipped open to display my black lingerie.

I'll never be able to forget the arousal that gripped Eliezer's face. He roamed my body with his rough hands and filled them with my breasts. He caressed them forcefully.

"On second thought, I don't think I like the black either."

"Before I could give the slight a second thought, Eliezer brushed the *hanfu* that was hanging from my shoulders aside. He savored the silks that guarded the booty he had discovered. He took off my bra and pulled down my panties.

I wanted to strip him too... to rid him of his shirt and his briefs that shamelessly marked his firm erection. Playing on the dividing line maintained equity between us, but he would not allow it. He took hold of my hands, raised them over my head, and forced me against the metal doorframe even more. The feeling of cold metal eased with the heat of my skin.

He didn't have to struggle to find the space between my legs. Among the rush of feelings, I began to watch him, to study him. His seriousness confused me. Some moments he seemed to enjoy the pleasure, other times his face would change, as if he were angry with himself for enjoying what he was doing. His lips gently caressed my sex. His tongue punished me with fury. Timidly, I tried to control my moans, which was impossible with the unequaled pleasure that Eliezer's maneuvers caused. My body was flooded by an overdose of that man.

Am I liberating you from your demons, with this, Clausell?

"I like the sound of your voice when you moan."

He paused while he took off the only piece of intimate clothing he was wearing. It was the perfect moment to get away, and I didn't. I prolonged it. It was the first time that he admitted liking something about me.

He roamed my body with kisses and caresses, as I swayed like a suspension bridge, from side to side. For as much as I wanted to regain control of the situation, it was impossible. Eliezer was in charge of every one of my sensations… my moans… my quivering.

He moved my legs up around his waist and moved my hands over my head once more.

He penetrated me without warning, suddenly and furiously, without stopping, every time more deeply and more forcefully.

"Defenseless," he whispered in between movements.

There was no compassion in his attack. He showed no mercy. I would not have wanted it any other way.

By the time sanity returned to our rooms, it was too late: there were only traces of what we had done without crossing the dividing line. We found ourselves on the floor, on our sides, each with a pillow, sharing Eliezer's bed comforter on the carpet of desire, exhausted, speaking in silent glances, letting regret rest between us, right on the dividing line.

***

I woke up in my bed, clothed.

The door that connected to Eliezer's room was shut.

Eliezer

"She fell in your game. Or did you fall into hers? Dummkopf[2]!"

Chapter 15

$\mathcal{T}$he warm air of Christmas Eve overwhelmed Medika and the city. Many had said their goodbyes the day before, others were lucky enough to be on vacation for a week, and a few worked until mid afternoon. I was not among any of those people. It was seven in the evening and there was still no end in sight to the list of emails that I had to send out before taking a few days off. I didn't want to leave anything pending.

I looked away from the monitor to rest my eyes when I noticed a circle of light that lit the area outside my office. By the position of the light, I figured there was someone in Eliezer's office.

Forgetting about my email, I tiptoed that way and found him at his desk, reading documents and reports from who knows what companies. He looked tired. His shirt was unbuttoned half way down the collar, the sleeves were rolled up, and his forearms were exposed. My memory was playing pranks on me, and suddenly I remembered how those forearms had held my hips and prevented me from crossing the dividing line between two rooms at a hotel in China.

I turned to return to my office and his voice called out

to me. I shut my eyes.

"Hello, Wise. What plans do you have for tomorrow? Something special, I imagine." I turned and Eliezer put down the papers. He looked at me. It took me a few seconds to process the question and respond.

"Nothing."

He shrugged.

"May you enjoy doing nothing."

He smiled and went back to his pen and papers. I was about to make a mistake: to invite him to anything or for him to be part of my Christmas Eve routine, but I overcame the impulse because, somehow, I knew it was one of those potentially life altering moments. I let his answer stand–an answer like that did not deserve any more thought–and I returned to finish my tasks.

As long as I can remember, I always connected Christmas season with sadness. I couldn't help a feeling of envy in my heart, though I was not proud of that. I knew that I should be happy for those who could celebrate big, surrounded by family and friends. Be that as it may, my heart cried out year after year: my family circle was diminished and consisted of strangers, namely Norman, Margaret, and Alex.

Perhaps my eternal feeling of loneliness was the reason I did the things I did on Christmas Eve and Christmas: looking for new meaning in those days, always spending Christmas Eve alone at home after dinner with whomever invited me, and Christmas lunch with Norman.

***

The thought of having Eliezer as my companion during my Christmas tasks was with me all night. I could barely sleep. What persistence!

He was the perfect candidate for the position of "suitable company." There was nothing between us, at least not as long as we lived in the real world. Once outside of it, alone and separated from our daily affairs, we would transform into other people. It wasn't that he was a different man, but it did take a huge effort to silence his demons, his traumas, that hunger to be unfaithful to the terrible loneliness that haunted him for so many moons.

At nine in the morning I took the cell phone, looked for his number in the directory, and mustered the courage to touch the screen and start dialing.

"Miranda."

"Clausell," I said, greeting him and taking the necessary time to repeat the sound of his voice saying my name in my mind. When I spoke again, my voice was high-pitched, "Good morning!"

Eliezer's response made me think that he had installed hidden cameras in my room and in my mind.

"Very good morning. Was it *that* difficult for you to call?"

I could not allow him to think that he was right, that I had been thinking about him for so many hours, so my response was quick and clear, although not very convincing.

"No, no. I pulled my telephone out of my purse and I accidentally dialed your number. It's not polite to hang-up on a call without saying good morning."

"Is that the best excuse you have, Wise? Let me tell you that you are not very creative."

I took a deep breath and by the slight, odd noise I

heard at the other end of the line, I imagine that Eliezer was smiling. I took off my armor.

"Would you like to go with me somewhere?"

"And what makes you think that I would be interested in going anywhere with you?"

I smiled and bit my lip.

"The fact that you still have not ended the call."

Eliezer laughed.

"Should I wear my pants?"

This time, I was the one laughing.

"If you feel more comfortable, yes."

My eardrum caught the muted snort of his muffled chuckle.

"Will we get into trouble, Ms. Wise?"

More than we have already would be difficult, I thought, but I said, "Worried, Clausell?"

"Not at all. Time and type of clothing?"

"I'll pick you up in 60 minutes." I was about to hang up when I remembered another detail. "Clausell!" I yelled so that he could hear me and not press the darn red button.

"I'm still here, Miranda," his voice calm.

"It may not be prudent for you to not have your pants on, and on tight, with a belt."

I pressed the button to end the call before hearing his laugh or his declining the invitation. I got out of bed and while I showered and put on my make-up, I fantasized about possible scenarios during the day. All of them, absolutely all of them, led me to two versions: either the day would turn out fine, almost perfect, or very bad, a tragedy. It was that simple.

With Eliezer nearby, there was a rule: every event that involved both of us began and ended badly... *usually, in bed, Miranda Wise.*

It was Christmas Eve, for heavens sake. Something out of the ordinary would be appropriate. I put on my favorite jeans and a blouse with pink shades that I had not worn yet.

***

I dialed Eliezer's number while parked in front of his imposing residential high rise. It rang three times when someone suddenly tapped on the window next to the passenger's seat of my car. My heartbeat quickened.

Outside, Eliezer was waving his iPhone at me, showing me the display where there was only the letter "W" to indicate an incoming call. I smiled and ended the call. *So "W" is how he labeled me on his cell phone. At least it wasn't International.*

Just as I was opening my door to get out and greet him, I could see Eliezer's expression change. No more smile. There was a woman on the sidewalk facing him. He turned around and walked over to her. They spoke for a few minutes. It appeared as if they were smoothing out a disrespectful conversation. At first, they were both talking at once, but then he was silent and listened. While the woman talked and talked, he sneaked a few furtive glances at me. It seemed as if his eyes were telling me that he had been surprised by the situation. He tired after a few minutes, and left the woman mid-sentence, abandoning the unfinished conversation. He walked back to my car, I unlocked the door, he opened it, and sat down. He fiddled with the side buttons on the phone. He put it in his pocket, sighed, and turned towards me with the same smile as before.

"Hello, Miranda. Where are we going?" He rubbed his hands together–an expression of enthusiasm in the face of uncertainty.

I looked out and around. The woman had disappeared. I turned to look into Eliezer's green eyes and I thought, that if he didn't give me any explanations about what had happened, there was nothing to worry about. I moved the stick shift without disengaging the brake.

"It's a surprise."

"Didn't you have anyone better to keep you company?"

With a quick head movement I threw my hair back and gave him a flirtatious look.

"Options one and two didn't accept. They weren't available."

The smile that had accompanied his suggestive questions vanished.

"So, I'm number three," he remarked with a grim voice, tasting the feeling of not being my first choice. "You know, next time invite all three of us ahead of time. Something that involves four promises to be very interesting."

I continued his game.

"I'll take that into consideration."

He continued the game.

"So plan the next invitation."

"That depends on how you behave today, Clausell."

208

"I'll wait for that invitation, Wise." He had the malevolent look that transported me to other encounters where there were no inhibitions between us.

I let my foot off the brake.

***

It wasn't very far to where we were going: about ten or fifteen minutes with traffic. I stopped at the gate that guarded the building entrance and we were quickly allowed to enter. The car slowly neared a large house with toys in the front yard. Surrounding it were swings and huge plastic castles where children pretended to be knights and princesses. Eliezer didn't smile, say anything, or react at all.

"Welcome to the Santa Maria Home, Mr. Clausell."

Eliezer looked around and lowered his head.

"Did you grow up here?" he asked cautiously, his voice sounding somewhat intimidated.

"Bingo!"

There was confusion on his face. I don't know if it was because of my outburst or my cheeriness. I tried to explain why we were there.

"I do this every year, Clausell. I bring these children a small Christmas party... some happiness. I like to share with them."

"Don't you think that if I, a complete stranger, had the need to be with children, a visit to the park would have been sufficient?"

Before I could respond, he exited the car and slammed the door. *This is going to be difficult,* I thought to myself. I exited and asked him to help me with the boxes that were in the trunk. When he approached me, I looked him in the eye.

"Listen to me, Clausell. Your needs don't matter here, just theirs. If you want to leave, go ahead." I took the things, turned and walked towards the home. "But you'll have to find your own transportation because I just got here." I wouldn't let his stupid words ruin my day, nor my excitement. Why did he always make my life more complicated? And why was he determined to do it so often?

"If I wanted to, Wise, it wouldn't be difficult to find a way to leave," he whispered at my side with four boxes in hand.

***

Don Jose greeted us. He had worked as handyman at the home for as long as I could remember. He could do plumbing, carpentry, cabinetry, and construction. The years had not treated Don Jose well. At sixty something, his walk was slower, his hands were shaky, but his mind and memory seemed to be unaffected. We affectionately called him "Grandpa Jose." He was the father figure to our Santa Maria family and home.

Grandpa Jose hugged me and squeezed my cheeks – a gesture of affection that he had for me and all the other children he had seen grow-up.

"Wow, my love! You're so handsome!" I flirted.

"I look younger every day. Don't I?"

We hugged each other again in a happy embrace.

"Grandpa, this is my friend Eliezer."

There was no reason to give him details. Grandpa looked intently at whom I had introduced as my friend.

I know he was doing an instant profile of him. He half-closed his eyes.

"Eliezer, son of Moses? Do you know that your name means, 'God is help'?"

"Yes, but this Eliezer is son of Norman," I offered that bit of information. In my mind, a joke that was not very funny: *and to deal with this one, I sure need God's help...*

"Oh! This one is more handsome than the last one you brought!" he said with a smile, satisfied with his comment.

I couldn't help thinking, *swallow me Earth! How could you say something like that?*

"Grandpa, please!"

Eliezer didn't take Don Jose's indiscreet announcement too well but he was able to disguise it. When he spoke, he did it tactfully and courteously.

"Don Jose, it's a pleasure." They shook hands. "It's good to know that Ms. Wise's taste is improving." He looked at me with a sneaky look. "And thank you for the info. When we least expect it, we learn something."

The men shared some chuckles that eased the uncomfortable tension. As they moved away, Grandpa adjusted the shoulder straps of his overalls.

"Well, no more formalities. Come in. Come in. The children are waiting for you."

We met in the playroom. There were dozens of them. More than when I was there. Some of the older ones ran toward me when they saw me. They smothered me with hugs and kisses... each time pushing and jostling forward more. Each one of them wanted a moment with me.

Eliezer almost yelled out, startled when the children

wrapped around his legs. He didn't know what to do. He gave me a pleading look and I came to the rescue.

"Well, children, I brought you a new friend. He is Eliezer and he is eager to play and enjoy the day with us. Treat him well because he is a little grumpy."

I made an angry face and the children laughed boisterously. They went to Eliezer and they pulled him by the hand taking him to the ball pool. There they pushed him and jumped on top of him, on his sides, and some on top of each other. I heard his laugh among the smaller laughs, which told me that he would be fine.

Grandpa, one of the nuns, and I placed the gifts under the Christmas tree. Then we prepared the table with the sweets. The interior of the playroom had not changed, although there were a few more technologically current games. Inevitably I'd be transported back to my childhood… to those years when I was one of the children waiting eagerly for visiting strangers bearing gifts. One of those Christmases was when I met Norman.

I thought he would never come back again, just like many others, and if he did, that I wouldn't see him until next year's holiday season. It didn't turn out that way. There he was, day after day. He would take me to school and pick me up afterward. Some afternoons he would ask for permission to take me to his office. Every other weekend he would come up with outings, trips, going to the movies. *I couldn't avoid asking myself: why didn't he ever make my adoption official?*

"Miri! Darling!"

It was Sister Aurora, the nun who'd been in charge of the orphanage for 40 years.

"How are you? I missed you so much…" She hugged

me and I felt my blouse becoming damp.

I didn't think that seeing me there would bring out such emotion in her. I don't remember ever seeing her that way. I suddenly became worried: what if something was happening that I didn't know about? Sister Aurora was mercurial: she was either very affectionate or very cold. There was no middle ground for her. She was very strict. As a little girl and as a teenager I tried to play pranks on her, but I never succeeded. She had a knack for always turning the tables on me.

"I'm fine Sister Aurora." I tried to give her my best smile. I think I gave her the kind I give when I'm tired. She didn't seem to notice it and remarked mischievously:

"I see you brought company."

"He's Norman's son," I whispered to her while shielding my mouth with my hand.

Sister Aurora's big eyes got even bigger.

"My! How did you manage to bring him?"

"It's such a long story that it calls for good coffee." I tried not to give her any clues in my tone or my eyes. I'll never know if I succeeded.

"So then we have a date. I'm definitely interested in that story." She winked.

We laughed and I looked up. I saw Eliezer almost drowning in the ball pool.

I excused myself and went to rescue him.

"How much have you paid these children to get rid of me for you?"

"If only it were that simple!"

I dived into the pool and started an enthusiastic ball

throwing battle with him. Every time a break was near, we'd start up again. When I had a moment of peace, I glanced at Eliezer. I wanted to get a feel for his mood. I figured that it wasn't too bad. The lines on his forehead were relaxed. That would only happen to him when he had me in his arms.

After the war was over in the ball pool, it was story time. At the insistence of some of the children, Eliezer was pressured into reading *The Lorax* by Dr. Seuss. I had never enjoyed that story much before. His voice, although he tried to soften it, was hoarse and unyielding to the intonations and feelings that a children's story demanded. At some point it went unnoticed that one of the lines made him look away from the book and at me for a brief moment: "It's not about what it is. It's about what it can become."

The story was over and one of the older children, Rafael, asked me to tell a story.

"Please, Miranda!" the boy begged.

Telling stories is the worst thing I do, but I couldn't refuse, so I told the only story I knew by heart at that time.

"Okay, okay... Let's see… There was once a boy. He did not have the opportunity to grow up with love. Because he didn't know love, and he didn't know what it felt like to love and be loved, he blamed others for his feelings of unhappiness and for always being so alone."

One of the younger girls, who must have been around six years old interrupted:

"Did that boy turn into *Shrek*? Is he a real ogre?"

"Well... one would say he is. However, instead of having green skin, he had green eyes."

I cast a slight glance at Eliezer only to realize he was

already staring at me.

One of the other girls asked, "And when he grew up he became old and ugly because he didn't have love?"

"One could say that. The boy grew up and did a lot in life, although he was never happy and never found love. He had money, homes, and nice clothing. But his heart was a hundred years older than he."

The children's jaws dropped and they let out a gasp of surprise. One sitting next to me asked:

"Was his heart ugly and wrinkled?"

"Yes, my boy, ugly and wrinkled."

Chapter 16

$\mathscr{I}$ looked up to see the real Shrek in the room, but Eliezer was no longer there. From the doorway, Grandpa motioned to me that he had already left. I said goodbye to the children and hugged Grandpa and each one of the nuns.

Eliezer was smoking outside. I had never seen him smoking before. He was leaning against the trunk of my car. When he heard the sound of my shoes shuffling the pebbles on the dirt road, Eliezer's eyes met mine. He took one last puff and tossed the remaining cigarette on the ground. He put it out with a stomp, walked toward the passenger door and got in the car. The uncomfortable silence between us confirmed that I had crossed the line. The evening had been a disaster. *Mea culpa.* A few blocks from his home, I broke the silence.

"I'm sorry if the story made you feel uncomfortable. This morning you said something that was very true: creativity is not my forte."

"Why should it make me uncomfortable?" he asked.

I'm a businesswoman. I know how to read people's tone of voice, and his conveyed dissatisfaction and a lie.

"Then I hope you had a pleasant day." I smiled and

looked ahead.

"It wasn't unpleasant."

My eyes suddenly had a life of their own and they rolled rudely. *Why? Why can't he ever respond with simple answers?* I broke hard in front of his apartment. I smiled at him again.

"Thank you for joining me, Eliezer. I hope you have a wonderful Christmas."

He didn't respond. He was pensive. His gaze was fixed on the window in front of him. Outside, the world continued in a frenzy as always, cars frantically moving from one place to another, lights flashing in the streets, passersby, the light rain that left drops like decorations here and there. Inside the car there was peace, or at least a strange peacefulness that contrasted with the city. I took a deep breath. I was inebriated by the peculiar scent from Eliezer's skin. I felt that my heart would stop beating if I didn't inhale again.

"Do you want to go somewhere with me, Wise?"

Hmmm. That story with the same script: I already knew it.

"Should I keep my pants on?" I asked.

Mischief took over his half smile, and it wasn't enough to hide his obvious nervousness. He was rubbing the palms of his hands on his thighs. He looked me in the eye.

"Pants are optional, Miranda."

The warmth that traveled through my neck and settled on my cheeks made it impossible for me to produce any words. Eliezer tried to help me find the words.

"We haven't had anything to eat... " He paused,

smiled, and clarified, "adult food in the last six hours."

"Are you inviting me to dinner, Clausell?"

"Don't expect too much, Wise. I just want you to try the best sandwiches in this city."

"Always so modest," I moved the stick shift. "Which way do I go?"

Eliezer signaled to the far right with his finger.

"Towards the visitors sign."

"Are we walking?"

Eliezer laughed.

"Can you think of a better way to get to the seventeenth floor, Wise?"

My jaw dropped open but there was nothing else to say.

From the parking lot we took the elevator, which took us directly to his apartment door… or rather, *his penthouse door*. As I walked through the door, I got goose bumps. That was familiar to me too. Entering a room alone, any room, always ended in reason going on strike and desire dictating our actions.

The foyer in Eliezer space was modern and showy: roomy, well lit, and white marble floors with two white cushion-less chairs. Further in, the living room opened up with a black sofa, gray loveseat and blank canvases. Unquestionably, it had an atmosphere of solitude and masculinity.

I wanted to see more color, but the kitchen was eerily similar. The cabinets were a true work of art in cabinetmaking, as black as onyx with a black granite countertop. The edges of the furniture, as well as the handles were white. LED lights illuminated the undersides.

I sat on one of the white stools. Eliezer opened the white refrigerator and after slowly and carefully selecting the ingredients he placed them on the counter.

"How do you like your sandwich, Wise?" He exhibited a range of ingredients, which allowed for many possibilities.

"It's up to you, but no onions or cucumbers." I hated cucumbers and onions were not appropriate for the occasion.

"So then it won't be up to me, Wise." He enjoyed the look of resignation that I gave him. "Perfect... a sandwich the way I want it, but no onions and no cucumbers."

He took out vegetables, cheese, and cold cuts out of their packages.

"I know. I already said it, but I want to do it again. Thank you for going with me today. It was a lovely afternoon."

He stopped cutting the bread. I could see his eyes looking for mine and then avoiding them. He sighed and continued slicing the bread and the rest of the ingredients. I thought the conversation would end there. Within seconds, he let out his feelings with a burst of angry words.

"You want to play mind games, Miranda. I noticed. Do you think that exposing me to those children is a type of 'treatment' for my illness? Or better yet, 'my insensitivity,' as you call it. Do you know why I left before the storytelling ended?" He moved the knife away from the bread that he was cutting with more force than was necessary. "Do you have any idea? Allow me to enlighten you." He spoke very slowly. "Because I did not want the memory of those children's faces etched in my mind when we said goodbye."

He returned to slicing the bread. Suddenly, I felt like I shouldn't be there, but hiding underneath a rock far away from him instead. I placed my hand on his.

"It was not my intention to make you feel uncomfortable. I just wanted to share something with you that makes me happy and re-energizes me."

He shook his hand away from mine. He moved it to the tomato and began slicing.

"We are very different. You think you are doing those kids some good when the real reason is your doing it for yourself."

I couldn't blink anymore, perhaps because I was stunned by his response. Why was he attacking me for no reason?

"I think that people perform social and community work and service to others as a type of quota to fill to make themselves feel better with respect to others. Tell me the truth, Wise. Do you truly believe that the lives of those people or those children were changed after what we did today? No. To me it's just plain hypocrisy." He took a slice of tomato and put it in his mouth.

Although his way of thinking bothered me, I knew that, in the end, he was somewhat right. I had been on the other side of the fence. I had been one of those children, and I saw how strangers would arrive suddenly with gifts and would spend a few hours with us. At the end of the day, after the difficult goodbyes, nothing had changed. Our lives continued on the same as before. Theirs? Who knows? Many never came back. Some perhaps cared a little more and would return every year.

"I had not thought about it that way. But hypocrisy or not, you can't deny that the children had a great time, that we gave them a few moments of fun and happiness."

Eliezer laughed again.

"And why give them happiness? You can't miss what you never had."

My thoughts weren't clear. I watched and observed him, trying to understand why I insisted on pretending that he could change... that he could become more humane.

"Would you prefer that those children grow up not having any happiness because that way, they'll never miss it?"

"Does that make sense or not?"

Anger consumed me. How could Eliezer simplify the children's experiences into such a cold statement? "What you don't know, you can't miss." The disappointment made me want to leave and feel like it was not worth arguing about.

Eliezer was a lost work of art that I was determined to restore, but not because of the obligation I felt in paying my debt to Norman, but rather because deep down I wanted him restored for myself, and to relieve him of the weight of each of the images on his back. It was impossible to not think of him or of those images. It was too late. I had come to know him too well.

The food was delicious, but I put it down after just one bite.

"I need to go."

Eliezer wiped his mouth covered it with the napkin

while he spoke.

"Didn't you like the sandwich? It doesn't have onions or cucumbers."

I tried, but it was impossible for me to smile.

"The sandwich was fine, thank you." I took my purse.

He took my arm.

"So then, it's the chef?"

I shook his touch off of my arm just as he had done it earlier.

"Let's just say it was his methods," I whispered.

"Do you have other commitments?"

He bit the sandwich a second time. Did he feel victorious or did he want to challenge me?

"No... Well, yes! Yes, I have another commitment. It's important... I forgot."

Eliezer smiled. Ethan's tactics didn't work on him. I wasn't a good liar. He left the sandwich on the counter and walked towards me. Again, he gripped my arm. He held it tightly–that impulsive gesture of his that I hate.

Sometimes, I recalled in my mind.

"Stay," he shut his eyes and he exhaled. "Stay... please."

He released my arm. Silence filled the kitchen. There was only one reason why I felt I should stay, and it wasn't necessarily so that we could have another one of those conversations where he easily upended my thoughts, my beliefs, and my morality.

"What for, Eliezer? If we can't even have a conversation where we agree in the slightest. That's not the only thing that bothers me about you. What bothers me even more is that you force me to think differently, to rethink my ideas and my philosophy. I feel that, with you, I'm lost."

My confession caused his eyes to relax.

"Miranda Wise, if you hate so many things about me, why do you waste so much of your time with me?"

I shrugged my shoulders.

"Because I like self-flagellation," I said nothing more.

We looked into each other's eyes. I smiled and he smiled. He bit his lower lip.

"You know, picturing that in my mind is very tempting..."

I didn't think twice. If he could say and do what he wanted, then I could too. I approached him, my skin radiating heat. Eliezer took two steps back. He avoided the collision of our bodies. Standing at a distance, he repeated himself.

"I'm still waiting for an answer, Wise." He licked his lips. He spoke more slowly, with a huskier, more seductive tone. "If you hate me why waste a single minute of your life with me?"

He approached me again. It was my downfall. My eyes traveled over his provocative chest that heaved boldly with each breath, until I remembered his beautiful eyes and watched him. I approached him. It was his downfall. Desire had us eating from the palm of its hand, and he was overwhelmed with it.

Without looking away from those lovely and lustful emeralds, I reached out and unzipped his pants. I placed my hand inside feeling somewhat like an intruder, and I began to stroke the instrument of passion that he was hiding. I

224

noticed that he was enjoying our silent conversation. I was using a new strategy: provoke the prey so as to bring it out of its hiding place and once it was exposed, pounce.

As I carried out the laborious task of providing him with caresses, Eliezer's eyes slowly transformed. The peculiar green color of his eyes was dissolving into a diamond-like tone. He knew the day would end this way. I suspected it too, but neither of us imagined it like this.

I pulled out his manhood from his pants, feeling like I owned it. I held it tightly so that he could feel me. I took it to my mouth and caressed with my tongue. Eliezer took me by the hair. He wanted to guide my movements. Every time I took him deeper into my mouth, Eliezer would curl his fingers in my hair even more, he would let out groans, moans and almost imperceptible lustful curses. Arousing so much pleasure in a man had never excited me so much as that night. I felt like I was losing control with only light strokes.

Eliezer moved away. With his fingers still entangled in my hair, he picked me up and moved me close to his face. He sought my lips and kissed me passionately, carelessly, limitlessly. He wanted to bite my lips off. He scraped the skin around my mouth with his beard.

He moved away from me once more and took me by the hair to the black couch in the living room. He removed my pants and underwear. His face moved to the space between my legs to tend to the fire he had ignited. His tongue and fingers were the combination that made me lose my judgment and my morals. From below, Eliezer stared at me intently with the sweet rage that adorned his pupils. When I could no longer take the insistence of his touching and his glances, I shut my eyes and allowed my body to be at his complete mercy, to take whatever course he wanted. After the quake, I caught my breath and I looked at him again. There he was, in the same position, watching what he was capable of doing to me.

With his hands he brusquely took me by the hips and sat me on his thighs. He swung his waist until he felt himself inside of me. We opted for silence. The union was perfect—so unique and necessary, that neither one of us wanted to ruin it with the kind of awkward words that we would blurt out in conversations.

His burning fingers embedded in my skin and his hands swayed me to and fro in a raging ocean storm. The groans of pleasure were deafening. Once more, I felt as if I was floating. This time as I came back down, I knew I was in love.

Eliezer moved a little to fall back down on the couch. I was on top with him still inside me. Our hearts were beating together. The sweat of our bodies was the only thing between our skins. His right hand was tenderly caressing my hair. With the other hand he held my chin and turned me to face him. He broke our pact of silence.

"You drive me crazy."

I had no idea my heart could beat faster than it already was, and at that moment I realized how wrong I was. I sighed.

Should I say something? What? There was no word that wanted to be spoken. I never imagined that something like that could happen. I froze under his increasingly strange look.

"It started the moment that, thanks to your clumsiness, you ruined my shirt with your coffee." He raised himself a bit and I with him. He leaned his elbow on the couch. With the fingers of his free hand, he moved a strand of my hair on my sweaty forehead. "You know it Miranda. You know you drive me crazy and you enjoy it."

I was still unable to speak. I was drawing every possible response on what little canvas was left blank on the skin of his back. Suddenly the situation seemed more confusing.

"Don't you have anything to say, Miranda? Here I am trying to figure out my thoughts and you have nothing to say?"

I looked down. I spoke softly.

"It's not that I don't have anything to say, Eliezer. I don't know how to react or what to say. Out of so much I'd say, I don't know what to say." I looked toward his chest. Sincerity took hold of me.

Eliezer took me by the chin again. He moved my lips to his. The kiss was rushed but it saved me. He looked into my eyes. He wanted to surround himself with more of my confessions. I didn't want to disappoint him.

"I hate so many things about you, Clausell. To name a few: your arrogance, your pompousness, your insensitivity, and you smoke, and honestly, these months I have done nothing but ask myself how the heck I can't stop thinking about the only person who irritates me so frequently on a whim, and with the slightest provocation, even with just a look."

He half smiled. Sarcastic and absurd: that was his kind of reaction. It was the confirmation he needed that his feelings, whatever they were, were reciprocated. He moved his face close to mine again. While he sighed, he kissed my forehead. This time, I felt he was grateful.

The cell phone rang, interrupting the moment. Eliezer held his gaze on me.

The cell phone rang again.

Eliezer got up and went to the kitchen. He returned to the living room in short steps, with a dark cloud over his head, yelling and cursing.

"I don't want any visitors! Shit! Why did you let her in?"

And without waiting for a response, he hung up. His face had transformed. No more sweetness, just anger.

"What's wrong?" I asked while I picked up my clothes from the floor and dressed, worried about the unexpected visit.

"Isabel is in the elevator." He began to put on his underwear.

"Oh, God!" was the only thing I could say.

I couldn't let that woman see me here. If she thought I was an intruder at first, I couldn't imagine what she would think if she found out that I sleep with her son.

"Calm down" Eliezer noticed my worry. "Why don't you go to the bedroom and take a shower while I send her off?"

I couldn't have thought of a better idea. He finished getting dressed.

"Where do I go?"

"Second door on the left."

I headed for his bedroom. He kissed me and slapped

228

my behind.

The room was very big–bigger than the living room and more unsettling than the rest of his home. Everything was white: the floor, the walls, the carpet, the headboard, the sheets, the linen, and the chair near the window.

There were no cologne bottles or containers on the white dresser! It was driving me crazy! Nothing that wasn't white! Nothing with color, besides the red cushions on the bed!

There was also no mess. Every object that was part of the space had been placed in a precise location. Was Eliezer obsessive compulsive?

The private bathroom was also white. Against the wall at the end was a square shower enclosed by clear glass that allowed viewing from any side.

I heard the voices outside and I turned on the faucet. I couldn't resist. So, wrapped in a white towel, I went back to the bedroom door, opening it slightly to see.

"What do you want, Isabel?"

"You are my son. I came to wish you a Merry Christmas."

"It's not a good time."

"Is something going on with you?" Isabel asked.

Eliezer responded before she could finish her question.

"I have company."

"I don't want to intrude, but do I know her?"

"I don't think who I sleep with is any of your business."

The way Eliezer spoke to his mother told me that he

had no respect for her, and barely any affection. I didn't think him a miscreant at all, but he had no trace of the admiration that children usually feel for their parents... the kind of admiration that I felt for Norman.

"You're right, and I don't want to intrude. I'll leave." Her high heels could be heard as she walked away... she paused. "One more thing, Eliezer: make certain that these kinds of encounters don't ruin our plans."

"Merry Christmas, Isabel," he concluded in a sarcastic tone and closed the penthouse door.

I ran to the shower and nimbly covered my body with soap, to make it look like I had not been eavesdropping. Eliezer's silhouette cast a shadow through the clear glass. He wasn't wearing pants.

"May I join you, Miss Wise?"

"Of course, Mr. Clausell... as though we were in your house, and this were your shower, and your soap."

As soon as he was in the shower, he began to caress my back. His lips neared my neck.

"What am I going to do with you?" he asked.

What has gotten into him?

Something in Eliezer's psyche had changed. It was obvious. He appeared relaxed and no longer uncomfortable with me. I turned halfway around and embraced him, caressing his back and each one of the inked emotions. It was then that I knew that every second that I would spend with Eliezer would not be enough to save him, to save myself, to calm my hunger to be with him.

"For the moment..." I bit my lips, lost in his nakedness, experiencing short circuits deep inside. "What about repeating what we just got through doing?"

230

MIRANDA

He made that idiosyncratic smile that he would make when he gets excited.

He imprisoned me in his arms to the point of hurting my breasts.

That's how the rest of Christmas Eve went, and that's how we began Christmas: wine, sandwiches, a few hours of sleepiness, and a lot of sex. Neither of us questioned anything. Neither of us wanted to solve the enigma of what was happening.

Tomorrow would be another day.

Eliezer

"What are you doing?"

Chapter 17

$\mathcal{W}$e woke up in his bed, our souls stripped of their differences. I looked at the clock. It was ten in the morning and Eliezer Clausell was asleep. In deep sleep he appeared so defenseless and so peaceful.

It took me several minutes to understand this new state of affairs... us. I didn't know whether it was a sure thing or whether the hours of sex lent it to us for a few moments, or if this was, essentially, the beginning of something less sporadic, or at least sensible, because I couldn't see anything logical to these sparks of passion that ignited between us.

His mother's comments, "don't ruin our plans," and the argument with the woman on the street circulated through my mind. What plans could there have been, if he could barely tolerate her for a minute? I didn't feel like I had the right to question it, nor did I want to ruin the moment.

As soon as I placed one foot on the floor, he woke up.

"Where do you think you're going?" He grabbed me by the arm, his voice hoarse.

"I was trying to escape."

"I thought so." He turned around and looked at the clock on the nightstand. The morning tone rose in volume. "It's ten o'clock already?"

"Surprised, Clausell?"

"Enough…" He scratched his head. "I don't remember having slept until ten in the morning… ever."

I thought he was joking.

"Never?"

He didn't answer.

My cell phone rang. It was Norman. I hesitated to answer, until I remembered that it was well into the morning. I couldn't avoid the call. We would have lunch together every Christmas. That was our family tradition. I thought that this year we might break the rule. The events during the last few months made me feel like, perhaps, I was no longer one of his priorities.

"Good morning, Norman! Merry Christmas."

He sounded more excited than I did.

"Merry Christmas, Miranda my love!"

That very moment, Eliezer's cell phone also rang. He looked at it and looked at me confused about the coincidence of the two calls.

"Where are you?"

"At home."

"Yeah? I just rang your doorbell, but you didn't answer."

I couldn't lie to him, nor tell him the truth, so finding

something in between was what was necessary.

"I just woke up."

Norman was silent. He knew me too well. I heard a sigh.

"Are we going to lunch today?"

"To tell you the truth, I thought that we wouldn't be having a lunch this year. You know, after the…"

"You're mistaken, girl. The food will be served at one in the afternoon."

I smiled.

"I'll see you at one."

I hung up. Eliezer was no longer talking on his phone. He had his silent look planted squarely on my naked chest.

"Let me guess. Lunch is at his house at one in the afternoon."

"You guessed it. Are you going too?"

"That was Isabel." He made a gesture with his hand that held his phone. "She has something up her sleeve. I was also invited."

"Are you going?" I asked while I put on my bra.

"I don't think I'll have a choice."

"The truth is, you do."

It infuriated me that Isabel exerted a certain control over Eliezer. And I couldn't understand why deciding not to go would be complicated and carry negative consequences for him.

"We'll see what I do. You'll find out at one."

I shrugged my shoulders. I got up off the bed. I put

on my pants that I supposedly would not have taken off.

"I need to go. I need to go home, shower, and change."

I looked at his eyes. The time had come. *Now what?* I needed to be brave and willing to hear Eliezer's response, even though it may not be what I'd want.

He walked me to the living room.

"Now what?" I asked.

His green eyes became misty. He stroked my lips with his fingers. I had to control my body.

"We'll see... We'll see..."

He opened the door.

I got to my car. My cell alerted me to an incoming text message.

"Let's enjoy the moment"

I didn't know what to make of the message, so I decided to follow the advice, at least for the day.

***

I got to Norman's house and the first thing I saw was the white GTR parked near the enormous entrance. Eliezer had decided to come too. I would pretend that nothing had happened between us, but, in any case, we would at least treat each other cordially.

A new maid greeted me. *How things have changed,* I thought. The woman walked me to the room where various people were already gathered. This was not the traditional and familiar lunch with Norman to which I was accustomed. For the first time, Medika put on a big show. For a few seconds, I was stunned and didn't react. Before me there were silhouettes with names and faces: Norman,

MIRANDA

Isabel, Ethan and his wife, Eliezer, and… who was she?

I don't believe it. The woman with whom he was arguing yesterday!

As soon as Norman was aware of my presence he got up with the aid of a cane, then Isabel rose, holding one of his hands and the other supporting his back so that he would not teeter and fall. The gesture didn't seem sincere to me. The moment turned strange. Even Ethan, in his surprise, shot a look of confusion at me. Suddenly, just as Ethan saw me, the rest turned their eyes toward me. I became the center of attention.

Norman approached. He caressed my face, from my cheek to my chin. He smiled while he moved his hand into mine to hold it firmly.

"It always pleases me when you come," he said, and I smiled.

"How could I not, Norman?" I responded, looking at his eyes, filled with a mixture of happiness, hope, and a few traces of some emotion that I've never seen him experience, and that I could not describe.

Even though my mind tried to decipher Norman's sentiments, my eyes outsmarted me and escaped to look a few meters further away to where Eliezer was intently watching our interaction. The moment those green eyes, stuck to my memory like screen protectors, met mine, he looked down because they were interrupted by what appeared to be his companion speaking to him. I couldn't hear her, but only noticed that Eliezer gave her his attention.

One of the servants of the kitchen approached Isabel and spoke into her ear. Immediately afterward, she announced that the table was ready. Norman still held my hand. The group began walking with me now acting as Norman's support. Isabel paused in between the foyer and the dining room. We approached her, and she smiled, but her face wasn't friendly. I took it to mean: *you shouldn't have come.*

"Thank you, Miranda. I'll take him from here." She took Norman's hand away from mine.

In the dining room, at the insistence of the man of the house, I sat next to Norman. I looked up and took note of who my nearest neighbors at the table were: Eliezer and the female he was with. Isabel sat her next to him.

The scene seemed like piece of Dali surrealism. For more than twenty years, the luncheon had been with only Norman and myself and no one else–at the same time and in the same place. It seemed unbelievable to me. That evening, the house seemed packed with too many people, and I struggled to understand the reason for the presence of each one of them.

"Miranda, we haven't had a chance to introduce you." Isabel put on a courteous tone like a mask. "She is Vanessa, my friend, moreover, a very good friend of Eliezer."

I smiled, not to be cordial, but to override the remorseful anger that engulfed my being. At least I would no longer have to call the anonymous female, "the woman in question," rather "Vanessa." I tried to not to put much stock into the sarcasm that every one of Isabel's words carried, but there were three words whose significance I couldn't overlook: *very good friend.* Certainly, the definition of "very good friend" could mean different things. In this case, it seemed like Isabel had left out two words: *with privileges.*

Vanessa wouldn't stop talking to Eliezer. She followed

every one of his moves with her perky, insistent eyes. When he would raise a glass to his lips, she would follow his hand–the same hand that had been deep within my most intimate parts a few hours ago–with her eyes. He, on the other hand, would project a calmer demeanor. I knew that he was not that calm. Something made him uncomfortable, perhaps it was one of the people present: Vanessa, his mother, his father... me? There were many possibilities. I, in my eternal complex, was hopeful that the uncomfortable one would interact with me. At least, that way he would think of me, even though he would be hearing the words of another.

With a gulp of red wine, I exerted force against the lump that was forming in my throat where columns of unanswered questions were assembled for a parade. Why the hell did I feel angry the moment I spotted the redhead within Eliezer's comfort zone? Why am I here? Why do I feel so inadequate... so bad? Why does this luncheon carry such a heavy atmosphere? Why do I feel that the relationships between the Clausell men and myself don't feel the way they used to?

Norman, on the other hand, whistled and expressed happiness and gratitude on his face. Nonetheless, I knew that happiness that he was showing wasn't real. The familial reconciliation was no more than staged, a farce... a circus. Yes, it was difficult to decipher who was in on it and who wasn't.

Norman resumed holding my hand, which lay on the table after putting down my glass of wine.

"Tell me, Miranda, did you go to the home yesterday?"

The volume of his voice was sufficient for the people seated nearby to become interested in the conversation.

My answer was simple. Hopefully, perhaps, that way, he would get the message and stop asking me questions.

"Yes."

"How wonderful! And who did you seduce into going with you this year?"

I could have sworn that he knew the answer to that question. He made it very easy for me, and it was the moment for which I was waiting since I arrived to launch my attack.

"No one of importance. In fact, the third choice on my list."

The words could not have come out any better. With them, I felt that I opened the escape valve of a pressure wave. Norman belted out a belly laugh and my attention returned to Eliezer in front of me. I enjoyed how every one of the lines of his forehead deepened while we stared at each other. Within seconds, after I had already retreated, and just before taking a sip from his cup, he launched his attack.

"You must have really bad luck, Wise." He took a sip of wine, which surely helped make his mouth more acidic for the words that he planned to unleash against my response.

"Perhaps," I responded with a sarcastic half smile.

"They say that people attract those whom they most desire."

Oh, I thought, we'd leave it there… that he would set aside his pride and accept my comment. This was not the place to instigate a melodrama–not with all these people around.

"Certainly, Clausell. Perhaps that should be one of my

New Year's resolutions."

He raised his cup and, with that look that irritated me so, made a toast.

"To your New Year's resolution!"

I had no choice but to raise my glass. I went back to being the center of attention.

"Miranda, tell me more about this home. Is it where you grew up?"

I didn't know whether Isabel's interest was genuine... or sinister.

"Yes. I grew up there," I answered candidly and innocently.

"So it was where Norman rescued you."

Within that comment there wasn't a bit of interest in knowing more about the home, rather it was in screwing me over and ridiculing me. I had to think twice before letting my words go. The first few options were neither decent nor appropriate for the setting. I was already accustomed to being the center of attention, but it also felt unpleasant enough.

"He didn't rescue me from the place, rather from a future with few opportunities in store. That home is my home. It's where I grew up. It's where I was loved, and we'll always be appreciative of Norman's help and for the other noble hearts that provided for us."

My heart beat a million times a second, and even though my words broke the attack that Isabel had been brewing against me, the pause lasted only a few brief seconds.

"And tell me, dear... you never knew your parents?

You know nothing of your past?"

Anyone else might have believed the card she was playing, but not those who knew her. Her bad vibrations were capable of penetrating my skin and forcing me to remember the day when the curiosity to know about my parents was so strong, I couldn't contain it…

Soon I'd be fifteen years old. Norman had been asking me what I wanted for a gift for months. I didn't know what to request, until the day when I said:

"May I ask for anything?"

"Except for a car, a house, or permission to marry." He *answered the question in a jocular tone but without diverting his attention from the computer."*

"I want to know who my parents are." His fingers stopped *typing. His face remained fixed on the monitor. He fought the sudden disconcerting feeling that invaded him upon hearing my request with a sigh."*

"If that's what you want."

***

Eliezer sneezed and I was back to reality. I looked at the others. All eyes were on me.

"No… and no." I said to Isabel.

"I'm sorry, dear?" She didn't understand my short answers.

"The answers to your two questions are: No, I didn't know my parents, and no, it's not necessary to understand my past, well I've always lived in the home, so *that* is my past."

Just as she was about to launch another question,

Eliezer interrupted her. For a moment, I thought that he would come to my aid.

"Does anyone want to share their New Year's plans?" he asked, to which I asked myself: *since when is this egotist so interested in what other people do?*

"We're going to Colorado," Ethan said.

"That's a good place for the occasion," his wife completed.

Eliezer made a gesture of approval and looked at me. I could see it coming…

"And you, Wise… Where are you going to get bored on the 31st of December?"

I resolved to follow his game.

"Well… really… I'd love to get bored in New York, and it's not that parties and hustle and bustle excite me, because they tend to make life complicated…" I began to say. He knew to what I was referring and I could notice how the slight smile unsuccessfully tried to escape from the prison bars of his lips when he drowned it with another gulp of wine.

"And what is it that excites you to make you want to go there?" he interrupted.

"Being part of an iconic event… being part of history."

Isabel didn't lose the opportunity to insinuate herself in the conversation.

"Interesting."

A voice I didn't recognize spoke.

"And you, Eliezer… What are your plans?"

The redhead opened her eyes like a girl who's been

offered candy. I perceived the reaction as evidence that between those two there was something more than a "very good friendship."

"Nothing. That's a day like any other. My life at midnight and one second on the morning of the first of January will continue being the same as it was at eleven fifty nine on December 31st."

For the others, those words were the typical arrogant and conceited Eliezer, but not for me. I felt every trace of pain and unhappiness that served as a canvas for what he was expressing.

"Colorado promises to be too interesting a place for your life to go on unaffected. Don't you think?"

The redhead had proposed an invitation to him in public. The evening was becoming more interesting every time. Thinking that I knew him more than the others, I tried to imagine the possible affirmative and accepting answers that Eliezer could give her.

What an idiot! Having sex like an animal can't bring you to really know someone...

"Perhaps. I'll consider the three options, as well as a fourth, if it arises," he said.

Wine splattered the faces and clothes of the two turtledoves, but unfortunately, the cup that fell from my hand onto the table didn't injure anyone. I could have been in worse trouble.

Chapter 18

*E*liezer shot a deadly stare at me. He grabbed the closest napkin and wiped his face with it. At least he swallowed the insults. The redhead didn't. Isabel rose and also joined her with her rude shrieking while she helped wipe him down. I said nothing; rather I lost myself in illogical thoughts.

Norman's voice brought me back to reality. My subconscious, moreover, ordered me to. My reason sometimes prevailed, even though, in reality, it hadn't been that way during recent days as long as there was a bed and Eliezer around at the same time. Norman had to have noticed the tones of sarcasm and the word games. He became the voice of harmony for the rest of the luncheon, setting the subjects of conversation, and marginalizing Isabel's intrusions.

I became desperate to leave such a horrible date. Seeing the redhead act like Eliezer's sidekick–following his every move–made me nauseous. I hated the looks of anger she threw at me even more. When Ethan and his wife were saying their goodbyes, I took advantage of their exit and did the same.

I approached my car. Instead of going home, I went to

a restaurant with a bar. Contrary to my expectations, the place was almost empty. I took a stool and ordered one craft beer after another. Sometimes, after work, I would go there, and not only because they had a good selection of craft beers that I so love for their distinctive flavors that awaken the senses, but also because I knew the bartender from the home where I was raised, so we always had pleasant topics of conversation between us. That evening we talked sporadically about the basketball game on the TV screens.

Shortly before nightfall, after befriending another waiter and some men that sat next to me, I heard someone say my name. No, it wouldn't have been the voice that I wanted to hear, so I didn't turn around to look. The voice repeated my name. I turned my eyes to toward the direction of the voice. I couldn't contain my laughter.

"Would you mind if I ask you what's so funny?"

"Hello, officer."

There was no doubt. Definitely, hell had taken upon itself to send a fallen angel of temptation at a very delicate time: inspector Carlos Hernandez. He began speaking again, this time, more seriously:

"How many of those have you had, Miranda?"

"However many I needed to make it hard to stop laughing."

He took the vacant seat next to me and got comfortable. Not a trace of contagious laughter could be seen on his face. Hernandez looked so serious, I took a gulp of air to dilute the alcohol in my blood. When I exhaled, my inclination to laughter intensified.

"At some point will you tell me what is making you

laugh so hard?" His eyes relaxed. He was beginning to feel comfortable.

"You, me, here, this place... what brought me here. Everything is so funny! But let's forget about what's making me laugh." I wanted to guide the conversation toward another topic, far from what could bring me to tell him my heartbreak over Eliezer, or, worse still, make me have a romp with him as though he were really Eliezer. "How are you, inspector?"

He let loose a smile.

"Very good, Miranda." He played along. "And you?"

"Perfectly fine, thanks. Will you join me?"

He analyzed the possibilities before answering.

"Sure, but only to assure myself that you get home safely."

Oh, now I had to negotiate. *For God's sake, Miranda. How could you have drunk so much?* It was only one beer... I didn't like it when I was subject to conditions. Growing up with Norman had exposed me to being in power, enjoying it, to be the one to set the rules and conditions. A few beers were not going to shake my pride.

"Great! So, what will you have to drink?"

"Whatever you're having would be fine."

My friend, the bartender, served us the beers and placed them on the counter in front of us. I took my glass and, with a gesture, prompted Hernandez to take his.

"A toast to chance." It was the best my intoxicated

mouth could say.

"A toast to people who believe in chance."

That was cute.

An hour later we were still there, with three more beers on our tab. The attraction was showing. He was also a basketball fan, and he couldn't believe that he was having such a pleasant and complex conversation with a female.

Suddenly, he took his cell phone out of his back pocket. The tight jeans certainly fit him really, really well. He looked at the screen and made a gesture of annoyance.

"I have to go. I forgot that I have an engagement." He got up.

"In that case, it was a pleasure to talk with you and thank you for sharing a few beers with me."

"Not so fast, Miranda. Did you forget that we have a deal?"

The truth is that I did, in fact, forget about that. I didn't want him to know.

"Don't worry, Carlos. That's not necessary."

He put on his serious face again.

"A deal is a deal, Wise."

"I can go alone. Calm down, because I'm not drunk."

Hernandez confronted me like a member of a SWAT team. He fixed his eyes on my pupils. His tone of voice was low and firm.

"I know that you are a good person, and it would be hard for you to do someone harm."

Where does this guy want to take me? What is he

talking about?

He continued.

"I'm an officer charged with preserving the public order, and protecting and looking after others is my responsibility. If I turn around and leave, I would not be doing my duty and I'd be in trouble." He turned his head lightly. "You don't want to cause problems for me, right?"

Carlos Hernandez didn't have the slightest idea what kind of problems he was tempting me to cause him. I smiled.

"Have they told you that you have an admirable power for persuasion and negotiation?" I frowned while I looked for the key to my car in my purse.

"I live off that, my dear Miranda," he said with a look of sweetness.

"If you ever find yourself out of work one day, or you want a change of scenery, let me know. You'd be really usefull on my team."

His smile exposed the dimple on his right cheek.

I called out to my friend at the other end of the bar and gave him the key to my car.

"They'll come for it in a bit."

He nodded his head and gave me a smile that I returned. I raised an arm toward Carlos.

"You're in charge, Mr. Officer. Shall we go?"

We walked in total silence. The situation ended up a bit uncomfortable, but fun. We got close to an all-terrain truck and Hernandez, in a gesture of chivalry, opened the passenger door.

"Where do I go, Miranda?" he said when he got in.

"Do I really have to tell you?" He looked at me like he wanted to understand the question. "Isn't it understood that you know where I live? Isn't that part of your job?"

He laughed. He had an attractive, contagious laugh.

"You haven't answered my question." I stopped laughing. I accept a certain level of responsibility. "So, I leave myself in your hands."

What the hell did I just say? That I'm in his hands? How many ways could he interpret those words? Let's see... that I trust him, that I appreciate the gesture of making sure that I wouldn't leave my thirty two years of life hanging from a tree or at the bottom of a ravine... or, perhaps, I was indeed in his hands, literally, and that he could do with me what he wanted. Everything he wanted...

I raised my hands to my head.

Shit! Another event to add to my list of embarrassing moments!

Hernandez deciphered my thoughts and the redness of my face, because the heat that was rising in me was definitely from embarrassment. He laughed a milder laugh than before. He imitated my comforting words.

"Easy, Miranda. This isn't my first time. I'm an expert in bringing people home who have had too much to drink."

What an ability he had to ease the tension during suffocating moments! Fifteen minutes later and we were in front of my home. If the man didn't want to spend the night with me, at least I had an excuse to have him with me for a few more minutes.

"Do you have any news on the Norman Clausell case?"

I didn't take my eyes off him so as to analyze his reaction.

"The case is closed."

When he spoke, his tone was controlled. I took note of a look of annoyance in his eyes. He didn't convince me, because he also looked away toward the steering wheel.

"Why would there be no longer any interest in knowing what caused the accident?" Hooray for me: I definitely caught him unprepared.

Something made him feel uncomfortable. Since I met him that morning in the trauma waiting room, the way he would look around worried me. I could understand the constant state of alert because of the nature of his work and the number of enemies that I imagine the years have given him. Maybe it was the alcohol, maybe not. The reality was that, at that moment, I noticed a significant increase in the frequency of those scans of his surroundings.

"I'm sorry, Miranda, but I can't give you information about that." He still wasn't looking me in the eye.

"If you discovered the truth," I leaned forward in an effort to come into his view. Why is it that silence allows the soul to hear words better? "I don't think that telling me would do anyone any harm."

"Clausell is very important to you?" he asked, cautiously. That time, he made it a point to have his eyes fixed firmly on mine.

"Are you referring to Norman?"

Without thinking about it in advance, I let slip that commentary that ended up being more illuminating and revealing for me than for him. Now there wasn't one Clausell in my life, rather there were two, and both, one way or another, in different ways, were important. I concluded with a vague response.

"Yes, Clausell is very important."

"I can't give you details," he paused and hesitated to continue, "but I can tell you that you also are for him. Why don't you ask him yourself?"

There was no more to say. Norman knew the reason for his accident and didn't tell me about it. A feeling of disappointment came over me. I was no longer that important to him. Why did he profess otherwise?

Hernandez was in a bad situation. I didn't want him to risk himself for me, nor did I want to be left with so many unanswered questions, much less put him in an even more uncomfortable situation. Though, how should I say goodbye? The truth is that I didn't want to, and that, in particular, was not good.

Why did I have the two Clausell men on my mind?

"Thank you for driving me." I managed to say, finally.

The heat of his lips burned me before I could touch them with mine. It was a brief kiss–one of those that feels good… until reason enters the consciousness.

"Oh! Oh! Sorry!" I squealed.

My chest and my face heated up from so much embarrassment. Hernandez didn't take his eyes off me.

254

MIRANDA

He kept savoring the sensation that my lips left on his.

"Miranda," he sighed, "you are a beautiful woman, and you have a heart of gold…"

I was taken aback. That opening was evidently the beginning of a rejection.

"I would have been delighted to get to know you at another time in my life, but now I am engaged to a marvelous woman. I can't reciprocate."

Remorse made its smug and triumphal entrance. *What a bitch you are, Miranda! How could you think of tempting such a decent man?*

"I… I'm so sorry." In a move of desperation, I grabbed the good man's hand. His hand, even though it looked rough, had delicate and tender skin. It took me by surprise. "Please forgive me." I scolded myself in my mind: *But what are you doing, idiot? You keep provoking him?* I let go of his hand. "I have to go home now."

I reached out to give him a regular handshake. He did the same.

"Taking me home was kind of you. I regret my indiscretion."

The dimple returned to his cheek.

"It was a pleasure to be sure that you got home in one piece. I also ask that you forgive me for my part in this."

I stopped looking at him and shaking his hand. I left the vehicle as fast as I could.

"Miranda!" I turned to look.

"Yes?"

His eyes spoke to me before his lips did. The way he deliberately controlled the rhythm and sound of his words forced me to decipher them slowly.

"Be very careful."

That was not part of any protocol. It was a warning.

Chapter 19

$\mathcal{H}$ernandez was no fallen angel sent from hell... more like an angel from heaven. If he hadn't put the brakes on the seduction, I would have ended up in bed, keeping the sheets warm with the tenderness of his voice.

For God's sake Miranda! Anyone would say that you sleep with every man that crosses your path!

I went toward the door and... darn! I noticed that I didn't have my key because I would always use the garage to enter the house. My car was far away and the remote control was in it. I thought that technology was fabulous, yes, but when we least expect it, it makes life frustrating. I had no other choice but to squat to open the garage door and force it open to get inside.

The damned thing was heavy! Why wouldn't one of those gossipy neighbors come around to help me? I would have to overpower the door by myself, but I succeeded in accomplishing the task with efficiency.

It was really dark, and the light switch for the garage was inconveniently located inside the house, but I knew my way around. I got up to the water heater hidden in a closet, and I felt for the emergency key that I hide behind it. My absent-minded moments are so numerous that, on various occasions, I lock the door and forget the keys inside.

I struggled to insert the spare in the keyhole of the connecting door to the house. My intoxication, the darkness, and the sweat on my hands made it so that the key fell to the floor. *Is so much bad luck on the same day possible?*

I took my cell phone out of my purse and, using the flashlight feature, I searched and searched…

Then I heard heavy breathing… there was someone else near me!

I got goose bumps and screamed. A hand touched my shoulder and I started screaming again from the terror. I fell to the floor backwards on my rear, ready for whatever it was.

"Calm down woman… it's me!"

I could barely pronounce the name.

"Eliezer?"

He offered me a hand, but I ignored it. It was like there was no alcohol in my blood anymore. That's how potent adrenaline is. He was holding the spare key. He opened the door and motioned to me to go inside. I turned on the lights and took note of how much Eliezer enjoyed the mishap. His presumptuous look irritated me so much that I could not contemplate niceties.

"What are you doing here?" I said while taking off a shoe.

"I would prefer it if you would thank me for my help."

"And since when do you care about gratitude?" I threw the other shoe at his feet. "What are you doing here?

258

What do you want?"

I went to the refrigerator. I grabbed a bottle of water and took a drink.

"Can I tell you something? It's not safe to keep that key there. Anyone could find that hiding place. Anyone with malicious intentions, that is."

I smiled a smile that would have turned to laughter, but when I gulped down the water, I didn't feel like laughing anymore.

"Thank you for the advice, Clausell. If you don't answer my questions, you can go. I don't need you here." Why was I being consumed by uncontrollable anger?

Eliezer had leaned against the counter, crossing his arms and legs, observing me–trying to understand why I was getting angrier.

Breathe, Miranda. Inhale peace... exhale anxiety... I would repeat in my mind.

I controlled my anger. I imitated his pose. I crossed my arms and legs and leaned my weight against the counter in front of him.

"Are you going to tell me what brings you here?" This time my friendliness was sneaky.

"Was that Hernandez? The inspector handling Norman's case?"

I looked at him perplexed. How did he know who had driven me?

"Were you already here when I arrived?" There was a vibration visible at the corner of his mouth. "And you didn't help me raise the damned door?"

The way he was looking at me made a perverse

transformation.

"I thought about doing it, until I remembered a certain kiss, and my mind became occupied with that thought."

Then it hit me… *the kiss!*

"You are an idiot!"

"Is that the best you can think of telling me, Miranda?" I said nothing. "I have been given worse excuses. Go ahead… surprise me! Answer me!"

I lowered the tone of my voice.

"What's the question?"

He got close. The heat of his body caressed mine. He brought his lips to my hatred.

"Weren't the kisses I gave you last night enough?"

I pushed him away. I would not tolerate insults.

"Do you know about red amnesia?" Eliezer examined me from head to toe, probably asking himself what the hell I was talking about. Since he didn't answer, I made myself clearer. "Red amnesia is the temporary amnesia that women get when they see the idiot that they had fucked all night going to a luncheon they would both be attending, accompanied by a flirtatious redhead."

An intermittent glow in his eyes told me that he would push the envelope again.

"Fucked, Miranda? That's what you did all night? Fucking?"

"Check your words with me, Eliezer Clausell!"

"Me? You check your words with yourself. I feel sorry for the guy you fucked all night."

"And what did you do last night, Eliezer?" I raised

260

my eyebrows and smiled.

His emeralds dropped to the floor and I could tell how his chest sank. I longed for a response, but got silence.

"This is my house, Clausell, and if you want to remain in it one second longer, spit out some kind of answer."

He looked up. The more attitude I added to my words, the more his eyes turned to anger.

He stepped back without taking his angry look off me.

"I thought we should make a few things clear." His voice was halting, but cold, like the water I was drinking. I gave him space to continue. "Today's luncheon was more than a disaster, Miranda. I should have imagined that something like that would happen…"

"But you didn't imagine it. Why didn't you tell me that you would be going with someone? Why didn't you tell me that you were seeing someone? The last thing I want is that kind of problem, Eliezer. I don't know what the hell is going on between us, if there is something going on between us, but I don't play those games."

Eliezer got close and put his index finger on my lips.

"I am not here to give you explanations, Miranda Wise. I'm here to tell you the rules of my game."

How convenient and lovely! I'm talking about "something between us" and he thinks he's the referee of a "game." *How convenient indeed!*

"What game are you taking about, Clausell… the *fucking* game?"

He covered my mouth with his hand.

"Stop saying that, Miranda! You sound like a vulgar

whore."

He pushed harder… and noticed that he had just put his foot in it all the way. He withdrew his hand and wiped his forehead with it, as though with that he would find a way to undo the damage done. However, he couldn't find a way of making up for the lack of respect and tact.

Eliezer was, definitely, a man incapable of breathing life into emotions that aren't based on self-absorption and arrogance. *How did you get here, Miranda? How did you succeed in being as intimate with this iceberg as you have never been with anyone else?*

"You have to go, Clausell. There's no need for you to lay down your rules because I'm not going to be playing anymore." I tried to project firmness, and I would have succeeded if the words hadn't boomeranged and hit me in the chest.

His shoulders fell along with his breathing a sigh, a clear signal of surrender. They didn't drag across the floor because his well-defined muscles held them in place.

My tears lined up in single file, ready to make their majestic entrance, but I didn't allow it. I walked to the door and pointed to it. Even though I hoped he wouldn't, Eliezer made every step resonate. He went out the door and paused. He turned and we were face to face.

"Can you look me in the eye without looking away for a moment? Only a minute, Miranda."

I batted out a pair of tears with my lashes. I raised my eyes until they met his emeralds. I could look at those pupils for the rest of my life, if he let me.

"Miranda… You are the only person in the world with whom I would want the least bit of any kind of relationship.

This thing that happened to us wasn't planned, at least, not on my part. If there is anger in my words, it's because that's what I feel about myself for having gone along. I also think that you hadn't planned this jumble of emotions, and that makes me even angrier. We should have been more prudent before… getting to this. We're very different, Wise. Your life is simple. You see everything through rose-colored glasses. My life is not at all simple, as much as it seems otherwise. I carry very heavy baggage and broken glasses of many, many colors."

The confession tore my soul to pieces. Why couldn't I tell that I would fall in love with him from the beginning? Why did I have to figure it out right before he would tear my heart to shreds?

Eliezer restarted our conversation.

"My life is complicated, yes. But I assure you, Miranda Wise, that the redhead doesn't have any place in it." The declaration patched up one of the torn pieces of my soul. "I don't know how to reciprocate your friendliness, because that's not how I was raised. Since Panama, I asked myself what the hell you see in me, if I am your opposite. My rants, filled with sarcasm and my ire, must shock you to the point that you dream about clobbering me. I tried to find one reason, only one reason, that would assure me that having a relationship with you would be the best for both of us, but, shit… Wise! To this day I couldn't find one. And a few hours ago, during the luncheon, when I saw the way Isabel tried to expose you to ridicule and give you a hard time, I felt that it wasn't right, but I was powerless. I was supposed to be the one who would protect you… who would defend you.

His words had me in the lead car of a roller coaster.

Climb, Miranda, climb… now… fall, Miranda, fall! I wiped away a careless tear.

"I didn't ask that you do any of those things, Eliezer."

He wiped away another that fell unexpectedly.

"One thing that you have to understand, Miranda. Your life will no longer be the same. My presence and that of Isabel have changed everything, and will continue to do so. You have to be very, very clear about that.

I tried to decipher the codes embedded in every one of his words that frightened me and, at the same time, fed me crumbs of hope. I knew how the conversation would end, because I had been through it before. The last goodbye wasn't the final memory that I wanted of him. This time, I was the one who approached and dared to put hands on him. I hung a finger on his lower lip. I held back any other desire to continue the conversation.

"If you're going to end this, Clausell, let's at least do it the way it started."

Eliezer closed his eyes, got close, placed his lips against mine, hugged me tightly around my waist, and that way, wrapping me in hugs and kisses, he took us back inside the house and closed the door behind us.

Our clothing littered the hallway of my home as evidence. That night was different: no more roughness and savagery… only tenderness and affection. It made me tremble more than usual, of course, but it didn't make things easier.

We made love.

***

I woke up in mid-morning and he was no longer in bed. The key to my car was on the nightstand along with a brief note.

Wise, it is against corporate policy to leave company assets unattended. Do you know that using Medika property while intoxicated is sufficient cause to give you the boot?

I wanted to laugh, but tears betrayed me. Naked, I wrapped myself in the bed sheet tightly against my chest where a freezing winter was slipping through.

Eliezer concluded with a memorable farewell.

Chapter 20

*I*t was hard to get out of bed the next day. No calls, no text messages, not even smoke signals. It's not that I'm complaining, no. I was disillusioned with myself and down. That's how good the sweet goodbye tasted. The days passed with no rhyme, no reason, and no novelty.

I took the opportunity of the holiday season to visit some acquaintances and to exercise in the evenings. Running cooled the heat I would feel between my legs every time I remembered nights with Eliezer. At home, I did nothing but lie in bed. I liked torturing my mind with ridiculous romance novels: a tasteless cliché, I know. At least it helped me understand my situation. What was the baggage that Eliezer was carrying that weighed him down so? He understood the significance of the presence of his mother in my life perfectly, but how could he be a risk to me?

***

December 31st.

8:45 in the morning

My cell phone rang to tell me that I received a text message.

Sleepy and grumpy, I reached out and grabbed the

device.

> I'll see you today at the airport. One in the afternoon.
> Private flights section. Eliezer.

I re-read the message. *Am I dreaming?*

I sat up in bed suddenly, laughing out loud, with hope agitating the butterflies that once again fluttered in my stomach. Oh! How I missed those hyperactive butterflies! They only let me get to the sink, where I vomited over and over. The scene was neither pleasant, nor sexy, and was a prelude to hot and cold flashes... leading to a major worry.

The malaise passed quickly. I went to the kitchen and made coffee. I returned to bed. Should I respond to the message? Confirm the meeting? Turn it down? Leave him waiting?

I got out of bed again. I turned toward the wardrobe, opening it wide. What to wear? What to take? For how many days? Weeks? *No... it couldn't be a trip lasting for weeks....*

The cell phone rang again. I put the cup halfway on the nightstand.

> Don't make it complicated, Miranda. Wear jeans.

I laughed. *And how does he know me so well?*

I prepared a carry-on suitcase with a rolled up pair of jeans, toiletries, and various jackets. I would take only one pair of shoes.

After packing, my stomach started making strange noises and my head started spinning. I ran to the bathroom– this time to the toilet. My stomach protested for the second time. Suddenly, an idea crossed from one side of my mind to the other, like a deer crossing a street on a dark night.

No, no, no, Miranda Wise! No!

I left my house in a hurry, on foot, sure that the fresh air would alleviate my discomfort. At the pharmacy, I bought a pregnancy test. I ran back home.

Before starting, I read the instructions exhaustively. I never had to resort to such an instrument. I never before let myself leave it to the spur of the moment; I would always use protection. It was a different story with Eliezer. Neither of us had spoken about the subject–a very irresponsible attitude on both of our parts, not only because of the risk of an unwanted pregnancy, but also because of the risk to our health. He knew nothing of my sexual history, and I knew of his even less.

And if the flirtatious redhead is on his list? God no! Disgusting!

Supernatural agility... I followed the directions. I waited the required minutes, which seemed like hours. How strange life can be! How disruptive the result appearing on a three-inch long white stick can be!

I took the "future changer" in my hands, sat down, and felt like I was being born again.

I closed my eyes and opened them. I closed them again. I opened them. I needed to assure myself that there was only one line on the stick. One line. There was no doubt. I read the instructions on the packaging again. One line: not pregnant. I exhaled–one less worry.

I drank a home remedy for my discomfort and left the house, suitcases in tow. I was arriving at the airport when

I got a call from Norman.

"Miranda…" He said… unenthusiastically.

"Hello, Norman. Are you alright?"

"Yes, yes. And you? Where are you?"

And since when does Norman ask so many questions?

"I'm fine…" I had to pause to make up the following statement. "I'm taking advantage of the day to take care of some errands. And you? And why are you asking me these questions?"

"I wanted to be sure that you were ok. You know you are my favorite spoiled girl. And I know that the Christmas luncheon was not what we both hoped. I apologize."

"Don't worry, it was fine… I'm fine."

"Can I ask you one other thing?"

"Another?" I chuckled.

Norman made a sound with his nose. Was it the sound of a suppressed laugh?

"Where are you going to celebrate New Years?"

"Well… at… my home." I lied. Maybe he suspected something about Eliezer? "And you, what are you going to do?"

"I'm also going to stay at home. I'm too old for parties and the hustle and bustle."

I took a deep breath. What stress! Was Norman really suspicious?

"I seems like a good idea to me. After all, you're still recovering and you have gotten very bold in the last few days."

"Yes, yes, yes… Well, I'll let you go before you

continue with the sermon. Has anyone ever told you that you seem like an old lady?"

"Yes, a number of times. And yes, if my mind doesn't fail me, each time it was you. To be precise, you always remind me about it when you don't want to hear my sermons."

"Miranda, you've had thirty two springs. Live! Happy New Year! Hugs."

"I wish you the same, Norman…!"

He hung up without giving me the opportunity of refuting his order.

During what little time was left to go, one of his words reverberated in my mind, "Live!" and, on the other hand, the words of his son, "Your life is simple."

Could it be that the Clausell men were colluding to give me messages? Was it time for my life to become complicated? My time to live? How much longer should I complicate my simple life?

When I arrived, he was already there, in the private lounge, looking out the enormous glass wall of windows facing the runway. I wanted to run to him, to breathe again. I suppressed my impulses.

Eliezer turned around. Upon seeing me, he straightened his posture. He took a few steps and paused when we were face to face. He gave me a gesture that approximated a smile, and pointed the way to the plane.

"Punctual, Wise. Congratulations," is how he greeted me.

"Surprised?" I responded.

The plane was not the Medika jet, rather another

slightly older Gulfstream, which accommodated a larger crew. It had a black leather interior with four seats that formed pairs in front of a sofa for four. I took one of the seats with Eliezer by my side. I observed each detail of the curious plane and, before asking, Eliezer was already giving me an answer.

"It belongs to a friend. It's not an official trip, so we should not be using the corporate one."

He was right, but...

"How do we categorize this trip?"

Pensive, rummaging through the nooks and crannies of his mind for an answer, he furrowed his brow. The answers he considered, undoubtedly made him uncomfortable.

"A work of charity?"

I elbowed him in the ribs, and he let out a groan.

He elaborated on his explanation:

"Let's say that I was moved by the banal wishes of a bored woman."

"So you assessed your options..."

He leaned in toward me. The plane was taking off, the sound of which was making it difficult to hear him.

"Let's say I took your advice, Wise. I was friendly that evening. I already knew which option to choose in advance." He winked.

He went back to reclining in his seat, leaning his head back and letting it rest on the cushioned backrest.

Why can I never find a way to respond to his

complements?

He broke the silence and said:

"What size do you wear?"

"Excuse me?"

Eliezer got close again, thinking that I didn't hear him well because of the noise.

"We need to get you more clothes or you're going to freeze."

"Medium," I answered quickly. "I only need a coat."

Eliezer leaned back and smiled. His reaction to my confusion was to make another face of confusion.

"What is the matter with you, Miranda?"

"It's that this is unusual."

"That you get a trip as a gift?"

"No, that it would not be me buying my clothes."

I said no more, and then noticed that my comments hit him hard. His face straightened out.

"So you are used to getting trips as gifts?" Sarcasm clothed his words.

"I've only received two surprises in my *simple* life, Eliezer." I emphasized the word "simple," so that he would not forget that fundamental aspect of my life. "When your father…" I noticed that he became uncomfortable when I mentioned Norman's relationship to him, so I corrected myself. "… excuse me, when Norman enrolled me in school, and when he paid for college."

He blew a fleck of dust off his pants, crossed his legs, and gave me a look.

"So, miss Wise, I hope this gift meets the criteria for

being included on such an exclusive list."

I shot a smile at him.

"It's certainly on the right track. Your last name is Clausell."

"Fine." His face shined with an air of pride, because he already knew me so well that he understood the joke. He took out a blanket and a pillow for me from the compartment below his seat. "Why don't you relax and enjoy the flight."

I took them as my own.

"Invitation accepted."

I put the pillow behind the nape of my neck, and the blanket over my legs. I took my tablet out of my suitcase, in case I could concentrate with him by my side and read something. In minutes, I restarted the conversation, more to ask a question than to break the tension.

"Eliezer, when are we coming back?"

"We haven't arrived yet, and you already want to come back? I know that I could never have better company, but…. is being with me so bad?"

I wanted to tell him, "If you knew that if it were up to me, we'd never come back," but I thought that would be imprudent.

"Can we reach an agreement?" I had to make an attempt to guarantee that the hours or days to come would be tolerable.

"We are at an altitude of fifteen thousand feet on the way to fulfill your dream, with me engaging in the most charitable act of my life, and you want to negotiate? Don't you think it's a little late for that?"

"Is it possible for you to put sarcasm aside for the duration of this charitable act of yours?"

His smile faded. He bit the inside of his cheeks and his lips several times. For a moment, an expression of resolution appeared on his face as he weighing the alternatives.

"And what do I get in return, Wise?"

Let's see... What can I offer him? Sex, passion, lust? Fucking? *For God's sake! What am I becoming?!*

"I'll try to look at life through some glasses that aren't rose-colored."

That rose-color that you detest, I completed in my mind. I would have wanted to express those words out loud too, still it was difficult to know how far to go with him. It was too hard to keep myself on the other side of the line beyond which the most intense emotions could be triggered in him. It was like the tide: constantly changing. A few hours in one place, and then somewhere else.

But there was a crucial difference between the tides and Eliezer Clausell. The tide lives in an eternal love triangle between the sun, the moon, and the Earth. Eliezer still had not succeeded in figuring out what controlled him, what moved him, and what made him live.

"And why in hell do you want to do that?" The man analyzed me, as though that way he could try to understand the nature of my words or understand, perhaps, where the conversation would take us.

"Because I want to complicate my life a little."

He laughed silently.

"You don't know what you are saying, Wise. You don't have the slightest fucking idea how your life can be complicated by the simple act of being here with me, at this instant."

An alarm rang in my subconscious, an alarm with screeching and sinister sounds that was fighting to overtake me. Was it part of his act, or did he really intend for me to know about those details?

"I regret to inform you, miss Wise, that at this time, the terms of your proposal are not appropriate to reach an agreement that would benefit both parties."

With those words, he tried to smooth over the warning that he inadvertently let out without really understanding the consequences. A whirlpool of questions formed in my mind. I could swear that my face did not show any expression.

"Hey!" he suddenly screamed. It made me return to my senses, my mind clear, back to reality, to the plane that was flying over the Atlantic Ocean.

"And how much more can my life be complicated? I ask so that I can have the fucking slightest idea."

"Oh, please, Miranda." He raised his hands up to his head. "Don't do this. Not now. Not on this trip."

"Don't you think it was a very vulgar thing to say? Do you hear me say vulgar things like that?"

His gorgeous eyes became like that of a puppy dog

scolded for breaking his owner's most precious possession.

"I'm sorry." He reached out and put his hand on my leg and, in a low tone of voice, said "Let's come to another agreement. I'll try to control my sarcasm and vulgarity. In return, you forget about everything else."

I thought about it a little.

"Before responding to your proposal, tell me something else. Why would being with you here and now complicate my life?" While I spoke, I looked at his eyes without wavering. I wanted to verify the answer, whatever it may be."

"Come on, Miranda, you're not so naïve. I'm your boss–the one who would make up any excuse to fire you. Remember? Moreover, you know that Isabel detests you. Ah! And let's not forget about the redhead. Do you think that your dear Norman would approve of this?"

I couldn't stand it, and I hit him in the arm with my fist.

"Damn! That definitely hurt."

"I don't give a shit what other people think about me." My voice stumbled between breaths because I was trying to talk while alleviating the pain in my hand. "Agreement accepted."

He took the hand in question and placed it between his hands, caressing it.

"You need to recognize your limits," he said.

I gave him a chastising look.

"Excuse me, that was just a little teasing," he added.

"A little."

We both laughed.

Eliezer planted a kiss on the palm of my hand, rested his head on the backrest of his seat and we kept ourselves, in silence, sleepy, side by side, in touch with each other's hands, until we landed at Macarthur airport in Long Island.

A black limousine waited for us. We arrived at the Hotel W, in the heart of Times Square. The smile and tears of emotion that formed in my eyes, but never came out, were evidence of that indescribable sensation that being there and then caused in me, and being with Eliezer even more so.

The elevator was going up... 30th floor... 40th floor... 50th floor... 57th floor: a luxuriously decorated suite extended before us, surrounded by walls of glass that allowed us to appreciate Times Square. Eliezer had his bag taken care of. I... I only contemplated the surprising view up close. If it wasn't for this arrogant and, at times, self-absorbed man, I would never have been able to imagine something so fantastic but so real.

I felt his breath on the back of my neck. The hands that wrapped around my waist gave me goose bumps.

"There's a good chance that you can be part of history from here. Excuse me for wanting to avoid the hustle and bustle that fascinates you so. I don't think that it would sit well with us on a night like this."

We shared a smile. Eliezer spoke of us, in the plural... of both of us.

"It's perfect, Clausell, perfect!"

Without caring about the high heeled boots that I was wearing, I climbed onto the nearby sofa to be at his level and look at his face, which I caressed with my hands, as if, that way, I could transmit all of the affection that I had well kept in my heart to him. I kissed his affectionate lips, enjoying every contact between our two skins, quenching the thirst that I felt for the peculiar taste of his mouth.

That's how I noticed something odd. Eliezer tasted like Eliezer, and in that taste, there was a trace of sweetness that enchanted me… He hadn't smoked. His hands rested on my rear. The vulnerability reflected in his eyes gripped my heart.

Has anyone had the chance to look in Eliezer Clausell's eyes at this level?

"Thank you," I whispered.

He flung me on his back like a sack and threw me on the bed. He took it upon himself to remove my boots.

"Although you look very tempting, Miss Wise, I suggest that we rest a while and recharge ourselves for the evening. We don't want to miss the spectacle… or do we?"

After he took off the second boot, he did the same with his shoes. He lay down by my side. He took a pillow. He planted a kiss on my cheek and placed the pillow over my face.

"If you can't rest, I recommend a cold shower. It works."

I grabbed my pillow and threw it at him.

"Wise! I wasn't teasing. I meant it seriously."

He threw his arm over my chest. He pulled me toward him, leaving no space between our bodies.

"Rest." He repeated the order.

Chapter 21

$\mathcal{A}$ different Eliezer was getting dressed in the room: relaxed, smiling… happy? It was nine o'clock at night. We had decided to have dinner at the hotel restaurant. The food promised to be delicious. We ordered dessert to go, so that we could enjoy it at the precise moment of the spectacle.

I admit I didn't know how to behave that evening, at first. Was I part of a couple? Should I behave accordingly, or only as his companion? Without caring about which of those terms described me, I shouldn't neglect a most urgent subject of conversation any longer. I didn't want another scare like I had in the morning, so it was time to dot my "I's".

"We've been very irresponsible about… you know… no protection." I blurted out at the table after the waiter brought wines and appetizers. I thought his reaction would be different, maybe I would hear the screeching of a fork over ceramic… but it didn't happen that way. Eliezer wasn't surprised by my comments.

"Certainly," he said. He paused. He put one of his hands in a pocket of his pants. He took out a condom packet and put it on the table without caring about who could see it.

If I were another woman, what he did may have made me blush–but I enjoyed the moment. Eliezer couldn't have imagined my counterattack.

"You're so un-ambitious! Only one?" I smiled. I put my hand in my pocket and removed a box of condoms and placed it beside the solitary envelope. I hope I was right about the size.

He had no other choice but to break out in laughter. He took back what he had put on the table and took the box as well.

"I think I can put them to more and better use, Miss Wise."

Now that he had taken the initiative to take me to dinner, and pay the tab, I decided to take charge during the second part of the night, as long as he didn't have a huge plan, of course. During a dinnertime bathroom break, I had the hotel take care of everything. I had them place bottles of champagne and some strawberries on the table in the middle of the room facing the huge array of windows from where we would watch the year's end, New York style… where we'd watch me fulfill one of my dreams.

When we got back to the room, it was eleven thirty. I adjusted the lighting to be soft, warm, and seductive– allowing me to lose myself in Eliezer's gorgeous eyes while not making out the furrows on his forehead ow that so revealed the sorrows in his life.

I put the dessert in the room refrigerator, and I took one of the bottles of champagne, popped the cork, and poured it into two glasses, handing one to my companion.

"Thank you, Wise," he muttered while raising his cup.

"You're learning manners, Mr. Clausell." I winked. "You're welcome."

"It's hard to have manners with you, Miss Wise."

"What do you mean?"

He didn't answer. He put his glass on the table, took mine out of my hand, and came close enough for me to feel his breath. The playful tone he was using gave me goose bumps all over.

"I said… that it's very difficult… to have manners with you."

He put his hands on my breasts and caressed them. I bit my lower lip.

"Do you know I can interpret that as being vulgar?"

He pinched one of my breasts.

"And how would you interpret that you make me feel like throwing you on that sofa behind you, tearing off your underwear, and thrusting myself in you until New Years?"

I bit my tongue, because I was out of things to bite.

"I would say that would be vulgar on your part, and that there was no need to tear off my underwear…" I paused to allow the butterflies fluttering in my stomach to breathe, "…because I'm not wearing any."

I noticed how his lewd smile let his perfect teeth shine through. I began to take off my clothes and my morals: sweater, blouse, bra, pants…

"You lied. You *are* wearing underwear," he complained

with a look of forced offense on his face.

"You can't deny how provocative it was for you to imagine me without them."

It took little effort to remove the last article of clothing I was wearing–one that I wish I could have taken off first. I took my cup of champagne, bit into one of the strawberries, and lay down on the sofa as an overt invitation to my companion. Indeed, desire and obscenity were in his eyes. "And what do you suppose a vulgar man like myself would do now?" He tried to control his halting voice.

"You could join me and whisper some of those obscenities that you have in your mind into my ear."

Eliezer put his hand on his crotch and rubbed the bulge that was forming in his pants. He approached me with his hand still in its obscene performance and whispered in my ear.

"And what if I tell you that I'd like to imagine what you could do without me?"

This time, the blush did make its appearance. *Oh! He wants to see what I can do with myself.* No. Eliezer was not a man of insinuations. He was asking me.

He moved back with a smile on his face and took a seat facing the sofa. He again put his hands between his legs.

What the hell am I doing? How do I start? Into what sort of predicament have you gotten yourself, Miranda Wise?

Eliezer figured that I was nervous and he smiled.

"Nervous?" I didn't answer. "Relax, Miranda. Imagine

that you're alone and bored after a long day at the office."

I closed my eyes, but I didn't feel the same, so I opened them. I needed to see his face up close. I needed inspiration. I closed my eyes again. I imagined him caressing my bust with his rude hands, exploring my most intimate parts with his tongue.

I opened my eyes again. I found myself with him and his grimace of excitement. His eyes were fixed on my hands that were desperately rubbing my flaming sex. He remained in his chair, with one hand on his thigh and the other hand holding the glass of champagne.

I accelerated the movement with which my fingers rocked and concentrated on my breathing. I felt his hands open a path between my legs. This time, I wasn't fantasizing. Eliezer touched me with the same desperation. He caressed me and introduced his fingers. He helped me accelerate my rhythm, introducing me to energetic, shameless sensations.

Then came the orgasm. I started moaning. My whole body shook involuntarily. My brain rattled. I controlled my breaths again until the air started to clarify the blackness of my imagination. I came back to my senses and there he was, seated by my side, naked except for a condom.

"You've done an excellent job, Miss Wise. It would be an honor for me to take it from here."

Those words were what I needed to lose myself in the feeling that his lips provoked as they caressed my vagina. I lost myself in the enduring sensation as his tongue followed its path to the right spot.

The licking went from delicate to rough. Within seconds, I managed to lose myself on my way to that murky place so removed from reality. He was merciless.

It didn't matter to him that I was recently satisfied and a little drained: he took me by the hair to the windows. He forced me to remain standing and backed up near the window. He closed in, pressing my back against the glass. He grabbed me by the waist and kissed my neck, shoulders, and breasts. When I least expected it, he paused.

"You can't miss this, Miranda Wise."

He turned me so that I faced the window overlooking the grand celebration. Eliezer grabbed me from behind. He held me by the hips so that I wouldn't slip away, as I had not yet regained my strength. He spread my legs with his feet and penetrated me. His body didn't delay in coupling with mine... we became one.

His movements were reviving my lost strength. The fireworks on the outside with him on the inside were enough to drive me crazy. I welcomed the New Year in a suite in Times Square, while the man who stole my heart, made me his own.

Eliezer's face was reflected in the glass–his eyes were lost in me–though the sweat from our hands promptly dulled it and my breath fogged it. I didn't want to miss the moment when he would explode, so I turned around and pushed him toward the sofa. He fell, enjoying the sudden aggressiveness. I climbed up onto his lap. We again became one body. This time, my hips assaulted his. My vagina received him. It was already familiar with the sporadic vibrations that he induced. The intensity of his face was overwhelming and exiting. I predicted that soon he'd reach his climax, when he would squint, leaving only a little bit of green visible.

"This is what I don't want to miss," I whispered in his ear... and that whisper was detonating. One of his hands imprisoned my hips. The other did what it should on my rear. He put two fingers in a place he had never before explored. He unleashed a chain of sensations that provoked my vagina to strangle his sex inside of me.

We moved with force, out of control and aggressive between strong breaths and groans. We were prisoners of a powerful electric current.

God, this is heaven! How and why have I made myself dependent on this man?

Our bodies convulsed at once.

"I love you," I whispered, my head buried in his neck.

Shit! What did I say? I suppose that confession will remain etched in my mind! Shit! Shit!

Shit!

The weight of my words didn't allow me to draw back from the skin of his neck. His hands directed my face to his.

"I'm sorry, that shouldn't have come out of my mouth." I murmured too soon.

It wasn't true. I didn't regret expressing myself. I loved him. I learned to love him. I couldn't deny it. I didn't want to live without him for a second, and my big mouth had ruined the night.

He kept my face between his hands, looking into my eyes, processing every one of my crazy words. The more he seemed to consider them, the more the havoc they made in him.

"We'll pretend that the last second of this night didn't happen," I whispered.

Eliezer drew me close and kissed my forehead.

"Happy New Year." He smiled. "You are now part of

history."

I thought I should ease the uncomfortable tension even more.

"It happened as I had imagined it," I paused to wet my lips, "totally boring."

With a smile on his lips, he lifted me off him. He slapped my behind, got up out of the couch a bit, and reached for the table. He picked up the glasses of champagne and the plate with strawberries. The smell of sex, champagne, and strawberries were like taking nitroglycerine for slight dizziness. It made me nauseous. I got up off the sofa, ran to the bathroom, and slammed the door behind me. It was my stomach again.

"Are you ok?" He opened the door after hearing me flush. I was still holding on to the toilet.

"Yes." I reached out for him to hand me one of the towels that were hanging on the wall. "Next time, make sure to take me to a hotel that serves good champagne."

Eliezer smiled, but there was no happiness in it… rather there was worry.

"Are you sure you're ok?"

"If you don't get dressed quickly, I won't be." He didn't look convinced. "Don't worry, Eliezer, it's nothing that we'll have to worry about," I said in a clear tone of voice. This time he looked convinced.

He got up and helped me to my feet with both hands.

"Go take a shower." He winked at me. "You stink!"

"Is that supposed to make me feel better?"

I tried to seduce him into showering with me. He

MIRANDA

rejected my invitation with a subtle gesture.

"We only have twenty four hours left..."

Chapter 22

*H*is hands in his pockets and unshaved, Eliezer paced quickly from one side of the lounge to the other. I could hardly see through the fogged windows, where immense drops of rain were running down. A blurred light could be seen in the distance, and then, nothing. Only rain and more rain and gray. "Who thinks of traveling in this kind of weather?" I asked in a low voice, because I was talking to myself. I adjusted my hair back and smiled. "Who else?"

I turned. Eliezer was no longer pacing. He had leaned against a wall, in that posture that was so his own: legs and arms crossed, a man filled with defenses. It was his turn to wait. Two hours after departure time, and the runways were still closed–something about zero visibility.

My heels clicked until I was near him. I had to tell him. I wanted him to know. Both of us needed a sense of security. I touched his shoulder.

"I'm going to the ladies room." I caressed his chin with my hand and winked. "My period is a little early." Eliezer nodded silently, only half smiling.

When I returned, Eliezer's posture had changed. He was speaking calmly to a tall man with brown hair. He looked like he was about Norman's age.

As I approached them, the man began staring at my body. He gave me goose bumps. Eliezer noticed that his company was distracted and turned around. His expression quickly changed and he smiled timidly. His lower lips moved, as though his own mouth betrayed him because he realized that smile was inadequate. He reached out his hand.

"Miranda, this a business acquaintance of mine. His name is Paul." He paused in a way that seemed deliberate.

The man grabbed my hand and shook it. He finished saying his whole name.

"W. Hopgood."

I didn't have a chance to respond. A man came to us and told us that the runways had opened and we were welcome to board the jet. I said goodbye to Mr. Hopgood with a nod and left the trio, thinking Eliezer would follow. Then I heard a whisper from a distance behind me. It didn't come from Eliezer. I turned my head and noticed Eliezer's perennial face. No more tranquility nor hope for contentment, only annoyance… a great deal of annoyance.

Grabbing my bag and his, I went back and, with a look, forced him to excuse himself from the unfinished conversation. The mysterious man remained where we had left him, looking at us. Eliezer began to walk. I took him by the arm and, although I was unfamiliar with their private conflict, I commented:

"Don't let anything ruin the last forty eight hours."

Eliezer smiled.

We boarded the jet and as soon as we were seated, I took off my coat and my jersey and sat on his lap and kissed him.

And has this trip relieved you of your bad memories, Eliezer Clausell? Has it relieved you of your bad moods and grief?

Eliezer eased me off in a mixture of tenderness and rudeness.

"Wise, I don't think that it would be prudent for you to kiss me now that way. First, you are not in a position to satisfy my needs…"

I furrowed my brow and didn't allow him to continue.

"I have a marvelous mouth and two hands that work miracles." I kissed him again, my hand between his legs.

Eliezer's sex quickly responded. When he felt that he was on the verge of losing his judgment and tearing off my clothes, he separated his mouth from mine slightly. I felt his warm breath caressing my lips.

"Allow me to inform you, Miss Wise," he continued, caressing the rebellious hair that adorned my forehead, "that we've boarded a plane which, although not commercial, lacks privacy and we're at the mercy of various natural and human variables, as well as destiny." He smiled mischievously and fixed the strap on my blouse that had come loose, taking advantage of the opportunity to caress my shoulder and neck.

I was overcome with hot and cold flashes. I closed my eyes and my whole body surrendered to a mild earthquake. Eliezer tickled my ear with kisses, and softly asked me:

"If you don't get up in the next three seconds, Miranda, I'll have to go to the restroom in mid-flight and pretend to call for your help."

The roughness of his tongue invaded my mouth. Rude and shameless, he put a hand on one of my breasts and squeezed. So I was the one to move away.

"It sounds interesting, Clausell. The perfect way of ending this adventure."

I thought my words would excite him, but that didn't happen. The bulge in his pants lost its strength. His smile faded and he withdrew his hands from me.

"What happened? Was it something that I said?"

"Damn, Miranda! Is that what you think of this?" He said in a low but intense voice, as though it were fading in the fog of a rainy dusk. "A damn adventure?"

So that was the word that yanked away the smile from his lips and the arousal from his body. I was left baffled. If it wasn't an adventure, then what was it?

What puzzled me even more: *Why did he react so dramatically to an innocent comment, but didn't react so intensely, or positively, at least, when I told him that I loved him? This man is going to drive me crazy…"*

With both hands, I hooked my hair behind my ears and licked my lips.

"I didn't mean it that way, Eliezer, but now that we're on the subject, tell me, if it wasn't an adventure, what was it?"

Silence eased the roar of the Gulfstream engines that was preparing for take-off. Eliezer didn't take his eyes off me. I explained myself better.

"You said that we'd live for the moment. That's exactly what I'm doing, Clausell. I'm following your advice."

He stood up suddenly, without warning me. I was about to fall, and I don't know how my reflexes could have been faster than my reasoning. I grabbed one of the armrests and regained my balance. *Has he gone mad?*

Eliezer grabbed me by the arm. He pulled me toward him, turned me around and forced me to walk ahead, causing me to trip on the carpeting. We got to the restroom and he thrust me inside with a shove, followed me in, and secured the latch. He didn't stop squeezing my arm. My heart beat so scandalously, that not even the din of the jet engines silenced the thumping. That was the sensation that filled me every time he grabbed me that way.

The uncertainty of what would happen next took my breath away. His breathing was heavy and deep and his stare was cold. He gave me another light push and an order. With no time to think about what I was doing, I sat on the cover of the toilet seat. Eliezer grabbed the zipper of his pants with the hand that hurt my arm.

"Do you want to know how to end an adventure?" he murmured.

He drew down his zipper. He tangled his fingers in my hair and tugged, pulling me in, and just as quickly, he let me go and slapped the wall with his hand. We looked at each other without blinking. Our eyes were bright: his with fury, mine with sadness. This is not how I would have imagined it. Two tears ran down my face.

Eliezer became himself again and noticed my expression of fear and disappointment. He zipped his pants. He didn't apologize. I imagined the moment as if it were another brush stroke in the paintings that covered his back. Had he experienced scenes like the ones flooding my mind? Were they with other women? How many? I opened and closed my mouth, but not to speak. *What kinds of things has this man done?* I came out of my stupor. My eyes started itching. I got up.

"Move away from the door, please." I wiped my cheeks with my hand. I was blinking more than usual. Coldness enveloped my voice, but it wasn't due to our altitude. Eliezer made no other moves. He stayed quiet. Frozen.

"Eliezer, please. Stop ruining the best time of my life." I pleaded. The walls began closing in on my shoulders. With every blink of my eyes, the space seemed to become more and more confined.

He punched the countertop of the sink, which made me jump from the start. If I hadn't kept my mouth shut, my heart would have come out of my chest.

"Shit!" he yelled, and then, calmly, "I'm sorry, Miranda. Truly, I'm sorry."

I spoke quickly, without caring much about the meaning of Eliezer's words.

"Yes, yes. Apology accepted. Now, please, move away from the damned door." It wasn't the time to argue. I wanted to get out. I wanted to be out of his reach.

He moved, but not away, rather he got out of the way by moving in the other direction, toward where I had been standing. He sat down on the toilet, with his head in his hands. It hurt me to see him like that. His soul in tatters, a prisoner of frustration, but I couldn't do anything for him. Not this time.

I needed to move away and get out, to stop consuming myself so much with him, to console my soul. I turned the latch on the door, and stepped out. I left the door half-open. I collapsed in the nearest seat. Between tears, the smell of freshly upholstered leather and coldness in my chest,

MIRANDA

I dozed off. I don't know how long Eliezer stayed in the bathroom.

***

I awoke and he was by my side, in the seat nearest the other side of the aisle. He was asleep, or at least, he was trying. Seeing him there, with his face still twisted by the demons that pursued him, he confused me. I noticed that, with our breathing in sync, Eliezer was stripped little by little, once and for all, of all of those demons, while I... I had not noticed soon enough that all of that weight had accumulated, little by little, and more and more every time, in me.

I had no idea what would happen after landing. How should I behave at Medika? The next day? The next week? My whole life? It became clear that what we had done was no adventure, not for me, nor for him, and anyway, we had to keep this secret. *Isn't that another name for adventure? No, Miranda, for God's sake! It's another name for a discreet couple.*

It wasn't proper to give Medika employees something like this to talk about. Clausell was the boss; Wise was a dispensable employee. Nor was it proper for Norman to know. Thinking about him, about his son, about myself, and about this... secret... caused me to feel disgust and a slight dizziness. It could be said that having sex with Eliezer was practically a sin. Norman saw both of us as his children... We were his two children!

Nausea.

He had already warned me. He always said the same thing. "Miranda Wise, conquer the world, if you wish. Just take care to remember my advice: never urinate where you eat." That was his way of advising me not to mix business with pleasure, because business and pleasure, indeed,

297

don't mix. One is oil; the other is water.

Also, there was a woman named Isabel. I couldn't leave her out of the picture.

What do we do now?

I got up and approached him. I placed my hand on his head, as though that way I could surprise myself and discover what he was dreaming about. I caressed his smooth hair, it seemed like a piece of corduroy fabric that was kept suitably short and matched his unshaved beard. At my touch, he opened his eyes and looked at me. He gently took one of my hands—no more squeezing.

"You don't know how much I regret it."

I took one step forward. I leaned in a little and embraced him as well as I could, caressing his temple.

"I know. I know."

Chapter 23

"Thank you for the company," he whispered into my ear.

"Thank you for the invitation." I imitated his whisper.

Eliezer put my bag in the trunk. He took my hands in his and rested them on his hips.

Neither of us looked forward to the goodbye. New York had changed us. We needed each other. He was my dark side; I was his light. How could two forces in such opposition complement each other so well? Eliezer Clausell was the rock that would fall into calm water and release waves that would wake my sleeping demons.

"Drive carefully." He broke the silence.

He opened the driver's side door for me and I settled in the driver's seat. He pulled the seat belt across for me, secured it, and closed the door. I drove off and was going down the avenue when the cell phone rang. It was one of his text messages.

Is it possible that I already miss you, Wise?

The confession gave me a big smile. I took advantage of the red light.

That can be solved, Clausell.

Within seconds, there was another message.

Even though it's exciting to know that you also miss me, don't send text messages while driving. It's against policy.

I laughed, and then I got another message.

Even worse, I couldn't forgive myself if something happened to you while you were thinking about me.

I smiled again, tenderly this time. Eliezer began to worry about me.

Don't you think it would be a romantic way to die?
Thinking about you?

The texts ended and the phone rang.

"You don't like following orders, do you?" He was speaking in a scolding and teasing tone.

"Let's say that I enjoy living on the edge, and I am not used to being given orders."

"I'm not kidding, Wise."

"Neither am I, Clausell."

"I want you in my office at seven in the morning," he said emphatically, "healthy and safe."

"That's a little early, don't you think?"

"Be prompt, and don't bring coffee, please. We don't want any accidents."

Annoyed, I sighed. Hearing him speak in that playful authoritarian voice drove me crazy. It made my mind do somersaults thinking about what that man could have up his sleeve. Does he have a plan for us? I wet my lips.

"Fine, Clausell. I'll be there." I ended the call.

***

I woke up before dawn. I had cramps that made me writhe in pain. Nevertheless, I got to Medika a little before seven in the morning.

7:15

Nothing.

7:30

And what if something happened to him?

8:00

Should I call him? What do I tell him? Margaret is there. Should I ask her to call him? No, I shouldn't..."

8:30

To hell with waiting.

"Hello?"

"Good morning," he answered after the second ring, his voice dry and halting.

Silence.

"Are you alright?"

"I'm busy."

My face twisted with confusion. Busy? Busy?!

"Oh! How nice! In other words, I'm interrupting. And here I am so worried…"

I hung up.

***

Eliezer didn't go to Medika that day, nor did he call or leave messages, and much less did he come to my house that evening with a bunch of roses in his arms. As my dear Alex would say, "Eliezer Clausell, *missing in action.*"

The anxiety that Eliezer had caused in me was not pleasant. Who had I become? When had I begun to lose control of my emotions? When, exactly, did reason cease to be my guide? Why did I get used to that cold abyss that found its way into my heart?

Not one fucking sign. He's going to pay, I thought just before turning off the lamp on my nightstand.

***

The next day I didn't go to Medika. I called Margaret to put her in charge of excusing my absence with the proper authorities. It wasn't a day of rest or recreation. It was a day of vomiting, headaches, gastritis, and backaches. I spent most of the day in bed, watching cheesy soap operas on television.

It's been many years since my stomach had been so upset. The last time it happened was when I began my adventures in Latin America where I drank unfiltered water and ate everything that was put in front of me, then over the years, I became immune.

What if it's bacteria that I got in New York? The thought made my eyes water. I didn't want to fall ill. I didn't want to be alone. *Why don't I have anyone to care for me at times like this?* I cried a little. I also didn't want to face the night alone. *Why am I suddenly in such need of human tenderness when I hadn't been accustomed to having it before? And why do I only think about Eliezer?*

If I died at home, no one would know and no one would care. Perhaps in a couple of days, someone would come, but not to cheer me up, no; rather to find out why I wasn't getting my office work done. What a thankless life!

The night seemed eternal. Nothing helped me feel better, not even browsing the scrapbook that Norman gave me for my eighteenth birthday. Who knows what hurt me more: my soul, or my body.

***

I didn't go to the office on Wednesday either. That day, Margaret insisted on sending someone to my house to take me to the doctor. I rejected the offer, but in half an hour, the doorbell rang anyway. There Alex was, Chinese soup in hand, glasses on his face, and a smile on his lips. I couldn't contain myself.

"Alex!"

I threw myself in his arms. I almost made him spill the soup.

"You look terrible," was his greeting.

I took his glasses off and looked at his eyes.

"You have no idea how much I missed you…"

He took the glasses back, and put them on again.

"Yes, yes, yes…" I nudged him and invited him in.

I took a shower after eating the hot soup.

Alex took me to Dr. Julio Gomez, my family doctor, the same one that attends Norman regularly. He was an agreeable man, but his secretary was something else. Every time she saw me, she would give me annoyed faces. She was never nice. I sometimes think that, secretly, she wished the doctor would give me bad news, the kind that would make people cry because they had little time left to live.

The doctor visit went by quickly. At least it gave us time to update each other on the latest news, except about

Eliezer, and time for routine examinations. He concluded that he needed to give me some blood tests. That way he could eliminate various possibilities. He would also give me a prescription for gastritis medication.

Alex also accompanied me to the lab, thankfully, because hypodermic needles aren't my favorite devices. After the bloody operation, I asked them to send the results to the doctor directly. I didn't want to be responsible for any more. On the way home, I asked my good friend about the happenings at Medika during the past few days.

"Has our boss inflicted any other casualties?"

I was watching the cars going in the opposite direction through the window. That way Alex would not suspect that the real reason I was asking was to get information about a certain insensitive man.

"Not many. We've survived without you."

I turned my head toward him, mouth agape.

"What is going on with the big chief?"

"It would be better if I didn't tell you. He's been insufferable for several days now. You need to put yourself back together and return to work. That way, he'll take out his frustrations on you, and leave us alone."

"Is he in that bad of a mood?" I asked, in the hope that he would say "yes," and tell me, in passing, that his foul mood had something to do with me and my absence. I don't know why the thought of it made me smile.

"You should do him a little favor." He winked at me and made a vulgar gesticulation by drawing his fist toward his wide-open mouth. "I think he needs it."

I laughed, as I would usually do, but we both noticed that my smile wasn't natural. Perhaps that's why he didn't

304

break out with his usual laugh that went along with his sexual comments. During the uncomfortable silence I thought: *I only hope that Donovan hasn't said anything…*

I know Alex so well that I know that he spoke again to avoid the crazy thoughts that snuck into his mind.

"I imagine that the bidding for El Salvador has you worried."

He was repressing his voice with a more realistic and serious tone. I didn't like him saying that, much less the way he said it. Something bad was happening while I was away: something that would change the future of Medika… something important, and no one had told me about it.

"What happened?"

Alex took one hand off the steering wheel and pushed the bridge of his glasses with his index finger. That meant that he was nervous. It was also something he did when he was upset at himself for saying too much.

"That means that you still don't know…"

"Actually, no, Alex." I paused. I adjusted my blouse that had bunched up because of the seat belt. "Why do I get the feeling that I'm not supposed to know about this?"

Alex responded immediately. This time, he was the one looking through the windows at the opposing traffic.

"He ordered us to not tell you."

"Who is *he*?"

The answer came in a murmur, as though he didn't want to say it.

"Who else, Miranda? Our damned substitute chief,

the grand Clausell child."

He expressed that last bit along with ugly faces and gesticulations. I laughed a little. Alex always found a way to relieve uncomfortable situations.

"Who does he think he is? Allow me to remind you that I'm your immediate superior, so you better finish telling me, in abundant detail, about what's going on."

Alex, when he wants to, can be a man who speaks little but says much.

"They're contesting the bid and they're suing Medika at the same time."

It was impossible to keep my gaping mouth closed. *This can't be.*

Alex spoke of an eighty million dollar bid. For the first time in twenty years, we had been able to take the place of a supplier that, for years, had prevailed through better scheming rather than better bidding. That is, they corrupted themselves to stay on top.

"We knew this day would come."

My calm tone couldn't elicit the same peaceful reaction in him. He twisted his lips in a grimace. Something else was worrying him.

"Let's see, what would you do if I put my hand in your pocket and took the only eighty dollars that you have? Keep in mind that you don't have any more."

Another silence. After a few seconds:

"I would desperately do everything I could to make you give them back."

We laughed. My headache intensified. I put my hand

on my forehead in the hope of alleviating it.

"You are screwed," he teased.

I explained myself better.

"Alex, now they are desperately doing everything they can. They are begging… not for eighty dollars, but for eighty million. And note that they are not begging Medika. No! They are begging some person in the government."

Alex was pensive until he found the words to convey his cautious businessman strategy.

"I'm collecting information that has come out in the media, and I'll update you tomorrow as to whether we have to take any action."

"That seems fine to me. If you have something today, send it to me. I need to be up to date. These matters should not be left to themselves. And you, dear Alex, know better than anyone." By the face he made, I knew that he did not appreciate the scolding. "Does Norman know about this?"

My friend shrugged his shoulders and stopped the car in front of my house. He removed his glasses and looked me in the eye.

"Stop worrying. Save that for tomorrow." He got close and planted a kiss on my cheek. That smell of ostentatious cologne that he always wears got to my nose. I remembered, for a brief moment, that crazy night we had in college. "Miranda get out of my car and go rest. I need to go work. We're not all lucky enough to be sick."

I smiled.

"Thank you, dear."

He made a joke without skipping a beat.

"I hope that you take this into account when you draft

my year-end professional evaluation."

I took his hand and kissed it.

"*You* weren't the one who thought of their desperation strategy."

I closed the door and made a gesture for him to get going.

Alex drove away with a smile.

Chapter 24

$\mathcal{T}$he next morning, my eyes were heavy and my head was on the verge of exploding. I had not been able to sleep all night. I woke up to the ring of the cell phone under the pillow. I accepted the incoming call without even checking to see who was calling me at such an inappropriate time.

"Good morning. Miranda?"

At first, I didn't recognize the voice.

"She's speaking."

"Miranda, it's Julio."

My fatigue and heavy-headedness subsided. I sat up a bit. I cleared my throat, out of which my voice oozed out almost one octave lower than normal.

"Julio?"

The doctor didn't have time for games.

"How do you feel?" His voice exuded worry, he murmured, apparently trying to be discreet.

"Worse than yesterday."

He didn't seem to care about my answer.

"Can you come to my office?"

"Today?" It was more of a feeble whine than a question. I looked at the clock that hung on the wall in front of me. "What time is it?"

His voice confirmed what the hands indicated.

"Nine o'clock in the morning, Miranda. Come as soon as you can, please."

The doctor hung up and left me with, at least, three questions at the tip of my tongue.

I imagined the possibilities. *Hepatitis A? Hepatitis B? West Nile virus? Yellow fever? Let it not be AIDS, by God! Nor syphilis, nor gonorrhea. And what if it is syphilis or gonorrhea?*

I shot out of bed toward the closet, took out my blouse and pants, and threw them over the chair.

I only hope that damned Eliezer Clausell hasn't infected me with something…

I grabbed my clothes and went into the bathroom.

***

In the examination room, while I bit my nails, there was nothing more than loneliness on the cold vinyl examination bench. Julio entered and closed the door. He placed the white binder he was carrying on his desk and didn't open it. He put his pen in his pocket and turned around.

"Miranda, you're pregnant."

My heart skipped a beat, and during those eternal seconds I couldn't see, nor hear, nor feel anything.

"What?"

He opened the binder, pulled out a sheet of paper, and

raised it for me to see. It was the results of the blood test.

POSITIVE. That was the conclusion.

I hope someone has a defibrillator. I think my heart may stop beating.

I laughed and laughed.

"It can't be, Julio. I'm having my period! Plus, I already took a home pregnancy test, and it came out negative."

Julio put the document away. He sat down and held my hands.

"That worries me, Miranda, and it should worry you too. Perhaps you're experiencing symptoms of a miscarriage. Perhaps you've had a miscarriage and you're not aware of it."

I was silent for a while. I couldn't decide what news was worse.

"Now your secretary would definitely have reason to be upset at me." Julio didn't understand the joke and gave me a look of confusion. "It's that I don't know how to get down from this bench without collapsing, and the waiting room is full of people."

He smiled.

"This baby wasn't planned, or am I wrong?"

The understanding need few words, and the observant need few details.

My body trembled. My eyes teared. My skin crawled. A shocking cold took hold of my body, which became unresponsive to my will.

"Could you be mistaken?" I lowered my head while

tears rolled down.

The doctor put his hand on my back.

"Relax, Miranda. Take one step at a time. First, let's perform a second blood test to make sure. If it's positive again, then I'll see how advanced the pregnancy may be and the condition of the embryo. Then, I'll recommend a gynecologist whom I trust. Is that all right?"

No, it's not all right. Nothing is all right! I am pregnant! Pregnant! From a man whom I barely know!

I buried my head in my hands and began crying.

***

The next morning was the same story: insomnia, then a phone call. It was the doctor's office. The results indicated that, in effect, I was far along in my pregnancy. The blood tests were otherwise normal. Well, without another explanation, the bleeding made me another data point for the statistic of women who experience bleeding during the first gestational trimester.

Rest. Get a lot of rest, at least two weeks worth. That was the prescription.

Uh huh! And how do I explain that? Shouldn't I take advantage of my absence to pack my bags and disappear from the lives of both Clausells once and for all? And why not?

I got to the park where I would sometimes run alone. I sat on the bench where I would have a lot of alone time. I love getting out to people-watch during my sad days. It was a pastime and a lot more: the only activity that helped me clear my thoughts. People's faces tell stories. Some are faces of pain, some of success, and others… others belong to people living life… people living life and nothing more. *How should I live now?* My life had been turned upside

312

down.

I'm so lonely! I need a shoulder on which to cry, someone who'll hug me while I break down… Norman. I need Norman. At a little over thirty, I felt like a child. That immature child I had never been who commits acts of stupidity that have terrible repercussions.

Think, Miranda Wise. How would you run your life if it were a business? Like that company after the eighty million dollar contract in El Salvador, what wouldn't you do to keep your freedom? What are your choices?

One-Tell Eliezer. He regrets treating me badly. He comes clean with me. We live happily ever after. End of story. Probability: low.

Two-Tell Eliezer. He distances himself. I continue living my life with a baby. I die alone after a long series of failed loves. Probability: ridiculously high.

Three-Don't tell Eliezer. Don't tell anyone. Don't have the baby. Never have unprotected sex in your life. Probability: ridiculously high.

Life has such pitfalls…

***

Two long weeks and someone rang the doorbell. I would remain supine, staring up at the ceiling, the same thing that I had been doing during the past one hundred hours. Perhaps it was because I found an enormous, yet previously unnoticed crack filled with unexplored paths, or perhaps because it was the only thing I could do without losing my focus on not thinking.

With a jangling of keys, the front door opened and closed.

Norman, who was the only other person who had the

keys to my house, was the only one on the pre-approved visitors list.

I asked that he not come without telling me. But what if something happened to him?

I reached for my robe, tied the belt, and opened the door to my room. I hadn't fixed my hair. I stepped out. A face formed on a dark figure.

"What the hell are you doing here?!"

Eliezer got close. I backed up.

"Are you feeling better, Wise?"

I laughed. Is that how he comes to ask me for sex?

How dare he? More importantly…

"How did you get in? Did Norman give you the key?" I raised my voice. "Give it to me! Go away!"

He didn't dare take another step. He looked at the disaster of a woman that he had created.

"You definitely don't look good!"

I picked up a stray shoe on the hallway floor and threw it at his face.

"Did you come here to be an eyewitness? I'm feeling bad, very bad. You already confirmed it. Now go away at once!"

Having completed his inspection, he recovered his sense of self-confidence and resumed walking toward me while I continued backing away. He kept walking until I found myself sitting on the edge of my bed with him sitting beside me. He opened his hand and placed a key on my robe.

"I told you not to leave them in the garage. Just as I

could get in, so could anyone else."

"What do you want, Clausell?" Although calm, my tone reflected the anger inside. I wanted him to leave as soon as possible. I didn't know how long I could resist not falling prey to uncontrollable bawling. Eliezer spoke calmly, without sarcasm.

"To know how you are doing, Miranda." I noticed his jaw harden. Perhaps it was an attempt to suppress the pity. "May I know what's wrong with you?"

"And since when do you care about what's wrong with me?"

I already knew the story: it displeased him for me to speak to him that way. He inflated his chest. He took deep breaths. He wanted to maintain his self-control.

He leaned forward, resting his elbows on his knees.

He exhaled even more deeply.

"I know that you must be bother…" he began, but I interrupted him:

"That I must? That I must not! That I have every right to be furious!"

Eliezer gave me a look of surprise and disgust. Oh, it must be that he's never seen Miranda Wise furious, boiling on the inside, and on the verge of exploding.

I continued.

"You know? I feel creative today. Let's see if you can understand the situation through a story." I fixed my hair behind my ears and smiled. "A man made a date with a woman at a certain place and time. She had to get to that place at seven in the morning. Did I mention that she had to get there at seven? On the dot? In the morning?"

Eliezer couldn't find anything else to do. He nodded. I got up, because, if I didn't, I would have slapped him, and becoming violent with him wasn't a very good idea, not so much because of the sex that I would miss, but because of the baby that I was carrying. Eliezer watched my feet as I paced.

"So, the charlatan who made a date with her didn't come. Ever.... Ever! Can you believe that! Ah! Did I mention that the charlatan is her boss who she is in the habit of fucking?" He didn't respond, nor make a move. "Did I mention that?"

"No," he said in a cracking whisper.

"I didn't mention it? Well, now I'm mentioning it. The damned charlatan is her boss. Her damned boss! So, as a good employee, the stupid woman got worried. After an hour and a half, she felt obliged to call him. And do you know what happened next?" I stopped and stared at him. "I'll give you three possibilities. Surprise me!"

"That's enough, Miranda."

The quiet tone in which he spoke made me notice how loud I was.

"Wrong answer, dear. Try again." I winked.

He didn't say anything.

"Do you know, at least, what the man says when she asks him if he's alright?"

Eliezer turned to look at the floor. I walked up to him and raised his chin with my hand.

"The man answers, 'I'm busy.'" I stepped away, and continued my pacing from one corner of the room to the other. "That is, the charlatan isn't only fine, but also super busy. Can you believe a snub like that, Eliezer Clausell?" I paused to take a breath, because the heat deprived me of oxygen. I spoke in a lower tone, teary eyed. "Do you want to know something else? The charlatan has been super busy for two fucking weeks. Could he have been fucking for the last two weeks?"

He tried to grab me by the arm. I was too quick. I wouldn't give him the privilege of control. I moved my arm, and we were left looking each other dead on. The tension was building. The air was dense and reeked of sulfur. It was difficult to breathe. My hands were shaking like a vulnerable girl. The control that I felt over my thoughts and words vanished like ashes in the wind.

Eliezer bit his cheek and sighed. Was it out of guilt? Was it from frustration?

"Lately, things haven't gone as I had planned."

I smiled. In my mind, I said, *Oh! And you're telling me...*

He went back to looking at the floor. I wanted to see his eyes when he spoke to me. I wanted to scrutinize his pupils and look into them for the first sign of carelessness.

"I regret the misunderstanding," he added, and I felt myself becoming more infuriated.

"Misunderstanding?" I let out a gulp of air. "Do you know what's a misunderstanding? You being here. Get out!"

I took him by the arm and forced him to stand. I tried to pull him all the way to the door, which made a comical scene. It was like moving a wall. During the commotion, he managed to imprison me in his arms. His hands were shaking because mine were.

"Miranda, please, stop! What is wrong with you?"

I started to feel the disarming effect of his touch. That anger of mine melted into tears… tears that rolled down my cheeks.

"Go, please," I asked in a very soft tone. "I need to be alone." I paused. I don't know if it was to regain my breath or my strength. "I want to be alone."

Eliezer didn't follow my orders. Carefully, he slid his warm arms onto my shoulders, kissed my forehead, and waited for a reaction. It didn't come.

"Miranda, I can't go and leave you like this."

"You disappeared for two weeks, Clausell." I intended to break out of his lukewarm embrace. "You don't have any obligation toward me. Please, go already."

He lifted my chin. Was it an act of pity or consolation?

"I already told you. Things didn't go as they should have."

"And why don't you tell me once and for all how they should have gone?"

My hands lay motionless at my sides. I wanted to embrace him… but not like before… not like that. Anyway, I could hear the beating of his heart. Eliezer Clausell needed me as much as I needed him, but I couldn't save him… not like I was… in a state of chaos.

"It doesn't matter. Anyway, things won't be as they should… ever," I murmured.

When noticing that I wasn't returning his affection, he weakened his embrace.

"I'll go, Wise. I promise, but only if you tell me what's

wrong."

I didn't hesitate to answer.

"Physical exhaustion, Clausell. I need rest, a lot of rest…" I looked at his beautiful eyes. "…and tranquility."

The embrace was over. His hands dropped to his sides. He stopped leaning in toward me, and tilted toward the door.

"Fine, then I'll go so that you can rest."

That was another one of Eliezer's flaws. He gives up too easily.

He got up off the bed and moved away. I grabbed his hand.

"No, better yet, no." He turned around with the face of a suffering man. "I'd prefer it if you stay. At least tonight," then another uncomfortable pause, "please."

He went back to the corner of the bed where he was before and sat down. I rested my head on his lap. His hands caressed my hair, taking away the burdens that I carried.

Finally, after so many nights, I could rest.

Eliezer

"What is the matter with you? Don't judge me, please."

Chapter 25

$\mathcal{I}$t was 6:45 in the morning and Eliezer was no longer keeping me company. I was confined in a dwelling of mattresses, cushions, cold soups, juices that were past their expiration date, rest, and solitude. Before eight, I received Alex's daily call whose purpose was nothing more than following Margaret's required protocols and essentially verifying whether I was still alive.

"Good morning," he said.

"Today's answer is no. I'm still not dead."

"And if you were dead, dear, you'd be shocked right now, running around terrified."

I didn't allow him to continue. My mind felt very cloudy and distant to enjoy his silly jokes.

"Alex, I'm not up for this today."

"Sorry. I'm only trying to cheer you up a little and convince you to, finally, tell me the truth."

"The truth about what?"

"Don't play with me, Miranda. What's going on with you? Is it so serious that you don't want to share it with

The Great Alex? Your best friend?"

I doubted my resolve for a few moments. Beautiful words don't always convince me.

Except when they come from Eliezer, and even then, not every time.

I rediscovered the rudeness strategy.

"You haven't sent me the report on the correspondence and actions taken with regards to the bidding in El Salvador."

I listened to the silence that surrounded the other end of the line and the distant murmuring of those who deal in insults and rudeness.

"Fine. If you want to change topics, message received."

I insisted, but not because I was impatient.

"Where's the report on El Salvador?"

He sighed.

"Forget about El Salvador."

"What do you mean? How can I forget?"

He sighed again.

"Clausell's son ordered us to pull out of the negotiations."

I abandoned my fetal position. I got out of bed and stood up.

"You better give me the whys and wherefores, Alex"

I imagined how, just then, he was looking up at the ceiling, something he does when he doesn't want to follow an order.

"It's been a couple of days since Eliezer said so.

I wanted to tell you, but your state of mind and health haven't given me the opportunity to do it."

"Don't give me that story. The son of a bitch threatened you? He told you not to tell me, right?"

That was Eliezer's modus operandi, and the only valid reason for Alex to hide something so important from me.

"It's not easy here, Miranda. The strangest things have been happening. Decisions have been made that make no sense."

I didn't want to know any more details.

"We'll speak later, Alex."

I was on the verge of pressing the red button on the screen of the phone. The shout that came out of the speaker stopped me.

"Don't hang up yet, Miranda!"

"Just imagine. It's time for someone to put the imbecile we have for a boss in his place."

***

I didn't have a script in my mind, only determination and a question. Why would he want to do me harm?

I arrived with my face washed, sporting a long casual dress, high heel sandals, and a long lightweight coat. Margaret told me that Eliezer was in the boardroom. The pleading in her eyes–that I abandon whatever mission I was on–was fruitless. I couldn't even hear whom he was with. I took long quick strides and abruptly opened the door. My eyes found Eliezer and Isabel, both looking astonished.

I laughed wryly. *That's what I'd been missing.*

"Clausell, I need a few minutes."

The man gave his mother a greasy look.

"Wise. Can't you see that I'm in the middle of a meeting?"

I walked toward him. I raised my hand a little and spoke with a deliberate mannerism and a raised index finger.

"I need a few minutes. Now."

Despite the implicit threat and the strictness in my tone, Eliezer managed a mild, but nearly invisible smile, the kind that he likes to keep secret when he gets excited. Right away, the anxiety was reflected in his face. Isabel rose.

"Good morning, Miranda." I responded to the greeting sarcastically with a look of contempt. She responded with the first shot to begin the battle. "You can say whatever it is in my presence. I am the wife of the founder, mother of the CEO and, of course, your superior.

I walked toward her and put my hand on her shoulder.

"I prefer to speak alone with my immediate boss. It's my right," I responded with a smile on my lips. I withdrew my hand and Eliezer began to speak.

"Isabel is right, Miss Wise. Moreover, she's a shareholder in the company. We shouldn't exclude her

326

from Medika affairs."

I focused my eyes on the man. *Great! Two against one!*

I gave him the opportunity to redeem himself.

"Let's talk about El Salvador."

Eliezer leaned back in his chair and crossed his legs.

"Apparently, your team's loyalty is more powerful than my orders."

"Why did you do it?" I asked, when in reality I wanted to say, "Why are you doing this to me?"

Eliezer looked at his mother, who took advantage of the silence to sit down again, cross her legs, and smile from ear to ear. Then he looked at me very seriously for a few seconds and spoke: checkmate.

"I don't have to give explanations to my subordinates, much less share with them why I make decisions that are for the good of this company."

I noticed contempt in his words—that same contempt that he had for me the first day that he arrived. I didn't have to look at Isabel to notice how satisfied she was with her son's response. The atmosphere reeked with her malice.

If Eliezer and I were alone, the story would be different. We would have ended the conflict with strong words, insults, and a session of incomprehensible lust. Of course, that wasn't the case. Eliezer Clausell only made me feel anxiety, sadness, and anger. I had nothing more to say, nothing more to do. I turned halfway and abandoned Medika with my heels clacking.

After going out the door, I found the answer to my problem. I made a difficult decision. I leaned against the wastepaper bin outside the large glass doors of the main entrance. I felt a bit of nausea, but nothing more. That's what Eliezer Clausell had caused. How disgusting. Living nine months alone, unappreciated, devalued, and hated was not worth it. Much less was it worth giving such a father to an innocent child. You can't miss what you never had. Suddenly, those words of his reverberated in my mind. They made me reassess many of my ideas.

***

There it was: the most discreet place I could find with no Planned Parenthood sign on the outside. There were two women in the waiting room. The younger one looked relaxed and played with her smart phone. The older one, in her forties, was quiet. She hid her face behind large Christian Dior sunglasses that framed her Vanity Fair pose to perfection. I sat at the back of the room. I didn't go to the counter. I needed more time. What if I got over the anger and the will to go ahead with the act? In the middle of the turmoil of emotions, I received a text message.

What are you doing?

I looked at the shadowy door. There was no one there. I didn't respond to the message. Then another one came.

Where are you?

I looked at the door of the clinic again. There was still no one there.

Answer me!

I didn't look at the door any more. I had to shake the feeling of paranoia.

Get out of there, or I'll come in to get you.

MIRANDA

What the hell?

I looked up. Through the door, there was Norman, camouflaged by the frosted glass that hindered visibility from the inside.

> You have five seconds to get out.

But who do you think you are? What authority do you have to speak to me that way?

I began to key in a response. A sixth message appeared on the screen.

> This is serious, Miranda. If I go in, tomorrow we'll be on the front page of the national newspapers. My face is well known. And you are inside there. Get out!

The door began to open. So, I reacted.

Outside, I didn't have the nerve to look at his face. Churning in my gut was a mix of shame and anger. He walked me up to the vehicle that had driven him. He was wearing dark glasses. He ordered Donovan to get out of the car.

"How did you know where I was? Who told you?"

He spoke serenely.

"That doesn't matter. What were you doing there?"

"What were *you* doing there, Norman?"

Flustered, he threw up his hands.

"I intend to ask the right questions to avoid reaching the wrong conclusions."

I threw myself against the door on the other side and tried to open it. It was impossible, as was taking off my seatbelt. I gave Norman an angry look and then sighed in frustration. The old man smiled.

"Childproof, remember?"

"Norman, I am not a girl. I can do what I please without accounting to anyone. Much less, asking permission."

He looked at me carefully, a tender look, a look filled with a father's love. He knocked down the fragile wall that I had built to defend my privacy. My eyes, in a rescue attempt, tried to hide my shame. Still, as adult as I thought I was, I reverted to being a girl every time I tried to outthink him. In that moment, I became a stupid adolescent, again, the kind who gets impregnated by the first idiot who spreads her legs.

I leaned forward, embraced him closely and cried. I cried and cried. I cried even more when he held me in his arms. When he thought that was enough of an overflow of emotion, he removed his sunglasses and delicately detached my face from his arm. I was lost in his gaze. My soul so desired the company of Eliezer during these moments that I couldn't avoid...

"Miranda! What are you doing?"

With both hands, Norman held my arms and separated us, tearing my lips from his in another crushing deluge of embarrassment. My body began to shake. I started crying again. Norman only looked at me as though, that way, he could discover the source of my dementia.

"I'm sorry. I'm sorry. I'm sorry..." I whispered without pausing.

The good father covered me in another embrace, still stronger and warmer than the last.

"Tell me what's happening to you Miranda. You've

managed to scare me!"

Norman had never seen me cry like this. He had only seen me shed a few dumb tears when I fell off my bicycle, and when a boy whom I never saw again made fun of me in school for living at an orphanage.

"I need your support, Norman. Don't ask me questions, just keep me company."

He placed his hand on my back. That time I was conscious of the fact that I wasn't with Eliezer, rather his father who was also my father. Norman hugged me. We didn't keep track of time. I only know that it was becoming dark outside.

***

"Who's the father?"

I moved away a little. I wanted to avoid surrendering to the temptation to tell him the truth.

"*That's* what doesn't matter."

"Is the situation between you so bad?"

"I said that it doesn't matter."

He sighed.

"Does he know?"

"It doesn't matter, Norman!"

"Don't be immature, please!" He imitated my tone of voice. "I'm trying to help you."

"No one asked for your help. Furthermore, I've ceased to be your primary concern. I don't know you, Norman. It hurts me, but I don't know you. It's been some time since we've ceased to be family."

Silence. In seconds, he reformulated his approach.

"In a moment of desperation such as this, I don't want you to do something that you'll regret your whole life, my daughter."

More tears came out.

"Let's leave the sermon for later, Norman."

"In recognition of everything I've done for you, Miranda Wise, I demand that you tell me, at least, who the father is."

"That's none of your business–not yours, and not anyone's! This conversation won't take us anywhere." I tried to open the door again. "Please, Norman. I have to go."

He grabbed me by the arm and a freezing cold coursed through my veins. His touch was similar to that of his son: rough, rude, and irreverent.

"You're not going anywhere until you tell me what is going on." He continued holding me by the arm, just as his son was accustomed to doing.

The experience confused and so angered me that I lost control.

"Eliezer! Let me go!"

The pressure on my arm was relieved.

"Eliezer?" His voice came out in a murmur. The question was more of an assertion than an inquiry.

"I am sick of the Clausells thinking that they own my life! To hell with both of you! Consider my debt paid," I continued, screaming,

"God!"

Norman threw himself on me, he embraced me with such force that I felt like I was going to explode.

"I'm so sorry, Miranda…" he began to say. I pushed and kicked in response. He held my arms and tried to stop my crying with a penetrating stare. "Calm down, please. This isn't good for you."

"In these past months, have you given a damn about what was good for me, and what wasn't? Why has the paternal sentiment suddenly returned? You've only had time for, and a desire to tangle yourself up in who knows what with your wife. You've thrown our relationship in the trash!"

While his voice rose, I continued fighting my tears.

"I have neglected you, I know. Now I notice that I've been inconsiderate. I laid too much responsibility on you. That responsibility was mine and no one else's." He took a breath, and let go of me. He leaned back. "Does Eliezer know?"

"Your son is the most fucked up person that I've ever known." That is not the answer he was expecting, but the only one I had for him.

"Does he know?" he repeated with his eyes closed.

I shook my head.

"He has no reason to know."

"At least give him a chance to find out. I'm not going to judge your decision. I only… I only ask that you not rob him of his right."

"Things aren't that simple, Norman. Your son has not

earned that right. Your son is a disaster! Did you know? I still haven't explained how I fell into his clutches. Can you imagine what my life would be like if I had his baby? If, by chance, I remain by Eliezer Clausell's side?"

Without knowing it, I said the words that were key to making him start into another one of his sermons. This time, he rubbed the words in my face, and through them, the story that he had never told me before.

Chapter 26

"Miranda Wise, if it hadn't been for the bravery of your mother, you wouldn't be here today. Yes, I know her. Yes, I know who she is. The failed attempt to find them when you requested it of me as a gift for your fifteenth birthday was all a lie, a fabrication. Forgive me, please. I only wanted to protect you. I swore to never tell you anything about it because I didn't believe that knowing the truth would help you or change your destiny.

"Allow me to tell you a story, my daughter... the story of your life when you were still not yet self-aware. So, perhaps, you can forgive me, you can understand me, and you can perhaps rethink your decision and not return to a clinic like that. Realize what motherly love can do for you, because you, Miranda, can become an exceptional mother. You're afraid, yes, but you're not deficient in any way. Any way! And look at how I had to get you out of there! Miranda, you have an enviable job, a good salary, a life planned out. What are you worried about? You are, so to speak, a complete woman: educated and worldly. There have been women who have been more steadfast, and have not had even a third of what you have. So, let me tell you a story...

"I knew your mother, Laura, at the university. Isabel

and I were engaged, and they were friends. I was a friend of your father since I was a child. The four of us were living the life of university freshmen: parties, alcohol, and unbridled sex everywhere. We were free spirits full of energy and love—but we made some bad choices. So that's how our life stories intertwine even more.

"We had gotten so drunk that Isabel got pregnant with Eliezer. At the time, I thought we shared our reasons for deciding to keep the baby. After knowing her better in time, however, I came to realize why she had decided to embrace the pregnancy. First, she was never academically inclined, so when she had an excuse to drop out by having a baby, she did. Second, she could see that I was determined to make something of myself, so the baby was her way of ensuring my future financial support for her. Anyway, we came to an agreement: she would go live at her parent's house, give birth to Eliezer, and take care of him, while I would finish my university studies. During that time, when Eliezer was barely two months old, Laura got pregnant.

"Your parents had a more harmonious and stable relationship than I had with Isabel. Notwithstanding, as soon as Laura found out that she was pregnant and opted to fight for your life, your father turned his back on her and severed the relationship completely. She built up her courage and struggled against all odds. She didn't even tell her parents because she was so afraid of how your grandfather might react. He was a stubborn man with strongly held beliefs. I couldn't see her fight so alone against the world. Sometimes she didn't even have enough to eat decently, including when she was working full time with her protruding belly. She wanted so much for you! She dreamed of giving you everything you needed. In time, I realized that I lost my friendship with your father for having become Laura's rock and confidant. It hurt me, yes, but it didn't matter that much. I couldn't abandon her–such a fighter. During the final weeks of her pregnancy, symptoms of pre-eclampsia emerged. Then everything became even more complicated. She died during an emergency cesarean section that was nothing more than an effort to save both of you.

"Your maternal grandparents found out about the tragedy and the news because the university authorities notified next of kin. Certain people thought that I was your father: I would take her to lunch, to the gynecologist, and I would even take her to work when her feet would swell. I took a paternity test to certify the truth that I wasn't your father–because I'm not. I'm *not* your biological father. Isabel was jealous, of course, and she ended their friendship. We would fight almost daily. There was no way to convince her. Her sarcastic comments were something she would repeat every day: 'That stupid woman is your charity case. By now, you surely have earned your place in heaven…' She couldn't understand. No one could understand! I felt admiration for your mother. I had never before seen a woman fight so bravely. And yes, I admit: she filled the emptiness and loneliness that I felt because of the distance to and absence of my family. I also think that I filled the void in her that was caused by that imbecile. And understand that he officially acknowledged paternity because I threatened to tell his father that he had become a grandfather and that his son didn't even think about marriage. Your father hasn't been anything more than a coward his whole life. Your paternal grandfather also had told him: 'If you have children before you have a career, I'll disinherit you.'

"Your grandparents brought you back to their

hometown. I didn't know anything more about you until the evening when I saw you in the auditorium. You and Eliezer had reached the semifinals of the mathematics competition. He was a child of the privileged class, used to studying with the best teachers, the best books, and the best resources. You were a timid girl from a public school with worn out clothes and dirty socks. When I saw you standing there you were defenseless and fearsome at the same time. You reminded me of your mother. You had your mother's hair, her guts, and her mannerisms. So, when I heard your name, I was shocked.

"I knew it in my heart. You were my good friend's child. You were the child for whom she fought so hard. I was surprised and disappointed when you won the first place medal and your grandparents didn't show up to congratulate you. Instead it was two nuns. I found out later that your grandmother had passed away when you were less than two years old, and your grandfather didn't want to keep you. That's why I came. That's why I swore to protect you. That's why I swore to become the father you never had. Laura deserved that and more. You definitely deserved that and more."

Chapter 27

"*A*nd my father, Norman... Who is he? Is he alive?"

Naming the man wasn't a big deal. I knew his name. It was on my birth certificate, which I obtained from the public records to get my driver's license. Though, by that time, I had lost interest in taking the time to research him further: I was old enough to recognize how meaningless it would be since he had not played any role in my life. However, now that Norman was going into detail about my biological parentage, it wouldn't make sense to avoid talking about my father and leave a hole in the now more complete picture of my background.

Norman shrugged. He squinted and clenched his jaw, which was in significant contrast to the sweet demeanor he had when mentioning my mother's name. I could see doubt in his face. He didn't want to tell me, and when he did, he did so reluctantly.

"His name is Paul Wise."

Right, I know... Wait...

Although I had known his name for many years now, hearing Norman speak his name jarred something in my mind and made the pieces fall into place. The man who had bumped into Eliezer during our trip to New York was Paul W. Hopgood. Could he have been Paul *Wise* Hopgood? My heart began beating faster, because the more I thought about it, the more I believed it. The name began to reverberate in my mind like an echo. The image of his body and his face came to me out of the recesses of my memory and, like the memory, that unpleasant sensation that I felt in his presence came to me as well.

Eliezer knew him! They knew each other!

But… what do those two have to do with each other? How do they know each other? Why?

My eyes watered.

"I know who he is, Norman. He doesn't use his real last name."

Norman's face lit up with alarm and shock.

"You know him? How? From where? Did he try to harm you?"

The questions surprised me, but I didn't want to give him more to worry about.

"Where and how I know him isn't important. As far as I know, he hasn't tried to harm me. Why would he? And… what does that man have to do with Eliezer?"

Norman began to look very confused. I never imagined that Norman's face could be so expressive, because he had also learned from Ethan how to hide his most intimate truths.

"I don't know how nor why my son and that miscreant are acquainted, but it doesn't please me. In fact, there is absolutely no reason for it to have happened… at least not at this time."

"Not at this time? What do you mean, Norman?"

He fixed his eyes on mine. His chest sunk and he lost the little energy he had left for me. Then he began a second story.

"You've always asked why I allowed Isabel to take my son and sever communication with me. I think it's time for you to know the truth."

Chapter 28

"Eliezer was seven years old. I lived with them and had already founded Medika which took up much of my time. My relationship with Isabel cooled, and I accept that it was my fault. We talked about divorce on various occasions. I wanted her to be happier with someone who could take care of her like she wanted. She wanted money. She said that she wouldn't divorce me because she wouldn't allow someone else to end up with what was hers, and that she planned on living luxuriously all her life.

"Even though she didn't want a divorce and we lived together, we barely saw each other; but I still noticed that she began to neglect Eliezer who had more of a connection with his nanny than with her. In fact, I don't recall Isabel ever cuddling her son. I only ever saw his nanny do that.

"Our love had already died. That was clear. Nonetheless, my pride as a man and as a husband gnawed at me. I began to imagine her in other arms and with other men. I thought that if that's what her life had become, then we should get a divorce, once and for all.

"I hired an investigator. Within a few days, he came back with pictures... many, many pictures. I could never have imagined it. The scenes I saw would never have otherwise crossed my mind. My wife, the woman I had once loved so much, was unfaithful to me with the man who had been my best friend.

"Isabel was cheating on me with Paul Wise Hopgood. Oh, yes! That son of a bitch was slow, but he managed to exact his revenge on me just as he had sworn. 'This will cost you Norman. This will cost you…' he declared as soon as he attested to his paternity. That was the last time I saw him.

"I got home that evening with photographs and bank statements in hand. I was the one who put Eliezer to bed, and later, when I knew that he was fast asleep, I asked Isabel to meet me near the library.

"It was a heated discussion. She screamed and made her arguments, and I only demanded divorce. Nothing else interested me, not even recovering the money that she had spent with Paul. I wanted to have nothing more to do with her.

"Just then, when she realized that she would lose, she began to reveal more secrets. I don't know if it was to hurt me more, or because she couldn't help revealing them all after she had already revealed one. Isabel kept slapping me while crying out torturous confessions. She was saying that I had abandoned her just like Paul had abandoned Laura; that I had cast her aside to console another woman; that it was my fault; that she detested me; that I deserved the heartbreak and her revenge; that she wanted to see me fall, because she had fallen; and that I deserved to live a life of obscurity, just as she had when she left to live with her parents.

"She admitted that Eliezer knew, that she would take him along, that sometimes she would leave him in the bathroom of the hotel room where she would have sex with Paul, and that he would hear her moan but not say anything about it.

"I never thought that I, Norman Clausell, was capable of doing what I had done. I never thought that I'd allow myself to be consumed with rage. I never thought that, from one moment to the next, I could become another person, a person who, to this day, I detest.

"I lost control. I lost my mind. I responded to her beating and mistreatment. I unleashed my fury against her. How could she have committed such an atrocity on our innocent son? How could she? How?

"So, while beating her, I paused to look at the body of the woman who had fallen to the floor. That's how I noticed that my little Eliezer was there, in the doorway, clutching his plush toy truck to his chest, crying in silence, looking at a scene that would never, ever leave his mind.

"I still haven't forgotten the terror that had torn apart his little face. I still can't forget the horror and the disappointment. I can't forget it to this day. I still haven't forgiven myself. I still hate myself.

"Eliezer is very screwed up, I know. I murdered his goodness. I turned him into a different person. I, who was the closest he had to a hero, crushed his innocence and his potential.

"Isabel didn't turn me in. We both had much to lose. We came to an agreement that benefited her more than it did me. She would leave and would take our child with her so that I would have no contact with him, at least until he reached adulthood. Before leaving, she said that she wouldn't be seeing Paul anymore, and that he was only a plaything anyway, and that there were many other playthings to be had in the world.

"That's how I had sacrificed my relationship with my son for… for my company and money in my pocket! I don't want you to make the wrong decision. You would be making my mistake, and carrying that burden isn't living… it's hell. I beg you, please, forgive me for having been a monster, and I beg you, also, to speak with Eliezer.

"He is everything you say he is, but also, very deep down, he has a good heart. The little that I know about him confirms that he'll be a much better father than I was, and if the relationship between you develops, a great companion.

"Trust in me, his father… your father who loves you with all my soul…"

Chapter 29

I would find the cause of my misery in his office. It wasn't an appropriate place to broach the conversation; nevertheless, during the last few weeks, there had been no ideal place for us to speak, for us to be ourselves.

It was late at night. His car was the only one in the parking lot. I entered the office stealthily. Even though I would have wanted to make noise, I didn't have the strength to open the door with my usual brusqueness. I carried a heavy heart.

From the doorway, I saw him look over a few documents and crumple them in his hand. He had his back to me, attending to a call on his cell phone.

"That won't be a problem, I already told them... No, she has no fucking idea... No! Not her... but what are they saying? Norman no longer poses any risk, nor does he suspect. I told you, no! We've come to an agreement and we'll do it. I said so!"

He hung up. He turned around and threw the papers and the phone on the desk. I took a few steps forward and he lifted his head.

"What agreement are you talking about, my dear

Clausell?"

His eyes dilated and he quickly took control of his reaction.

Well, well… if this painter hasn't suddenly become an actor.

"What are you doing here, Miranda?" He looked at his wristwatch. I knew that he wanted to know what I had managed to hear.

"Eavesdropping. What else?" I answered, with a tone that was sarcastic and absurd like my life had been since the day I bumped into him. He relaxed his shoulders. I supposed that he found a way of managing the situation.

"What's wrong with you, Wise?"

"What agreement were you talking about, Clausell?" I walked up to his desk.

"Nothing of importance." He brushed his head with his hands. "Are you ok? Do you feel better?"

"Social protocol demands that I answer your question in the affirmative. But no, Eliezer, I'm not well, and I certainly don't feel better."

There was a strange brilliance in his eyes. He emerged from the space behind his desk and came up to me. He put his hands on my shoulders. The weight of his demons sunk me in his hell. I moved my shoulders so that he would remove himself because I didn't want him to touch me. He withdrew his hands, he was a bit confused by my indifference.

"If you don't tell me what's making you like this, I can't help you."

I pressed my index finger against his forehead.

"You've made me like this, Eliezer. I don't know what's

348

going on with you. I'm fed up with trying to decipher your thoughts. I'm tired of wanting to understand you."

My provocation didn't please him. If I had done this on the day we first met, I surely would have had my arm twisted and broken. He tensed his jaw enough to make it pop.

"Do you notice? Every expression of yours confirms that there's something more behind that face. This didn't begin well. Even so, I demand to know the truth. I'm prepared to hear what you have to say–the secrets that you have to reveal." I paused for a moment to reassure myself that I really wanted to say what I wanted to say. "I'm prepared, Clausell, for us to deal with and overcome that which divides us."

He took my hands in his.

"Miranda, I don't believe that now is the time for…"

"God damn it, Clausell! It's never the time! You know what? Us. That wasn't supposed to happen. That was the only bad time. It never should have been the fucking time. If you like, I'll start the explanation." He leaned back. "Miranda Wise, an orphan with a flawless life, living a lie, and stupidly in love with you."

Eliezer closed his eyes. I pushed him. I wanted him to look at me. I wanted him to see what he had destroyed.

"Miranda Wise was living a perfect and boringly happy life until she made the big mistake to not adhere to professional boundaries."

He was clothed in guilt. I could see it in his eyes. I sat down, and suddenly, I could understand the weight that he was carrying. What I couldn't understand was the reason for it. We were independent and free adults. What could be coming between us?

I wanted to give him the opportunity of freeing his soul so we could begin on a clean slate and paint our story anew… in another way. I needed to make him open up to me. That way, I could help him. Only that way could we help ourselves.

"Tell me, Eliezer: who are you?" His silence answered me. "Fine, it seems like I'm the one who wants to talk today. Would you forget about everything and everyone else for me?"

That was the key question. I needed an answer. I needed to know how far he would go for me. His eyes became watery. Was that a sign of pain? Why wouldn't he cough up what was making him choke. Why wouldn't he say anything?

"God damn it, Eliezer! It's so simple. Choose between two words. They're only two damned words: yes, or no."

Eliezer leaned back. He rubbed his hair and his face in frustration.

"It's not so simple, Miranda. Please, stop talking. Let's drop this now. We'll talk tomorrow. Today isn't the day. Now is not the time. Trust me. Please."

I closed in on him and pressed my finger against his forehead again. My voice cracked as I spoke.

"That's the problem. Unless we're rolling around in bed, I can't trust you. I don't want to trust you, because I don't know who you are."

Eliezer removed my finger from his forehead. He took the opportunity to touch me, to slide his arms onto me, and trap me in an embrace.

"I know, Miranda. I know." He kissed me on my

forehead. "Go home. Take a shower. Watch a movie. Calm down. Don't think about me. Don't think about us."

I removed myself from his embrace and wiped my tears.

"I gave you a chance. Only remember that I was the one who gave you that opportunity. Remember, always, that I was the one who gave us that opportunity. Tomorrow… tomorrow it'll be too late."

I made my decision that very instant. I would let both of the men whom I most loved in my life go: Norman, the father who hadn't abandoned me; and Eliezer, who had done who knows what for me. No, I wouldn't bring a child into this world who, ultimately, would be just as unhappy as those two. After all, Eliezer would agree: why bring more unhappy people into this world? I walked toward the door. I crossed the threshold and his voice made me pause.

"That's how you're leaving? That's how you're going to leave everything?"

I turned around and gave him a goodbye sigh.

"That's how I'm leaving, and that's how I'm leaving things. You're right. It's time to go home. I already know what it's like to be in hell."

***

My tears governed the route I took, not the lights nor the traffic signals. *How could I tell him that I'm expecting his baby?* No, that decision was mine and no one else's. Whatever it is, I would make it for me… only for me… and for the good of that… baby.

I opened the garage door, and parked the car. The ceiling light that turns on automatically when the door opens didn't work. I left the garage door partially open so that I would have some light when opening the door to the house.

Goosebumps... I heard someone else's breathing. In less than a second, I imagined Eliezer on his knees, saying 'yes,' boldly and clearly, but that was too much imagination for such a dark fairy tale. A hand covered my mouth and another restrained my hands. A shadow opened the door and suddenly my whole body flew up into the air. Someone threw me inside the house. My head cracked when it hit the concrete. Was it the floor or a wall? My eyesight darkened, a thick, dark liquid poured out of my forehead... dizziness... nausea... confusion. *What is this? What is going on? Please, someone help me!* Screaming overtook my thoughts because I couldn't manage to vocalize words.

Three men were attacking me... hitting and kicking. I managed to protect my abdomen by assuming a fetal position. I don't know why, just then, that was the only part of my body that mattered to me.

The light from the street lamps filtered through the curtains, forming the silhouettes of my attackers. Their faces were covered with black masks. One of them threw himself on me. He let his weight fall on my hips, immobilizing my legs. The second attacker restrained my hands again while a chunkier third bound them with tape, and wrapped another piece around my head and over my mouth. Then with a yank, he ripped the buttons off my blouse and, with a knife, cut through the bra I was wearing.

Intrusive hands squeezed my breasts and then moved to my pants. The man had no compassion for me. With a knife at my throat, he forced me to spread my legs, and he put his hand in my crotch. He hurt me. He squeezed mercilessly. Then one of the others pushed him aside. As soon as I could, I struggled to my feet, but then a kick sent me to the other side of the room. I fell face down. I stayed quiet. My eyes closed, I could imagine them gloating over me and relishing their next move. I wanted to die until I had a moment of lucidity. Although I had a gun in my purse, I had no idea where it was now, but I remembered I also kept one in my bedroom.

If only I could get there...

Their pause gave me a chance to stand up and run toward the bedroom while working my sweat soaked hands out of the tape that bound them. I just managed to get my hands free to tear the tape off my mouth when, halfway there, one of them managed to grab me by the hair. They put me up against the wall, took off my pants, and tore off my underwear.

"Kill her!" the one who was holding me impatiently ordered.

"No, not yet!" the other one said.

I heard the sound of a zipper opening.

God help me. Help me or let them kill me once and for all!

"Kill her! Quit being a jerk, and kill her!"

"No! She's too good to throw away!"

The wretch rubbed his disgusting penis against my vagina, looking for a way in. The moist taste of blood coming from my forehead and dripping into my mouth made me feel even more nauseous. Although they had me pinned against the wall, one hand was free enough to put two fingers as far as I could into my mouth.

My vomit shot out. The man that had me pinned threw me to the floor. The one who was watching stepped back so his shoes wouldn't get dirty. The last one, the one who wanted to invade my body, kicked me in the face. I rolled over onto something lumpy and turned over. It was my purse.

"I told you, asshole! I told you!" one of them repeated.

"Kill her already!" The other one said.

I took advantage of the discussion to try to open my purse. My hands were shaking. *Hurry up, Miranda. Hurry up…*

The shadow of one of the men hovered over me.

"Come here, bitch!"

The deafening sound of the shot shook the house. The evil bastard fell to the floor. The other son of a bitch shot at me twice but then stopped. Apparently his gun had jammed, so he and the third one ran, disappearing into the shadows. The gun fell out of my hands. My breath became short. Then there was silence and a brilliant darkness. It seemed like an eternity went by…

***

"Miranda! Miranda! Miranda!"

A light came on. Blood… there was blood everywhere. Eliezer ran to me and removed the pistol from my shaking hands. The man who lay by my side hadn't died. He was still breathing and began to rise. Eliezer got close to him and pointed the gun at him. He shot him twice and threw the gun to the ground. I collapsed. Eliezer came to my side, put his hands on my back, hugged me, and pulled me up.

"Miranda… What have they done to you? What the hell have they done to you?"

The little breath that I had left wasn't enough to speak to him… to tell him. With one of my bloody hands,

MIRANDA

I grabbed his. I placed it on my abdomen. His eyes were tearing.

"I know, Wise. I know."

I smiled… I couldn't find the strength to do more.

"No! Don't do that! Don't sleep! Open your eyes! Look at me! God damn it! Look at me!

No. I can't see you. It's too dark. Turn the light on…

"Miranda!"

Chapter 30

Rays of sunlight filtered through the bulging branches of the trees, forming abstract figures on my bare feet. I've always enjoyed the coolness that would find its way into the wood overnight. In the last few months, feeling it against the soles of my feet was the only thing that reminded me that I was still alive, above ground and not six feet under. The lawn still released an aroma from the rain that had punished it overnight–an unusual condition, considering that it wasn't the rainy season in Panama. The breeze was fresh. I could feel it with every sigh. My lungs wanted to give up, having declared a war on air. They no longer wanted its caresses. They no longer wanted those gifts of life that came with every breath.

Two or three months had passed since my arrival, I couldn't be sure. Before that, I had spent three weeks recovering in the hospital after the surgery to repair the damage to my collarbone. It had been hit by one of the bullets. The doctors didn't want to stop monitoring the progress of the first trimester of my pregnancy, and I agreed with them. Norman didn't leave my side for even a day. Margaret visited me every evening, and Alex from time to time, but no one else. No one else came.

The presence of my adoptive parents was suffocating.

None of them could scare away the darkness to which those soulless men condemned me that terrible night. Alex didn't ask questions, but only sat by my side, taking in my pain.

Hernandez owed me a favor, that's why he couldn't refuse when I begged him to get me out of that hospital so that no one would know about it.

"Don't you think it's risky to leave the country? And what if you have a medical emergency at 50,000 feet?"

"The doctor authorized it. I need to disappear. Moreover, I am not going to be flying commercial. The pilot can get us back to an airport fast enough if need be."

Alex, with Margaret's help, took charge of preparing my flight with a nurse and a specialist physician. He knew that it would put him in a difficult position with Norman, but the truth was that I didn't care about anyone or anything anymore.

We left that evening.

"Miranda, take this." Hernandez handed me a white envelope. "He asked for me to give this to you."

"Did you tell him?"

"No, but he knows."

Where is he? How is he? Why isn't he with me? Why hasn't he come to see me even once?

Hernandez must have interpreted my silence as sorrow. He tried to make me feel better.

"It's not going well for him."

"Don't excuse him."

Even though I was dying to know about him, I couldn't
358

bear the extra weight on the baggage I was carrying.

"Things have become complicated."

"Enough!" I took the envelope. "Take care of yourself, Hernandez. Thanks for everything."

Alex took my arm, and I began walking. Even though I had my back to him, Hernandez drew out his goodbye.

"Likewise, Miranda Wise. Likewise."

Before getting on the plane, I dropped the white envelope. There was no room on the plane for anyone else.

***

Some footsteps were softly coming close. It was Rosa. She paused by my side. She brought me a cup of orange juice. She placed it on the parquet floor and a hand of consolation on my shoulder, just as she had done every evening since I agreed for her to stay in the cabin.

Rosa's presence was the thing on which Norman and Luis Bartolome insisted as a condition to leave me alone after having learned of my escape. I agreed, not for their sake, but because I didn't feel like even getting myself a drink of water.

I turned toward her with a weak smile, and thanked her. She, Norman, Luis, Julio, Alex, and Margaret had stopped asking me questions and offering me words of encouragement. All of them gave up, allowing me to sink into bitterness, alone. They noticed that the only way they could support me would be from a distance.

I took the cup and barely could take a sip. The tartness hurt the wounds to my soul. I continued drinking, but not for myself. If that were the only reason, I would have already starved, or pursued one of those crazy ideas that, at times, seduced me.

Rosa left the house and, within minutes, I heard other steps approaching. I didn't want to turn around, not even when I knew the presence was unusual. They were firm footsteps and they advanced rapidly. I knew those footsteps. I knew them very well. They paused by my side and remained that way.

I didn't want to look at him. I kept my eyes fixed on the shadows that the sun was drawing on my skin. The breeze took it upon itself to confirm the identity of the visitor. That scent... that unforgettable scent. I closed my eyes. I imagined him sitting on the floor, by my side, because the parquet boards creaked distinctively.

"Miranda..."

He spoke my name as he always did, with that spicy sparkle that can be known only through the pleasure of hearing it. I knew that the day would come. I wouldn't have predicted it so soon. I wasn't prepared. Not yet.

"Everything is over, Miranda," he paused to clear his voice. "At home, we are very worried about all of you. You must return, take care of yourself, and seek help if necessary... please."

His voice exuded the same tone as always. It was the same icy voice that a few months ago could ignite every cell of my body. Could it be that man would never change?

"I may be the last person that you want to see. I understand. You have every right and, even though I refuse to accept it, you're absolutely right. Nevertheless, the others haven't been successful in their aims, and I can't keep my arms crossed."

I was incapable of reacting. I had turned to stone. Not

even my enlarged breasts moved with my breathing. Tears rolled down my cheeks, which surprised me, because I had come to think that I would never again be capable of crying–that I had no tears left in my eyes.

"Would you take care of the baby? Would you take responsibility?"

I tried to keep my voice firm. That was the only plan I could formulate: that Eliezer would give me his word that he would take care of the baby when born, because I wouldn't. I couldn't.

"That won't be necessary," he paused innocently. "He has both of us."

I laughed for the first time in months, but it wasn't exactly out of joy.

"Don't you realize how screwed up I am? I don't want the baby to have to live a shitty life with a screwed up mother like you had."

He got close and tried to give me a hug that I avoided with a scream and a look of anger, fear, and disgust.

Eliezer didn't give up. He tried to hug me again, using as much force as he could without hurting me.

"Let me go! Leave me alone once and for all!" I wanted to scream, but I could only muster murmurs. "If you had only hugged me like that a few months ago, Eliezer, that night in your office and those many other nights. It was so simple, Eliezer, very, very simple."

He squeezed me harder.

"I know, Miranda. I know! But please understand. You met me when I was a shit of a man, when everything was a mess. I wish I had done many things differently. I wish I had been able to protect both of you." His voice cracked.

"But it didn't happen that way, and I live cursing every second that I was incapable of making the right decisions. I live cursing that moment that I let you leave my office with so much pain on your face. Do you remember that Christmas day when I said that my life on January first would be the same as my life on December thirty-first?" He pulled away slightly and held my head between his trembling hands. "Miranda, that was the biggest of my mistakes. My life changed from the instant you uttered the words 'I love you.' Shit. And how could it not, since you turned my world upside down? No one has ever said 'I love you' to me, not even Isabel. Do you understand that? Can you imagine that?" He sighed. "My silence that night wasn't a gentlemanly rejection. No! It was caused by ignorance… not knowing how to love. I didn't know how to feel loved, and that night, damn it, I felt so many things that I felt like my emotions were going to suffocate me. Even today, I can't describe what I was carrying on my chest that night. There are no words to describe it. There will never be words to describe it, Miranda…. I should have… I should have told you how much I need you, how much pain I feel when you aren't by my side. I should have told you…"

I moved my hands to interrupt him.

"You shouldn't bother continuing, Clausell."

He took my hands, as he did so well on many other occasions.

"Please, listen to what I have to say. Let me tell you my side."

"There's no need. I have a thousand versions… a thousand damned versions, and I don't understand any of them. Another one won't help."

He placed a finger on my lips. He drew his face close to mine with that dangerous closeness that intoxicated me with his scent.

That scent…

"If you don't want to do it for me, don't do it for me."

He placed a hand on my abdomen. I so fantasized about such a moment. The tender touch of his roughness caused a sensation in me like the warmth of the sun on my feet after spending so much time in my personal winter.

"Do it for the baby."

He succeeded in breaking down my walls. I had no choice but to listen. After all, it was the least I could do for the baby that I was determined to not care for, and it was the least that I could do to feed my curiosity.

"I know that Norman told you the reason we left him." I nodded. He searched for the strength to mention the names of the two people who, one way or another, at different times in his life, had contributed to his cold personality. "When Norman had the accident, Isabel saw the opportunity to come back, to get the money she expected if he died. She wanted to be present to be sure that no one would take even one cent of what, according to her, belonged to us. Norman didn't die, so she began to weave her first plan: we would take control of the company and sell it. I was so blinded by the anger and hatred I had for Norman," another pause interrupted the story, "and you, that I agreed to be Isabel's puppet. You had robbed me of Norman's attention, time, and love. I needed to get you out of the way, and I was Norman's Achilles heel. What wouldn't he do for me? What would he, my father, not do for me?"

My father. It was the first time that I heard him say those words. I wished that Norman could have been there to hear them too.

"I didn't rob you of anything, Eli..."

He pressed his finger against my lips a little more.

"Listen to me, just listen to me... I grew up with that reality. That is the story that Isabel turned into my reality." He smeared his hands on his head and was teary eyed. "You don't know what it was like to grow up with her, Miranda. You don't have the... slightest... idea. My paintings were no more than a reflection of my upbringing. The pain that Isabel caused me was splattered on them. My sorrow was engraved on my back. Do you know what it's like to live like that? It's a constant reminder of how shitty a boy's life can be. Every time she would get drunk or inhale the white powder that she would lay out on the same table where we ate, she would repeat the same old thing over and over. She would repeat and repeat the same story: 'Your father doesn't love you, Eliezer. He loves some girl instead. That's why he abandoned you... because you're nothing.' What more could you expect from a child that grows up hearing that? Seeing that? What more can you expect from me, Miranda, if I continue being that child?"

For a brief moment, I understood. That child of whom he spoke was peering out through his eyes, and he was frightened, very frightened.

"I didn't understand why my father was no longer around, why my world had changed from one day to the next, because I only remembered a monster who was about to beat my mother to death, and not the affectionate man that existed before that terrible night."

"You had the chance to get close to him again."

"Yes, but that wasn't my motivation. I wanted to see him suffer. I wanted to hurt him just as he hurt Isabel, and just as he hurt me."

"All of these years you were tearing yourself apart..."

Again, he used the finger.

"I didn't realize." A tear fell. It was the first time that Eliezer displayed such strong emotion. "Until you came. I was doing nothing more than blaming the world for my unhappiness. I was filled with nothing and no one... until you came, Miranda Wise, with your rose-colored glasses, immune to my sarcasm, my insults, my offenses, and my insensitivity. You dared to walk barefoot over the broken glass surrounding my life. And, anyway, you had the nerve to tell me that you loved me. You had the character to show me how wrong I was about you, about Norman, about Medika. I, who later sought to destroy my father after destroying his insufferable company, in time began to appreciate its mission. Medika wasn't bad. I was the one who was behaving badly. In time, I discovered that Isabel was a schemer and that Norman was not the man I had imagined. You were the one who opened my eyes, who dazzled me with the possibility of living a different, perhaps pleasant, kind of life."

Nature was conspiring with him... The breeze carried every word he spoke and cleared the way for him to continue.

"I supposed, well, that at Medika's helm, I would be in control, that I could handle the situation, control Isabel's impulses, make her abandon her idea, or at least, give her part of the money that was hers so that she would leave us alone. So I met with Paul at the airport. On that day, I understood that Isabel was planning something worse than I had imagined."

"What made you think that?" I asked, but I answered my own question. "Ah, what he told you at the airport that changed your mood."

Eliezer agreed.

"Paul said, 'good work.' I didn't know to what he was referring, but it raised my suspicions. He supposed that Isabel's plan was our own alone. We would handle it, and no one else. I had known Paul a few years before. Isabel said that he was a businessman. They would meet at cafes, bars, and at home. She never wanted to tell me what business she had with him. Nor did I ask many questions. Isabel's life didn't matter much to me. When you and I were on our way back, when I unexpectedly saw Paul in New York, I wanted to confirm another link between Paul and Isabel. Norman said that he didn't know. I didn't believe him. Elizabeth, his sister, was the one who told me the truth. I was searching for evidence during those days when I disappeared that so infuriated you. When I found it, I confronted Isabel. She arranged a meeting for Paul and myself at her apartment. They had no other choice but to tell me about the plan that they had conceived so far. Paul wanted to kill you because you may get part of his inheritance. I couldn't believe what they were telling me, but I didn't show it. Together, we hatched the perfect plan."

"Together? Hatched?"

"Yes... I made them believe that I would support their plan. In fact, I offered a suggestion to make it 'better.' We agreed on the date, place, and method. As you can now imagine, everything went badly. Isabel suspected that I had stopped hating you. Apparently, I'm also not a very good actor and, of course, Norman... Norman committed a very grave error." His eyes looked at my face with tenderness. His hands fixed a few locks of hair that were coming out of my ponytail. "He confessed to her that you were pregnant and that I was the father. So Paul and Isabel's plan changed, and obviously they didn't tell me. The place remained the same, but the date changed, and their method would be more cruel, impersonal, and quick. I kept Inspector Hernandez informed. We had counterattack plan: gathering the evidence we could, arriving at the location right before it would happen, and sending them to jail for attempted premeditated murder. I wasn't cautious enough. I shouldn't have been so confident. They played me, Miranda.... They played me."

His fists held so much frustration that his knuckles turned white and looked as if they would explode. I put my hands over his fists, in an attempt to diminish the tension. It worked. I still had that power over him.

"That night, when you went to the office looking for an answer, I couldn't give it to you. There were so many things that I was hiding, that I couldn't give you a 'yes.' You marched away at my silence. Within minutes, Norman called me to follow up, thinking that you had told me about your pregnancy. He was sure that after speaking with you, you'd change your mind. I couldn't even respond to his cordial gesture. I hung up the telephone and went out to look for you. I had only your eyes filled with pain and frustration burned in my mind. I wanted to reach you, to tell you that I'd be there for you... for both of you... that I wouldn't disappear, that I wasn't Paul Wise, and that I... I love you, Miranda Wise." He closed his eyes, opened them again, and took a breath.

"On a corner of the block where your house is, there was always a black car. Did you notice it? Hernandez and I had your house under surveillance. We wanted to protect you, whatever the cost, 24 hours a day. I got to your neighborhood and stopped next to the contract bodyguard. That's how I noticed that looked like he was watching but wasn't blinking, and that a trickle of blood was coming down his lips. I imagined the worst. I reached into the window and took his gun. I went to your house, to the nightmarish scene. I think you know the rest, and there's no reason to make you relive it… You were on the way to the hospital when I went out searching for Isabel. There she was, in her apartment, drinking champagne with Paul. I snuck in and had him at gunpoint. Isabel screamed as always, as if she owned the world. I fired into the ceiling, and she got down on her knees and begged for me to not lose control. But I had already lost control. I gave her a blow to the face with the gun and she fell unconscious, gushing out blood on the floor. Then it was Paul's turn. I gave him a beating like I had never given anyone before. Now I have to go to court every few weeks, and I have had to bear the consequences of my actions for a few months. They are behind bars, but I think it's not punishment enough. She should rot in jail, and I should have blown his head off… Ironically, it was you and the baby that you're carrying that saved them. I thought of both of you. I can't leave you alone in this world that has turned to shit."

He touched my abdomen again, and the baby kicked. He smiled.

Chapter 31

"I'm no longer the same, Eliezer. You can't come here with your beautiful words and erase the memory... *my* memory."

"For the past five days, I've done nothing but watch you, because I didn't know how to approach you or how to speak to you. At 6:45 in the morning, you sit on the third step of the stairway to this terrace. By twelve, you had already gotten up four or five times, but you would always return to the same spot. When night would fall, you'd move to the big chair. You'd still be awake at midnight. I know by the frame of light that shines out of the bedroom where I had you for the first time. You still have hopes. I still have hopes. Come with me. Take my hand. We can give it a try.

"I'm not the same person."

"You are Miranda Wise... International," a tone of timidity and an attempt to smile colored that last word.

"I no longer know who I am."

"You are the marvelous woman who managed to awaken the will to change in me."

"Someone marvelous doesn't get into bed every night

thinking about a thousand and one reasons to not get up the next morning."

"I know what it is to be scared. You don't owe me any explanations."

"No, no. You don't understand. Marvelous people aren't dragged out of an abortion clinic. A marvelous person doesn't go with the idea of having an abortion."

"We aren't perfect, Miranda. Sometimes we don't make the right choices."

"I'm even afraid of my own shadow. The sound of my breathing keeps me awake. What have I become?"

He gave me a hug.

"I'm here, Wise. I'm here and I'm not thinking about leaving. I don't know what tomorrow, the next day, or the day after that will be like. I don't have the slightest fucking idea, but..."

My Eliezer had returned. I smiled to myself.

"I'm sorry, I shouldn't have...."

I put my fingers on his lips.

"Don't worry. I missed your expressions."

He kissed my hand.

I held his face and kissed his lips. I felt that, with that kiss, I brought life back to my body. I brought the shine back to that look... that look... that look....

If that's how, stuck to those lips, this damned life becomes complicated, I would never want to pull back, because I want to relive those moments over and over again, in which nothing and no one else exists other than us. Let it be nothing more than he and I alone... only he and his teasing, and I and my agitated heart and my frustration at hearing him.

Maybe it was a lie. Maybe it would be another act where the curtain would fall. Maybe it was a pause in time to get the answers to my questions. Maybe the most beautiful thing awaits me.

My savior's eyelids fluttered in a wave of victory. Eliezer let himself fall backward onto the terrace, my refuge. He reached up and said with a smile, "Come be next to me."

ELIEZER

Available in 2016

For the last two years Eliezer Clausell has made certain that the woman who gave him the gift of fatherhood, Miranda Wise, had the world at her feet. He has no doubts about having her by his side for life.

Meanwhile, Miranda has been silently fighting against the havoc in her mind caused by the vile attack. Her fears and anguish grow, but she is reluctant to seek professional help.

"Look only ahead to the future."

With those words as their guide, Miranda and Eliezer make a deal to find the peace and happiness they desperately seek. Nevertheless, even though they have a common goal, they seek it in very different ways, and as far as his wife and child are concerned, Eliezer thinks that the ends always justify the means.

What Miranda doesn't realize is that those repressed feelings are a time bomb that explodes when Eliezer decides to confront the cause of his love's unending nightmares: convicted criminal Paul Wise. However both are unaware that Paul is determined to take back what he thinks is his and will make use of the most terrible means to achieve his purposes.

In the sequel to *Miranda*, love will have to fight against intrigue, deception, and regret in an uncertain desire to survive. Ultimately, will the ends justify the means?

Thanks

Thank you to all those people who, one way or another, inspired, motivated, and believed in this craziness called, *Miranda*.

Pabsi Livmar, my editor and proofer for the spanish version, Hilda Naranjo, my translator, whom destiny placed in my path through a click on the Internet during one of those many sleepless nights. It's been a real pleasure and honor to work with both of you. You have no idea how much you've taught me. Thank you for making my story yours.

My little guinea pigs... you know who you are. I'm not going to mention your names to protect your reputation. What would others think if, being so serious, they knew that you read this story? Ha, ha, ha! Thank you for setting aside your complicated schedules and reading my musings. Your comments, observations, questions, and suggestions helped me nourish every one of my characters.

Shennen, when you reach adulthood, you can read what your mom writes, but not before.... nooooo!

Mikon, thank you for believing in me and giving me those kicks in the rear that gave me impetus when the road looked rocky. Love you!

To you, reader, who had the courage to give me a chance, and chose to read this story. I hope that you have enjoyed reading it as much as I did writing it. Thank you!

A special thanks to De Lorenzo Roman, my companion in letters, for putting his gorgeous poetry at my disposal. You can enjoy his work at **www.lahuelladelpresente.blogspot.com**

Thanks! Thanks! Thanks! Infinite thanks!

Visit **www.ssheeran.com** for more information about Sheila Sheeran projects.